ANOTHER VICTIM

Michael had discovered a damp pair of jeans and a shirt in his closet. It was clear he'd been sleepwalking in the rain last night, just as he had suspected. Now he had to find out where he'd gone and what he'd done.

His hands were trembling as he paged through the newspaper. There was an article about a woman who'd been murdered in Westwood. As he read the name of the victim, Margo Jantzen, his face turned white.

The phone book was still open on the coffee table and Michael forced himself to look at it. Margo Jantzen's name and address were right there in the middle of the page . . .

Books by Joanne Fluke

Hannah Swensen Mysteries

CHOCOLATE CHIP COOKIE MURDER
STRAWBERRY SHORTCAKE MURDER
BLUEBERRY MUFFIN MURDER
LEMON MERINGUE PIE MURDER
FUDGE CUPCAKE MURDER
SUGAR COOKIE MURDER
PEACH COBBLER MURDER
CHERRY CHEESECAKE MURDER
KEY LIME PIE MURDER
CANDY CANE MURDER
CARROT CAKE MURDER
CREAM PUFF MURDER
PLUM PUDDING MURDER
APPLE TURNOVER MURDER
DEVIL'S FOOD CAKE MURDER
GINGERBREAD COOKIE MURDER
CINNAMON ROLL MURDER
RED VELVET CUPCAKE MURDER
BLACKBERRY PIE MURDER
DOUBLE FUDGE BROWNIE MURDER
JOANNE FLUKE'S LAKE EDEN COOKBOOK

Suspense Novels

VIDEO KILL
WINTER CHILL
DEAD GIVEAWAY
THE OTHER CHILD
COLD JUDGMENT
FATAL IDENTITY
FINAL APPEAL

Published by Kensington Publishing Corporation

FINAL APPEAL

JOANNE FLUKE

KENSINGTON BOOKS

http://www.kensingtonbooks.com

KENSINGTON BOOKS are published by

Kensington Publishing Corp.
119 West 40th Street
New York, NY 10018

All Kensington titles, imprints and distributed lines are
available at special quantity discounts for bulk purchases
for sales promotion, premiums, fund-raising, educational
or institutional use. Special book excerpts or customized
printings can also be created to fit specific needs. For
details, write or phone the office of the Kensington
Special Sales Manager: Kensington Publishing Corp.,
119 West 40th Street, New York, NY, 10018. Attn. Special
Sales Department. Phone: 1-800-221-2647.

Kensington and the K logo Reg. U.S. Pat. & TM Off.

ISBN-13: 978-0-7582-8971-1
ISBN-10: 0-7582-8971-5
First Kensington Mass Market Edition: August 2015

eISBN-13: 978-0-7582-8972-8
eISBN-10: 0-7582-8972-3
First Kensington Electronic Edition: August 2015

10 9 8 7 6 5 4 3 2 1

Printed in the United States of America

CHAPTER 1

Hollywood, California

Carole Hart knew that her marriage was dead, but she was not the type to mourn. She had already shed her tears, many of them during the years she'd been married, and her resolve was firm. She still loved Michael, she'd never stop loving him, but divorcing him was her only chance to have a normal life. Her new husband, the one she'd marry after her divorce was final, would be a wonderful provider. And even if the passion she'd shared with Michael was missing, she realized that she was probably much better off without it.

Despite her resolve, tears threatened to fall as she folded her designer silk blouse, the only quality item of clothing she owned, and placed it carefully in her old red suitcase. The blouse had been a birthday present from Amy Weston, her best friend at work. Amy and the other secretaries who worked at World-Star Studios owned such extensive wardrobes that they were often mistaken for glamorous actresses.

Carole was the only exception. In the years that she had worked at the studio, no tourist had ever mistaken her for anyone. Her skirts, blouses, and dresses were relics left over from her single days, shortened and altered in a desperate attempt to keep up with the styles but never quite achieving that fashionable look. Carole hadn't purchased a single new item of clothing since she'd married Michael. Most of her salary had gone for necessities like the rent, the food, and the utility bills. Because maintaining Michaels's career was so expensive, any extra money was quickly allocated for his acting classes. And his SAG dues. And the glossy photographs he had to provide for casting directors. No matter how carefully Carole had economized, it had never seemed to make a real difference in their financial status.

Once, when the bills had piled up and Carole feared she'd never be able to pay them all, Michael had made a joke of it. He said that if they won just one major sweepstakes, they could get their heads above water. Carole had thought it was the funniest thing she'd ever heard. Back then.

Six years ago, when she'd married Michael, the couples in their Hollywood apartment building had formed an informal support group. They'd all been young and poor and on the brink of that first big break. They'd met for potluck dinners and either commiserated or celebrated, depending on their circumstances. Back then, Carole had been known for her cabbage salad. Cabbage was cheaper than lettuce because it wasn't seasonal. She'd chopped it and mixed it with an economical mixture of vinegar, sugar, salt, and black pepper. If Michael had worked that week, she occasionally splurged on red and yellow bell peppers to decorate the top. The first time she'd made her coleslaw, Michael had quipped about their salad days. Carole had laughed along with everyone else, but she hadn't understood the joke. Later she'd asked, and Michael had told her it was a quote from Shakespeare's *Anthony and Cleopatra.*

Looking back on those days now, Carole realized that she'd never had much in common with Michael. He was a college graduate, and she'd gone right to work as an entry-level secretary at World-Star the moment she'd finished high school. They'd met at an audition, where Carole had fallen in love with his voice and his handsome face. When Michael landed the part, he took her out for dinner to celebrate.

There had been many dinners when Michael was working. And even more lunches at hot dog stands when he was between roles.

There had also been long romantic evenings spent in his tiny apartment—the same apartment she was now leaving—listening to music and making love.

All the other secretaries, Amy included, had warned her not to get involved with an actor. She hadn't listened. And then, before she'd really thought about how terribly insecure their life together would be, she'd become Mrs. Michael Hart, the shoestring gourmet, bringing cabbage salad to potluck dinners where the men talked about artistic integrity and the women sat next to them and dreamed of all the things they couldn't afford.

At first, being married to an actor had been exciting. Carole had experienced a rush of pure pleasure every time she'd seen her husband's image on the screen. But show business was fickle, and it always took time for an actor to get established. The other couples had gradually traded their dreams for financial security. Most of them had decided the odds were against them, and they'd sacrificed their integrity to climb up corporate ladders. Couple by couple, they'd deserted their cramped apartments to make down payments on small houses in the valley where they could start their families. Then, one day during their fourth year of marriage, Carole and Michael had looked around and realized that they were the only holdouts from the original group.

Michael had never criticized their friends for giving up. The lifestyle of a dedicated artist was a tough one, and not everyone could endure the hardships it entailed. They'd kept in touch, and every time Carole and Michael had driven out to one of the rambling homes in the valley for a housewarming or a baby shower, the men had slapped Michael on the back and told him that they admired his perseverance. But their wives had gazed at Carole with eyes full of pity and offered to share their wealth. Here was the color television set that Tina's husband had replaced with a big-screen model. Since it was just sitting in the garage taking up space, they'd regard it as a real favor if Carole and Michael would take it off their hands. And Ellen's old Cuisinart, the old set of china that didn't go with Patricia's new wallpaper, the glassware that didn't fit in Yvonne's new dishwasher, and the answering machine that Tom no longer needed because he now subscribed to a service.

Carole had accepted the castoffs gratefully, even though she sometimes felt like their friends' favorite charity. She'd done her best not to envy the new bigger houses, the prestige cars, and the vacations in Europe. She told herself she'd have all those things someday. She had faith in Michael's talents, and she could wait. Then she'd held her friend's babies, and her resentment had started to grow. They'd agreed not to have children until they were financially secure, but how much longer would she have to wait?

Three months ago, on the morning of her thirtieth birthday, Carole had awakened to take stock of her life. Michael was an excellent character actor, and when he worked, he was paid very well. But there were those frightening dry periods between roles when Carole was forced to sit back and worry, watching helplessly as their savings dwindled. The stress of not knowing when her husband would land his next part had turned her into a nervous wreck. Their whole life was a series of ups and downs, regulated by the crazy whims of casting directors and studio executives. There were no guarantees in show biz, none at all. Carole had known this from the beginning. And on the morning of her thirtieth birthday, she'd finally realized that they'd never have the security she craved, not even if Michael made it big. He could be a huge success one year and box office poison the next. She'd seen it happen just that way.

Michael had arranged a surprise party with the old crowd, even though they'd been smack in the middle of one of their down periods with creditors calling and the rent two weeks overdue. That night, when Carole had arrived home from work, she'd found everyone waiting for her, armed with food and champagne.

After a toast to her birthday with expensive champagne, Daryl Forrester pulled both of them over for a little talk in the corner of the kitchen. Daryl had been a struggling young artist when they'd met, but now he was a corporate executive with a wife and a family and a big home in the valley. He told Michael that Amcorp needed someone to host daily motivational seminars for their salesmen, and he'd recommended Michael for the job. They'd pay sixty-thousand-a-year in base salary plus a percentage of the increased sales. Michael could pull in seventy to eighty grand annually, maybe more.

Carole shut her eyes and prayed. It would solve all their financial problems if Michael took the job. Then they could pay off their bills and think seriously about a house and a decent car and the baby Carole so desperately wanted. But Michael thanked Daryl for thinking of him and turned it down flat.

After everyone had left, Michael tried to explain. He was sorry that Carole was disappointed, but couldn't she see that hosting promotional seminars for a big corporation was the ultimate in selling out? He was an actor, not a company puppet. A job like that would kill him.

They'd gone to bed and tried to resolve their differences by making love, but the old magic didn't work. After Michael had fallen asleep, Carole had stared up into the darkness and realized that there was no future with Michael. As painful as it might be, she had to leave him if she ever wanted to live a normal life. But where would she go? And what would she do? She'd begun to make her plans.

With a start, Carole came back to the present. It was already eight o'clock, time to load the car and drive to Amy's. The bedroom was stifling, not a breath of air even though she'd opened the window as wide as it would go. Their air conditioner had gone on the blink two months ago, and they hadn't been able to spare the money to pay a repairman.

Her old red suitcase had a broken latch. As Carole tied it shut with a belt she promised herself that the moment she was remarried she march into Gucci and pick out a whole set of expensive matched luggage. Her lover had been shocked when she'd told him that she was pregnant, but she knew he'd come around. Her voice had held just the right tone of injured outrage when she said that of course the baby was his. And no, she hadn't confided in anyone. She'd kept their relationship a total secret, because she knew how important it was to protect him from the slightest scandal. Her only concern was to provide a normal family life for the baby, with a mother, a father, and nice surroundings. His son or daughter deserved the best, didn't he agree?

He was an intelligent man, and he'd quickly realized that she had him over a barrel. One word to the wrong person and he could kiss his career goodbye. They'd made a date for lunch tomorrow, and Carole was sure he was sitting in his office right now, figuring out the best way preserve his reputation and meet her demands at the same time.

Carole picked up the phone and called Amy's number to tell her that she was on the way. Amy must have been sitting right by the phone, because she picked up the receiver on the first ring.

"Carole!" Amy sounded worried, "Is something wrong? I thought you'd be here by now."

"I would have been, but Michael came in while I was packing."

"My God!" Amy gasped. "Are you all right? I can be there in twenty minutes if you need me."

"Thanks, but that's not necessary. He's gone now."

"Was it awful?"

Carole sighed. "That's the understatement of the year! I'll tell you all about it later. Right now, I want to get out of here before—" Carole paused as she heard a key in the lock. "He's back! Hold on, Amy. I'll find out what he wants."

Carole put down the phone and stood up. She was surprised to find that her knees were shaking, and she took a deep, calming breath. It was ridiculous to be afraid of the man she'd lived with for the past six years. Michael had a volatile temper, but he usually kept it under tight control. He'd probably thought it all over, replayed that ugly scene in his mind, and now he'd come back to apologize.

"Michael? I'm in here." Carole sighed as she headed for the door. There would be another scene. He'd tell her he loved her and beg her to stay. Maybe he'd even promise to call Daryl Forrester to see if that job with Amcorp was still open. She'd just have to tell him all over again that it was too late. Their marriage was over. He had no choice but to accept it.

The light was out in the hallway, and at first, she didn't see the gun. By the time she did, it was too late to scream.

CHAPTER 2

Ten Years later
Oakdale State Hospital for the
  Criminally Insane

Michael Hart had no idea what time it was. The dayroom clock had a dense coating of wire mesh over its face. He had been here for years now, but he still wasn't sure whether the metal cage around the clock was to protect it from possible damage or to keep him from discovering how slowly the hands crawled around its circumference.

On this particular morning, the dayroom was off-limits. The clock was safe from flying Ping-Pong balls and wads of paper. No patients from Ward B were allowed inside to use the rickety tables or the television set. Michael was the only exception.

He sat in a green plastic chair facing his accusers, the board of doctors and social workers. His hands were shaking, and he gripped the arms of the chair tightly in an effort to concentrate. His head felt like a balloon filled with helium, huge and lighter than air, nodding and bobbing uncontrollably as if someone else were jerking the string. The nurse had insisted he take his medication last night—no screaming, nightmares, or episodes of sleepwalking on her shift, thank you very much, even though he'd explained that he was up for review in the morning, and he had to be able to think clearly.

There was a clatter as one silver-haired man with aviator glasses dropped his pen on the tile floor. Everyone watched as he bent over to pick it up. It was a Cross ballpoint, and Michael wondered whether he had the pencil to match. A Cross pen and pencil set was a traditional high-school graduation gift. Aunt Alice had given Stan a gold set, and Michael had expected the same. Instead, his aunt had surprised him with a brand-new Volkswagen Beetle. Did Stan have it now? Michael almost laughed aloud at the thought of his sophisticated brother driving around in a beat-up VW Bug, but he caught himself just in time. He had to focus on what was happening here, in this room. It was opening night at the most important performance of his life. His role was to play a perfectly normal person, the type of man who'd work all week and spend the weekend mowing his lawn and cleaning out the garage. He'd be the typical man on the street, the sort of nondescript, ordinary guy you'd see on the evening news, answering some inane questions with a microphone shoved in his face.

Michael did all he could not to gasp out loud as his adrenaline began to race. That meant he was blocking. Something was there, a buried memory about the man on the street. But he didn't have time to explore it now. The head of the psychiatric division, Dr J. Bowman, was lighting his pipe. The curtain was about to go up.

Dr. Bowman had a brass name tag pinned to his lapel. Perhaps he wore it to remind him of who he was. Michael had asked his favorite orderly about Dr. Bowman. And Jack had told him that the doctor spent a lot of time locked in his office, drinking to escape the pressures of his job.

A dense cloud of gray smoke drifted toward Michael, and he took a deep breath before it reached out to enshroud his head. There was a red-and-white NO SMOKING sign on the wall under the imprisoned clock, but it applied only to patients. Dr Bowman could break any rule he wanted. He was the hospital honcho. And he had the power to set Michael free.

"Shall we start?" Dr. Bowman glanced at the clock just as if he could see through the mesh. Then he opened his briefcase and cleared his throat.

"Excuse me, Dr. Bowman," A frizzy-haired social worker raised her hand. Michael remembered seeing her in the halls when he went to therapy. "I believe you have the case histories?"

"I do? Oh, yes. Here they are."

Dr. Bowman passed out the red-covered folders. When Michael had asked, Jack had explained that red was the hospital's color code for convicted murderers. Everything was color-coded. It was policy. Michael wished his folders were a different color— blue, perhaps, even though that was the color for homosexuals, or good old paranoid–schizophrenic yellow. At least he knew what was inside the folders; no surprises this time. Jack had managed to get his hands on a copy, and Michael had memorized it during his allotted ten minutes in the lavatory. A good actor had to be a quick study, and he still thought he'd been a good actor.

There was a rustle of papers as the members of the board turned to the first page. Vital statistics.

"Now, er . . . Michael?" Dr. Bowman glanced at the case history. "Could you please give me your full name?"

"Excuse me, doctor?" The social worker interrupted again. "Shouldn't we inform the patient of the purpose of this hearing?"

"What?" Dr. Bowman looked startled. "Oh, yes. You're right of course." As he fumbled in his briefcase, Michael observed him very carefully.

Everything about Dr. Bowman was a bit rumpled. He was wearing a suit that had once been expensive, but now it was growing tight around the middle, and there were several large grease spots on his tie. His salt-and-pepper beard needed trimming, and it didn't match the color of his hair. Doctor Bowman was in his late fifties, and his hair was glossy black. That was unusual, unless . . . Michael bit back a smile.

The doctor drew out a piece of paper and studied it for a moment. There were bright spots of color in his pasty cheeks, and his nose was a road map of broken veins. Michael would have cast him in *Days of Wine and Roses*, but he certainly wasn't about to mention that. He might be crazy, but he wasn't stupid.

Dr. Bowman cleared his throat again and started to read. "As you may know, er . . . Michael, this board is charged with a solemn responsibility to make certain that you will be a contributing and law-abiding member of society in the event of your release. We are required to ask you a series of questions to assess your grasp of reality and your competency to make logical and reasonable assumptions. Now, where were we?"

"I believe you were about to ask the patient his name," the social worker prompted.

"Yes, that's right."

Dr. Bowman turned to face Michael and gave his impression of a reassuring smile. It wasn't very good. Forget *Days of Wine and Roses*. Dr. Bowman would never make it as an actor.

"Try to relax Michael. There's nothing to be afraid of. We're all concerned for your best interests. I want you to think of us as your friends."

Michael nodded and managed to keep the pleasant expression on his face. He had no friends here, not a familiar face in the bunch unless you counted the social worker he barely knew. Jack had petitioned to attend, but his request had been denied. You had to be in a position of authority to sit in on the review board. No orderlies allowed.

"Let us begin." Dr. Bowman picked up his folder and glanced at the first page. "Would you please give me your full and complete name?"

Michael opened his mouth, and the answer came out. "Michael Allen Hart." As several members of the board picked up their pens and began to write, he realized that he'd missed one already. Now he'd have to explain, and Jack told him not to volunteer anything, just to answer the questions and remember to smile. This would have to be an exception.

"Hart is my stage name, Dr. Bowman. I've been using it ever since I graduated from college. My legal name is Gerhardt, Michael Allen Gerhardt."

Dr. Bowman nodded, "Very good, Michael. I'm glad you made that distinction. Could you please give me your last street address?"

Michael hesitated. Surely, they didn't want the address of the prison where he'd spent his first few months. Or the hospital where he'd gone through the surgeries. He'd try the apartment. That must be right.

"Sixty-one fifty-five Franklin Avenue, apartment eighteen, Hollywood, California. I . . . I'm not sure of the zip code. Nine-zero-zero-two-six?"

Dr. Bowman referred to his notes. "It was nine-zero-zero-two-eight, but that's perfectly acceptable. This board doesn't expect you to be able to pass a postal service quiz on zip codes."

There was a titter of laughter, and Michael remembered to smile. Normal people were expected to smile politely, no matter how lame the joke.

"And what were your parent's names?"

"Robert Stanley Gerhardt and Cassie, that's short for Cassandra, Gerhardt."

"And your mother's maiden name?"

"Cassandra Michele Norman."

"Do you have any relatives living in the state of California?"

"Yes. My older brother, Stan Gerhardt, lives in Los Angeles and my Aunt Alice . . ." Michael faltered as he realized that Aunt Alice was dead. That was two he'd missed already, and the interview had just started. "I'm sorry, Dr. Bowman. I just remembered that my Aunt Alice Norman passed away last year."

"She did?" Dr. Bowman studied the folder for a moment. "Yes, that's correct. Michael. Now, do you know today's date?"

"September fourteenth."

"And the day of the week?"

"Thursday."

"Did you say Thursday?" Dr. Bowman frowned. Michael nodded, and the social worker spoke up again.

"He's right, doctor. Today is Thursday."

Dr. Bowman glared at her, and Michael hoped she wouldn't get into trouble. She was the only one on the board who seemed to be on his side.

"Let's go on then, Michael, who is the current president of the United States?"

Michael froze. How was he supposed to know that?

It wasn't fair!

"I . . . I'm not sure. Dr. Bowman. We're not allowed to watch the news on television because it upsets some of the patients and we don't have access to newspapers. I do know that nineteen eighty-eight was an election year, and the last time I heard, Vice President Bush was leading in the polls."

Michael winced as several board members made notes. If he'd known they were going to ask about the president, he would have found out from Jack.

"All right, Michael." Dr. Bowman referred to the sheet of paper again. "I realize that the following material may be painful, but we must have your complete recollection of the events that occurred ten years ago on . . . uh . . . what was that date again?"

There was an uncomfortable silence, and finally the social worker spoke. "October second, doctor."

"Thank you, Mrs. Gray." Turning his focus back to the patient, Dr. Bowman said, "Michael? Please answer the question."

Michael took a deep breath. He'd gotten this far before, but after he'd told them and exposed all his fears and uncertainties, they'd still denied his release.

"October second was the day my wife, Carole died."

"Died?"

"She was murdered. And I was convicted."

"Very good, go on Michael."

"I had an audition, but it was canceled, so I went straight home. And when I opened the door, I found Carole packing her things. I couldn't believe it when she told me that she was leaving. She wanted a divorce."

"And how did you feel about that?"

"I was shocked. And hurt. Especially when I saw the note, she'd written. It was clear she'd been planning on leaving without even talking to me."

"Did that make you angry?"

Michael winced, but he knew he had to tell the truth. "Yes, I thought I deserved better than that, but I tried not to let my anger get in the way. I told her that I loved her, that I wanted to try to work things out. I even suggested we go to a marriage counselor for help, but she wouldn't listen. She just kept packing things in boxes and repeating that our marriage was over and I had to accept it."

"She wouldn't tell you why she was leaving?"

"No. She said it was too late to even discuss it. The whole thing was so frustrating!"

Dr. Bowman leaned forward. "And was that when you killed her?"

"No!" Michael gripped the arms of the chair so

hard his knuckles turned white. "I . . . we had a fight, a terrible fight. And I left."

"Dr. Bowman?" The social worker spoke up again. "The patient is obviously agitated, and I feel we must have some compassion for . . ." Her voice trailed off as Dr. Bowman banged his fist on the table.

"I'm warning you, Mrs. Gray. I'm the chairman of this board, and I have the power to evict you from this proceeding. I'm sure Michael knows that no one in this room, including me, wants to cause him any unnecessary pain. Isn't that right, Michael?"

"Yes, Dr. Bowman."

"You're doing fine, Michael. Now take a deep breath, relax, and tell me where you went when you left the apartment."

"I went to a bar, Barney's Beanery, in West Hollywood. I was hoping to run into some of my friends. I needed someone to talk to, someone to tell me what to do."

"Of course you did. And were your friends there?"

"No, I sat there for a couple of hours, but no one I knew came in, so I left."

"And that was when you went back to kill your wife?"

This was the time Dr. Bowman wanted him to break down, to admit he'd killed Carole. But he hadn't! He knew he hadn't! It was Heller's *Catch Twenty-Two*. If he lied and said, he'd gone back to the apartment to murder Carole in a fit of passion, Dr. Bowman would pat him on the back for accepting reality and release him. He'd said as much in a staff meeting, and Jack had heard about it through the hospital grapevine. There were no secrets from orderlies. But if Michael told the truth and swore that he hadn't killed Carole. Dr. Bowman would decide he was still denying and keep him locked up with the caged clock forever.

Dr. Bowman was speaking again. Michael forced himself to listen.

". . . your own good, Michael. I want to help you, but my hands are tied if you refuse to cooperate. It's really quite simple. All you have to do is tell me precisely how you killed your wife."

Michael opened his mouth to play the game. It was the only way. Then he saw how Dr. Bowman was leaning forward in rapt fascination. His eyes were unblinking, and he seemed to be having some trouble breathing. The rasping sound of the air passing between his colorless lips reminded Michael of something in his past, something ugly.

It took a moment, but then he started to remember. Aunt Alice had taken them to a county fair. While she'd gone through the exhibit buildings, they'd explored the midway. Stan had gone off to buy them some cotton candy, and Michael had waited by the brightly colored posters advertising the wonders inside the tents. He'd stared at the pictures of the two-headed snake in a bottle, the half-man half-woman, and the bearded lady, wishing that he could go inside to see them. Then a smiling man had approached with an extra ticket. Would Michael like to go inside?

Michael had known he shouldn't. Stan had told him to stay put and not move. He glanced at the cotton candy booth and he could see that there were a lot of people ahead of Stan in line. That meant he had time to see the wonderful things inside the tent and be back outside before Stan even reached the counter.

It was just too much of a temptation for a little boy to resist.

As soon as the tent flap had closed, the man who had seemed so friendly had changed. He'd grasped Michael's hand and held it tightly. And pulled it forward to touch something Michael knew he shouldn't touch. He'd kicked and broken free, but he still remembered that the man in the tent had been breathing exactly like Dr. Bowman was breathing right now.

"Don't block it out, Michael. I know what's best for you."

Dr. Bowman moved his chair closer and reached out to take Michael's hand. "You'll feel so much better when you tell me all about it. Carole hurt you deeply. Of course, you wanted to punish her, to see her suffer. To cause her the kind of . . ."

The thought hit his mind like a sledge hammer. The perverted bastard was getting off on Carole's murder!

Someone must have jerked on the balloon string, because suddenly Michael was flying up out of the green plastic chair to fasten his fingers around Dr. Bowman's neck.

CHAPTER 3

The Law Firm of Gerhardt, Merrill, and Davis
Los Angeles, California

Stan stopped to glance at his Rolex and then resumed pacing across his new brown and gold Aubusson carpet. His secretary had put in a call to Jerry Bowman more than an hour ago, and the doctor still hadn't called back. No one ever kept Stan Gerhardt waiting that long!

As he covered the length of his large corner office, Stan was aware of the luxury that surrounded him. The offices of Gerhardt, Merrill, and Davis had recently been redecorated by Ralph of Brentwood, at considerable corporate expense. Several original oils hung on the walls, a secure investment that would surely double or even triple in the next ten years. Stylish but comfortable swivel chairs covered in natural chamois flanked the solid rosewood conference table. The floor-to-ceiling windows were draped in a heavy, natural silk that filtered in just the right amount of light, and a brass sculpture of

Lady Justice, complete with blindfold and scales, dominated the corner by the marble fireplace. The statue had been commissioned from a leading artist, and it glowed with a soft sheen from the reflected light.

Stan smiled briefly as he thought about his confrontation with Ralph. The prissy little decorator had strutted through Stan's offices like the Queen of the May, disturbing junior and senior partners alike with his palettes of paint samples and fabric swatches. At least he'd had the foresight to leave Stan alone—until that day when he'd actually interrupted one of Stan's weekly staff meetings with a crisis. A decision had to be made immediately between robin's-egg blue and pale melon. Stan had smiled and told him to go with the melon.

Since Ralph's work for Gerhardt, Merrill, and Davis would be featured in several prestigious magazines, the decorator had been a tyrant for absolute perfection. The furniture had already been selected, a painstaking process that had taken months. Every piece had to fit into Ralph's framework for the complete conceptual environment. When the receptionist's designer phone had been delivered in ivory instead of cream, Ralph had gone into a full-scale tizzy, screaming at the delivery man as if he were personally responsible. That was when Stan had decided it was time for a power play.

He'd left the office at noon and gone to a second-hand furniture store that advertised overnight delivery. When Ralph had arrived the next day, Stan had presented him with a phalanx of battered, decrepit, glass-enclosed lawyer's bookcases he claimed had belonged to his grandfather. Oh, hadn't he mentioned them before? An oversight on his part, his apologies. But surely Ralph was flexible enough to work them into his design. Of course, Stan was no expert on interior decorating, but he thought the bookcases should be dispersed, say one in each office? His heirloom antiques would lend a sense of tradition and continuity to his relativity young law firm.

Ralph had sputtered, and his face had turned red. Then he began to wheeze. It seemed Stan's "family antiques" had brought on an emotionally induced asthma attack.

Naturally, they hadn't used the secondhand bookcases. Stan had capitulated in the end, claiming that he had been swayed by Ralph's artistic judgment. But not before he'd given the phony little decorator some very anxious moments.

The intercom buzzed, and Stan hurried to answer, wincing a bit as his secretary's amplified voice echoed in his ear. There had to be a way to turn the volume down. He'd have her call a technician immediately.

"I have Dr. Bowman for you, Mr. Gerhardt, line five."

Stan sat down in his leather desk chair and held the phone a good three inches away from his ear. "Thank you, Joyce. Call a repairman for this damn phone system, will you? I want it fixed today. And you'd better tell Professor Zimmer that I've been unavoidably delayed. Offer him coffee or something."

"Right away, Mr. Gerhardt."

As Joyce clicked off Stan reached into the upper left-hand drawer of his rosewood executive desk to take out a fresh yellow legal pad. Michael had been up for release, and no one had told him. He had to get things straight with Bowman.

Stan jabbed the button for line five so savagely the phone jingled, yet he forced his voice to sound perfectly cordial. He knew Bowman would have to be replaced, but he wasn't quite ready to tip his hand.

"Hello Jerry, I understand you had a bit of trouble with my brother this morning?"

Stan's face looked even more haggard than usual as the doctor related the incident. There was a time when he'd considered plastic surgery to correct his prominent nose and the labial lines that were the curse of the Gerhardt's, but in the past ten years, since his brother hadn't been around, he'd shelved the idea. Michael had always been the handsome one, but where had it gotten him in the end? Stan had concluded that brainpower always won out over looks, and if people didn't agree with him, they were fools.

The doctor reached the end of his recital at last, and Stan put down his pen. "Thank you for sharing this with me, Jerry. Naturally, I'm relieved you weren't badly hurt. And you say my brother's sedated now?"

He listened as Bowman described the medications he'd prescribed and the restraints they'd put on Michael. Then it was time for him to play a little hardball.

"Something concerns me, Jerry. Why wasn't I notified that my brother was up for review? I thought we'd agreed that it was in Michael's best interest to keep me fully informed."

The doctor went into a lengthy explanation, and Stan's eyes narrowed.

"I see. New secretaries can be very unreliable. Perhaps, in the future, you'd do me the courtesy of making that call yourself?"

Bowman was really backpedaling now. Stan smiled at the man's obvious discomfort and let him rattle on for a moment. "Yes, Jerry, I'm sure you will. Sorry I don't have time to chat, I have a client waiting."

Stan ended the call and pushed the intercom button, remembering to hold the phone away from his ear as his secretary came on the line. "Joyce? Would you check my appointment schedule and clear me for tomorrow afternoon? I'll be out of the office from eleven on. And then you can bring in the professor."

He gave a sigh as his thoughts turned back to his brother's doctor. He knew Bowman was incompetent. It was no wonder he'd opted for running a state hospital rather than going into private practice. Stan planned to drive up to Oakdale tomorrow and drop in unannounced. It ought to be easy to find some irregularities if he arrived unexpectedly, and Stan had friends in high places. Perhaps the social worker who'd called could steer him in the right direction. While he was there, he'd visit Michael. Stan chuckled as he pictured his brother trying to choke the starch out of Bowman. Michael's actions might be crazy, but he'd certainly had the right man!

There was a knock on the door, and Joyce ushered in Professor Zimmer. Stan got up to shake hands. He remembered him only vaguely from Michael's trial, a thin, nervous man with thick glasses and an irritating habit of grinding his teeth. He had refused to say what he'd wanted over the phone.

"I thought I should come to you immediately,

Mr. Gerhardt." Professor Zimmer's voice matched his size, tentative and small. "Quite by accident I've come across some evidence that gives your brother an alibi for the night of the murder."

Through a supreme effort of will, Stan kept his expression neutral. Perhaps it was nothing. He seemed to recall that James Zimmer had been the excitable type.

"You say you have evidence?"

Professor Zimmer nodded and took a DVD out of his briefcase. "I've spent the past five years at Gateway University researching television news and its role in society. My contention is that networks set public opinion by choosing to air, or not to air, selected interviews. It's fascinating work, Mr. Gerhardt, simply fascinating. And naturally, it's of paramount importance to assess the influence the television medium has on—"

"Excuse me, Professor." Stan interrupted what was sure to be a lengthy monologue. "Michael was interviewed on television?"

"No, that's not it at all. You see, I gained access to the complete footage of the KLAX man-on-the-street interviews. The station donated them to the college. I studied the segments they ran, but I also viewed what they call the outtakes. Those are the segment the network decided not to run for various reasons, some of them mechanical, others because"—Professor Zimmer leaned forward conspiratorially—"if my contention is correct, the opinion of the interviewee did not fit into the preconceived framework of the network."

"I see." Stan took a deep breath. Professor Zimmer could be here for an hour, just getting to the point. "And Michael was the subject of one of those interviews?"

"Not the subject. Mr. Gerhardt. Another man was being interviewed, but your brother was in the background watching. Since a person can't be in two places at once, it proves he couldn't have killed his wife."

"Is this footage dated and time-stamped?"

"In a way," Professor Zimmer smiled. "The interview concerns the nurse's strike at County General, and there are several shots of nurses carrying placards. If you'll recall, that strike was settled overnight so the date has to be October second, nineteen seventy-nine."

"How about the time?" Stan leaned forward. Perhaps the professor really had something here.

"The time is a bit of a problem. There's no actual mention of the hour, per se."

Stan shook his head. "Without the exact time, Professor Zimmer, we don't have a prayer for an—"

"Wait, Mr. Gerhardt. I haven't told you everything. The interview takes place on the steps of the hospital. There's a bus that stops in the middle of the interview, and they have to wait for it to unload and load. The camera keeps rolling, and the number of the bus is clearly visible. It's a Rapid Transit Division Nine B."

"Go on." Stan leaned back. It was futile to try to rush the professor.

"I looked through the company records and discovered that Nine B was a special. It stopped at the hospital only at seven forty-five and eight fifteen."

"You've certainly done your research, Professor. But which one of these times was it?"

"Aha!" Professor Zimmer raised his eyebrows as if he were answering a question from a particularly slow student. "You see, Mr. Gerhardt, it doesn't matter. If your brother was in front of County General at either of those times, he couldn't possibly have murdered his wife. The drive from the hospital to his apartment takes over thirty minutes under optimum conditions. If your brother left the hospital at seven forty-five, right after the Nine B pulled out, he couldn't have arrived at his apartment before eight fifteen. And since Mrs. Hart's friend heard the shot and placed the time of death at eight o'clock precisely, that proves your brother is innocent."

Stan could do nothing but agree. "I see. And if Michael left immediately after the murder, he couldn't have arrived at the hospital before—"

"Eight-thirty." Fifteen minutes too late to be in the picture with the bus. Do you have a machine in your office? I want you to watch the footage for positive identification. I took the liberty of showing it to another juror, and we're both sure the man in question is your brother."

Stan watched the footage and was silent as he removed the disk. The man was definitely Michael.

"Well?" The professor beamed proudly. "What do you think, Mr. Gerhardt?"

Stan cleared his throat. "It does look like Michael, no doubt about that. Did you try to locate the cameraman who filmed the interview?"

"No, but I'll be glad to try."

"That's quite all right, Professor, you've done enough. I can take it from here. KLAX, is that right?"

Professor Zimmer nodded, and Stan took the

disk, dropped it in an envelope, and handed it to the professor.

"Could you seal this envelope, please, and write your name and the date on the outside? That's to certify that the disk in the envelope is the same one we've both seen today."

The professor signed his name and wrote the date. Then Stan took the envelope and buzzed for his secretary. In a moment, she appeared in the doorway.

"Joyce? Take this envelope and lock it in the safe. Log it in as Exhibit A. Michael Hart."

After Joyce had left with the envelope, Stan turned back to the professor. "I'd like to thank you for all you've done, Professor Zimmer. You've come across something that could clear my brother. Frankly, I'm surprised and pleased that you didn't go straight to the police."

"The police?" Professor Zimmer frowned. "I didn't even think of them. I came to you because you handled your brother's defense."

"And it's a stroke of fortune that you did!" Stan gave him a smile. "If you'd taken your tape to the police, they would have reopened their files. That always causes a flurry of publicity. The fewer people who know about your discovery, the better it is for Michael."

The professor looked confused, and Stan hurried to explain. "The evidence you've given me is almost certainly the basis for a retrial, but there's a lot of legwork to do first. I'll have to find the cameraman and get his sworn testimony that he taped the interview. Then I'll need an affidavit from the station stating that they gave Gateway University their outtakes. And a letter from Gateway administration explaining that you, as their employee, had access to this particular outtake. Of course, I'll attempt to locate the other people in the segment on the off chance that they might remember talking to Michael. Then I'll gather positive identification by expert bone structure comparison based on a freeze frame from the footage and photographs of Michael. Once everything's in order, it should be a simple matter to take this clearly exculpatory evidence—evidence that wasn't available at the time of Michael's conviction—and petition for a new trial."

"It's that complicated?" Professor Zimmer looked dazed.

"I'm afraid so. Let's just hope we can keep this thing under our hats until we have everything we need. It would be a terrible thing if the press got wind of it."

"It would?"

"Yes." Stan sighed deeply. "You see, Professor Zimmer, my brother's a patient at the Oakdale State Hospital. He had a complete psychotic breakdown shortly after his conviction."

"Oh, my!" Professor Zimmer blinked. "I'm so terribly sorry, Mr. Gerhardt."

"It was rough for a while, but they tell me he's doing much better now, finally adjusting to his incarceration. I wouldn't want to raise his hopes prematurely and then have them dashed again because we were turned down on some technicality. I'm afraid that he might . . . well . . . "I'd rather not go into that. Suffice to say, it would be kinder for Michael if he didn't know anything about this until it's a fait accompli."

"Of course, I understand perfectly. Mr. Gerhardt."

Stan cleared his throat. "And that's why I'm a bit concerned about the other juror, the one who saw the tape. If he or she mentions—"

"You can relax about that, Mr. Gerhardt," Professor Zimmer interrupted. "The other juror won't say a word."

"Yes, but perhaps it might be wise if I paid a call to stress the importance of—"

"No, I'll take care of it. You have my word that this matter will remain completely confidential. Now I've taken up enough of your valuable time. Goodbye, Mr. Gerhardt."

Professor Zimmer stood up and headed for the door. Stan opened his mouth to try for the juror's name again, but he didn't have time to say a thing before the professor was gone.

CHAPTER 4

Oakdale State Hospital

Michael Hart blinked his eyes as someone unlocked the door. The sheet they had fastened around him permitted no other movement. He was in a padded cell, flat on his back in a hospital bed.

"Hi, Mike. Feeling better?"

It was Jack. Michael felt better immediately. The big barrel-chested orderly had been at Oakdale almost as long as he had, and he was Michael's only real friend.

"Aw, for Christ's sake! They got you trussed up like a Christmas turkey. They must have figured you'd bang yourself up after I left last night. Hold still and let me get them restraints off you."

"Thanks, Jack." Michael's voice came out in a whispery croak. His throat felt sore, as if he'd been shouting for hours, and he was unbearably thirsty. He tried to lick his lips, but there seemed to be no saliva left in his body.

"You're pretty thirsty, huh?" Jack lifted something from his forehead, and Michael found he could nod. "Okay now, Mike. Don't try to talk. It'll just make your throat hurt. I'll get you some juice just as soon as I take off this other stuff."

It felt as if a great weight were removed from his chest as Jack lifted off the sheet. Another weight disappeared from his ankles, and finally his arms.

"That crabby nurse with the glasses gave you one of them yellow pills. Isn't that right, Mike?"

Michael opened his mouth to answer, but his throat was so sore he couldn't force out the word.

"That's okay. You don't have to talk. Just nod your head."

Michael nodded, and Jack sighed loudly. "I don't know where they find 'em, Mike. Maybe they dig 'em out from under old rocks someplace. Now, I'll tell you something, and it's God's truth. The only reason she gave you that pill was so you wouldn't pee the bed. Too lazy to change it. She didn't give a fiddler's damn about you, Mike. What d'ya say we slip one in her coffee and see how she likes it?"

Michael managed to laugh, even though it hurt. Jack really cared about him. Why weren't the orderlies paid as well as the doctors? They were a lot nicer, and they spent more time with the patients.

"Okay, Mike, I'm going to get that juice. Just lie there calm and easy, and don't try to get up until I can help you. I sneaked a look at your chart, and they shot you up with all kinds of drugs. You're going to feel like you went off on a cheap drunk last night."

The door closed, and Michael shut his eyes again. Jack was right. His head was pounding, and he felt sick to his stomach. It was a massive hangover, and he hadn't even had the pleasure of raising a glass. What had he done? It must have been something serious.

The door opened, and Jack was back. Michael struggled to a sitting position with the orderly's help and swallowed as Jack held a glass to his lips. Naturally, the glass wasn't glass. Only paper cups were used at Oakdale.

Michael made a face as he swallowed. Jack saw him and grinned.

"I know, I know. It tastes bad. Tomato juice with an egg in it and a handful of pepper. It's my daddy's hangover cure. When you can swallow better, I got a couple of Bayer's in my pocket. I lifted 'em from the nurse's lounge."

Michael nodded and took another swallow. Jack was an expert at expediting procedures. If Jack had gone through normal channels and asked the nurse for an aspirin, it would be tomorrow before Michael got it.

"Ready yet? The sooner you take 'em the sooner they can work."

Michael forced down the two aspirins. Jack's daddy's hangover remedy seemed to be working. His throat didn't feel so raw now. Perhaps the pepper burned out his pain receptors. He finished it off in one gulp and handed the paper cup to Jack.

"Good for you, Mike. Now just sit there a minute until your head starts to clear. One good thing about all them shots they gave you. You were out for the count, so you couldn't of dreamed your nightmare. Isn't that right?"

Michael nodded. If he'd had the nightmare, at least he couldn't remember it now. It always started with the courtroom, when the judge came in and banged his gavel. Then he rose to his feet. The jury had reached a verdict. Their faces were huge and hard, like sculptures of the presidents at Mount

Rushmore. Their eyes were flat, gleaming stones that accused him. Guilty. Guilty. Guilty. Over and over. How could they say that? They were wrong! Then he was moving, hurtling over the rail in one soaring leap, right into the jury box.

Michael forced his mind to back off, away from the nightmare. That was the point where he always woke up. And found himself not in bed, but somewhere else. The first time it had been in the hallway, only steps from the nurse's station. And then outside the dayroom, trying to get through the locked door. And once he'd been in the janitor's closet with all the mops and the brooms. Somnambulism, the doctors called it, their name for sleepwalking. That was why they gave him the nightly medication. To keep him from killing the jurors in his sleep.

At first, they'd tried something called reality therapy. They'd told him the dream wasn't right, that things hadn't really happened that way. They'd gone over it hundreds of times, the jury coming in, the judge banging his gavel, the foreman reading the verdict. They'd said he'd stood there beside his attorney, Stan. He hadn't moved at all until the two uniformed officers had snapped the handcuffs around his wrists and led him away. The part about hurtling over the rail had never happened. It was just what he'd wanted to do.

"Mike? Are you all right?"

Michael blinked hard and nodded. "Yes, I'm fine now. Do you know what I did, Jack? I mean, I must have done something terrible to end up in the rubber room."

Jack grinned. "Oh, you were impressive, from what I heard. The whole staff's buzzing. There's quite a few that think they should of given you a medal, but I guess Dr. Bowman doesn't see it that way."

"Bowman? Oh, Now I remember. I was up for review. And Bowman did something that made me so mad. What was it, Jack?"

"I don't know, Mike. I wasn't there. I just know what Mrs. Gray said. Bowman was trying to break you down so you'd say you killed your wife. From what I hear, he got real nasty, and you just sprang out of your chair and wrapped your hands around his scrawny neck. Surprised the hell out of everyone, except for Mrs. Gray. She said it took three guys to pry you loose."

"So now I'm in Dutch with Dr. Bowman?"

"I guess!" Jack shook his head. "But if I was you, I wouldn't let it worry me. The word's out that Bowman's gone. Any day now."

"He's leaving?"

"I guess you could put it that way." Jack chuckled. "My buddy on Ward C says your brother's here, raising all kinds of hell. He's been asking some real interesting questions, and lots of people are talking. He spent over an hour with Mrs. Gray, and then he went straight to the head nurse on Ward C. You remember her, don't you, Mike? The one that had the run-in with Bowman last year? She damn near got fired over them cakes."

Michael nodded He remembered her. She'd brought in little cupcakes in silver paper whenever there was a birthday. And star-shaped cookies at Christmas with red and green sugar on the top. She'd talked to him as if he were a real person, not crazy at all. And she'd made him believe it. She'd been the only reason he'd made it past Ward C.

"Believe me, Mike. There are people lining up for

a word with your brother. You can take it from me. Bowman's history.

"That's good. Jack. Is Stan coming up here?"

"Of course he is. Your brother wouldn't come to Oakdale without seeing you. You know that, Mike. Now what d'ya say we get you up and back to your regular room?"

"I'm sorry, Stan. I didn't mean to drag you all the way out here."

Stan reached out to pat Michael's back. "I was coming anyway. Don't worry about that. How do you feel?"

"Better, but I don't know how much longer I can take it, Stan. I mean, being locked up like this. They're not going to let me go. Ever!"

"Easy, Mikey. I hear what you're saying. I've already taken steps to see that Bowman is transferred. And when the new guy comes in—"

"That's not it, Stan." Michael took a deep breath. "I'm grateful you got me a place here. You know that. But it's almost worse than prison. At least there, I'd be up for parole. You don't know what it's like, sitting here day after day, staring at the same wall. If I stay here much longer, I'll be just as crazy as they say I am!"

"Mikey?" Stan leaned a little closer. "Keep your voice down and answer me. If I get you out of here, will you do everything I say?"

It took a moment for Stan's words to sink in. Then Michael nodded emphatically. "You know I will, Stan. But how can you?"

"I'll work out the details and get back to you." Stan put his fingers to his lips. "You'll be hearing from me in a day or two. Meanwhile, don't say a word, not to anyone. Do you promise?"

"Yes! But Stan . . . are you talking about a legal way, or—"

"That doesn't have to concern you at the moment, Mike. Trust me; I'll take care of everything. All you have to do is keep your mouth shut and be a model patient for the next couple of days. Can you do that?"

"Of course."

"Good!" Stan patted his brother on the shoulder and got up. "I'd better get going, Mike. There are a lot of things to arrange. Remember not a word. Not even to that orderly friend of yours."

Michael frowned as the door closed behind his brother. What did Stan have in mind? He was still trying to figure it out when Jack came in, an hour later with his dinner tray.

"Here you go, Mike. Its slops again tonight. They told me it's supposed to be creamed chicken on biscuits, and there's a pile of soggy cauliflower there on the side. But at least you got your favorite for dessert. Vanilla pudding."

Michael looked down at the food in disgust. White food. Everything on his tray was white. You could go snow-blind eating this stuff. What he wouldn't give for a greasy cheeseburger from one of those fast food places! Or maybe a plate of crispy French fries, and a chilidog. Well, he wouldn't have to eat Oakdale's food much longer if Stan came through. And Stan had always come through in the past.

"You look happy, Mike." Jack stuck a straw in a paper container of white milk. "Did you have a good visit with your brother?"

Michael opened his mouth to let Jack in on his

good news, but then he remembered. Not a word to anyone, not even Jack.

"Yes, he was here for a long time, Jack. And he promised to bring me some new shirts."

"The kind with them little alligators on the pockets?"

Michael nodded. "Stan says they've got a new line. With stripes."

"That's real nice, Mike. Gives you something to look forward to. Now eat that chicken or whatever it is. I gotta finish up with you fast tonight. That crabby nurse is on the warpath, and she thinks I spend too much time in here."

Michael shoveled some chicken into his mouth and swallowed. It didn't require chewing. In less than five minutes, he'd eaten everything on his tray.

Jack picked up the dishes and stood up. "Okay, Mike. Tomorrow's my day off, but I'll see you the next day, huh?"

Michael nodded. "Jack? You saved my life, you know. You're the only reason I'm here and not up on Ward D with the terminals."

"Aw, that's not true, Mike. There's lots of nice people here. Just wait until you get down to Ward A. They have dances, parties, and all that social stuff. And the nurses—" Jack stepped closer to the bed— "they're foxes, Mike. And I hear they got a real special way of rewarding good behavior, if you catch my meaning. Now, don't do anything foolish tomorrow. No black marks on your chart. Okay?"

"Okay Jack."

As the door clicked shut, Michael smiled. He'd miss Jack, but it would be wonderful to be out in the world again. And maybe, just maybe, he'd already be gone when Jack got back from his day off.

CHAPTER 5

James Zimmer pulled into his parking space in the faculty lot at Gateway University and shut off the engine of his gray Mazda. He'd purchased the car after a thorough review of the automotive section in Consumer Guide. Now the Mazda was almost ten years old, and it had never needed any major work. Some of the other faculty members had newer cars, but Professor Zimmer had decided the new prices were ridiculous. With proper maintenance, a car could last indefinitely.

There was a spring to the professor's step as he crossed the campus and headed for his office. A stolen hour with his lover always put him in a light-hearted mood. He'd gone there to discuss the footage and the need for complete secrecy, but that had taken only a few moments. Then they'd shared a glass of excellent Chardonnay and ended up in bed.

The square, in the center of the sprawling campus contained a lovely stonework cathedral. Gateway University was a religious institution. Professor Zimmer was sobered as he walked past the massive spires. If the administration ever found out about his lover, he'd be discharged for moral turpitude. No one could know, not even Mr. Gerhardt. That was why he'd refused to give the name of the other juror.

Once the cathedral was behind him, it was only a few steps to his office. Professor Zimmer climbed the stairs to the second floor and unlocked his door. Dorothy had left things spotless, as usual. The only item on the polished surface of her secretarial desk was a folder containing his airplane tickets and a neatly typed schedule of the meetings he was expected to attend.

Professor Zimmer turned on the lights in his private office and drew the blinds. No sense advertising his presence on campus. A passing student might see his light and drop in for an unscheduled conference. Normally he would have been receptive, but he didn't have much time to make his flight.

It took no more than fifteen minutes to collect the notes and materials he needed. Each subject was in a separate folder, clearly marked. They went into his briefcase, alphabetically for easy access, and then he was ready to go.

One last look around his office, and he reached out to turn off the light. Then he stopped, his fingers touching the switch, and sighed. The original footage of Mr. Michael Hart, the footage the station had given him, was in plain sight on his bookcase. Had he mentioned that the DVD he'd given to Mr. Gerhardt was a copy?

Professor Zimmer picked it up and started to put it in his briefcase. It would be best to take it with him for safekeeping, but that wasn't a valid option. One of his colleagues had come back from a trip with an audio tape of a lecture series in his carry-on luggage. When he'd attempted to play the lectures for his class, the audio had been garbled. It seemed that the scanners at the airport had been out of adjustment and damaged his tapes.

A desk drawer? Professor Zimmer pulled out his top drawer and hesitated. Dorothy always straightened his office while he was gone, and she might misplace the tape. There had to be a better place. If he'd had more time, he'd take it home for safekeeping, but that might make him late for his flight.

Professor Zimmer frowned. It was possible Mr. Gerhardt might need the original tape for evidence. These legal matters were so complicated. It was up to him to safeguard the footage while he was gone.

Suddenly, the professor smiled. Of course! So simple, and yet perfectly reasonable. It would take only a few minutes to secure the tape, and then he could be on his way.

Michael stifled a groan as the laundry cart was loaded roughly onto the truck. So far, so good. Stan's plan was working perfectly. When the nurse had given him his pill, he'd tucked it under his tongue and gulped the little paper cup of water. All gone. Yes indeed! He'd opened his mouth at her command, but she hadn't checked under his tongue. From the nurses' station, he'd gone to the lavatory, where he'd flushed the pill down the toilet. The pipes would sleep well tonight. No nightmares.

From the crack under his door, he'd been able to watch the nurses leave for their nine o'clock break. The pretty one with long red hair had been alone at the desk, reading a romance novel. Getting out of his room had been simple. Since he was a medicated patient who always slept like a zombie for at least eight hours, they never bothered to lock his door. He'd slipped out of his room, ducked past the nurse's station, and tiptoed down the hall to the laundry room.

This was the night for bedding. Piles of heavy sheets and blankets had been stuffed in the huge rolling carts. Michael climbed into an empty one and pulled a pile of soiled bedding on top of him.

The laundry men had come at ten to take the bedding. Michael had held his breath as two burly men wheeled him through the silent halls to the loading dock. And now he was inside of the belly of the truck, as snug as a bug in his evil-smelling cocoon.

The truck changed gears, and Michael winced. It was a rough ride, but they didn't expect to have passengers back here. There was a bump, another grind of the gears, and the truck slowed and stopped. They were at Alma's Café. Stan had told him that the driver always stopped there for a cup of coffee and a piece of Alma's apple pie.

The driver's door opened and banged shut. Michael heard the sound of footsteps crunching on gravel, and then it was very quiet. The driver's girlfriend worked at Alma's. He would be inside for at least fifteen minutes. All Michael had to do was get out of the cart and feel his way to the sliding back door. The driver never bothered to lock it. Who'd want to steal dirty sheets?

Michael's foot slipped as he got out of the cart and banged against the metal side of the truck. He crouched and froze. Had someone heard? He counted to a hundred, then two hundred just to make certain, but no one sounded the alarm. It was difficult to crawl through the darkness, feeling his way past the laundry carts. It seemed to take forever, but at last, his fingers touched the metal handle on the door. Freedom was just on the other side.

With trembling hands, Michael gripped the handle and lifted. Nothing happened. The door was locked! Michael forced himself to think positive. Stan hadn't been wrong about anything yet. Perhaps it was just stuck. He squatted and put his back to it, lifting up with all his strength. The door gave a protesting squeal, but it rose—only a few inches, but he had better leverage now.

Michael lifted again, and the door rose at least a foot. At last, he could see the outside! Silently, carefully he peeked through the opening. A big neon sign was directly across from the truck. It blinked on and off, "Alma's Café" in red and "Good Eats" in green. He could see the plate-glass door clearly, but no one was coming or going. He stuck his head out cautiously and glanced to the right. A camper. No one was sitting inside. To the left, three cars down, was a dark blue Ford. There was a cap hanging over the rearview mirror, and Michael's heart began to pound in excitement. It was the car Stan had rented for him.

Michael got down on his belly and slithered through the opening. No sense making any more noise. It was a drop of four feet to the pavement. The moment his feet touched the asphalt, his first instinct was to run. Stan had warned him of that. Don't do it, Stan hand told him. Stand there and

close the door. That way the driver will never know
he helped you to escape.

It seemed to take an eternity, but at last, the door
was latched shut. His heart racing wildly, Michael
walked toward the Ford. Walk, don't run. Stan had
cautioned him. Don't be conspicuous, whatever
you do.

The driver's door was unlocked. Michael opened
it and slid in behind the wheel. The keys were under
the mat, right where Stan had said they'd be. And
the map with his destination would be in the glove
box compartment, but Michael didn't have the
nerve to look now. He wanted to get miles away
before he pulled over to check.

Michael fit the key in the ignition and turned it.
The engine coughed once and then caught. Would
he remember how to drive? It had been ten years.

A moment later, he was pulling out of the lot and
onto the freeway. Driving must be like riding a bicycle, once you learned it, you never forgot. But he
had to keep the speedometer at fifty-five, no faster.
Even though Stan had promised to put a wallet with
phony identification in the glove box next to the
map, he didn't want to get pulled over for speeding.

The traffic was light, and after an uneventful ten
miles, Michael began to feel comfortable with the
car. He switched on the radio, expecting to hear a
song by a voice he recognized like Usher, or Alicia
Keys, but the music had changed in the ten years
he'd spent away from the world. It made him feel
strange and alien, like stepping into a time warp.

At least the freeway signs were still the same,
green with white letters. Michael braked as a car cut
into his lane, a new kind he'd never seen before. It

looked like a prototype, but it probably wasn't. Styles changed a lot in ten years. He felt a little like Rip Van Winkle as he kept his eye on his speed and drove along in the slow lane.

What else had changed? Would someone tell him what had happened to Tony on The Sopranos? How about Desperate Housewives? Was Marcia Cross still as sexy as she'd been when he'd seen her on the set in . . . no, he'd better not think of that. Could he fit into this new world? Could he blend in so well that no one would guess he'd been behind locked doors for the past ten years? He'd have to be very careful not to slip up. He still hadn't found out who was president. How would the driver in the next lane react if he said he didn't know the president's name?

Michael realized he had a death grip on the wheel. He had to find a way to relax. Pity he didn't smoke. A cigarette might help, but he'd never developed the habit. He'd didn't drink much either, so he'd just have to think himself into a calmer state. Take things as they came. Not borrow trouble. One day at a time. Those were terrible clichés, but they had a basis in fact. And if that didn't work, he'd think about Stan. His brother believed he could pull it off, or he wouldn't have gone to all this trouble.

Perhaps some music would help—his kind of music, not the new sounds that made his head hurt. Michael turned the radio dial until he found a station that advertised easy rock. He actually recognized the first song he heard. It had been popular during his last year in Los Angeles and he began to feel better. Yes, he could fit in. He'd been a fool to doubt himself. He was an actor, wasn't he? All the best actors were students of human behavior. He'd just observe other people and copy their reactions. Then he'd know what to do.

The song segued into Earth, Wind and Fire, and Michael smiled as he listened to "Got to Get You Into My Life," "September," and "After the Love Has Gone." Music had the power to calm the savage beast, or the savage breast, whichever it was. They really ought to use music at Oakdale. Perhaps, when Stan had managed to clear him completely, he'd write a letter to suggest it. He was certainly qualified to speak from the patient's point of view. They might just listen if someone who had been there told them what was wrong and how they could fix it.

Michael drove for more than three hours before the signs for Los Angeles began to appear. Things were beginning to look familiar. Just as soon as he got past the Santa Monica interchange, he'd pull over and study the map for his destination.

There was the turnoff for Ventura Boulevard. And after that Mulholland. The engine purred as the car climbed through the pass, and Michael began to feel euphoric. This was home. As he reached the crest and came down on the other side, the city spread out in front of him like a jewel box filled with glittering gems.

Michael rolled down the window and let out a whoop that disappeared in the wind rushing past the car. Free! He was free! No one to tell him what time to go to bed, no one to dictate what he would eat, or pick out which clothes he would wear. Stan was the most wonderful brother in the world!

CHAPTER 6

Stan swiped the phone card he'd bought and dialed the number. It was eight o'clock in the morning, the day after Michael's escape. He was standing at a wall-phone near the restrooms in Denny's Restaurant, five blocks from his office. Denny's was not Stan's usual habitat. The chain of inexpensive coffee shops had made their reputation by advertising good, cheap breakfasts. Two eggs cooked to order, bacon or sausage; toast and hash browns, all for under five dollars.

The smell of sizzling bacon made Stan feel queasy. He avoided bacon completely. Too much grease, and the smoking process was questionable, to say the least. His normal breakfast was a bowl of high-fiber cereal with half a chopped banana and six ounces of nonfat milk. Stan had become religious about watching his cholesterol, his fiber, and his carbohydrates. In his business, men in their forties were known to have massive heart attacks. Stress was the main factor, of course, but a proper diet played an important role in prevention.

He shifted from foot to foot as he waited for Michael to answer. He couldn't take the chance of calling from his apartment or office. The news of Michael's escape had broken an hour ago, and he had to take every precaution. It was a good thing he'd picked up the rental car and dropped it off at the agency last night. They would have no way of knowing what time it had come in, and they certainly wouldn't be suspicious. Gerhardt, Merrill, and Davis had a corporate account with the rental agency to provide transportation for out-of-town clients.

Stan gave an audible sigh of relief when his brother answered the phone. "Mikey? How are you doing?"

"Just fine, Stan. Do they know I escaped yet?"

"That's one of the reasons I called. I want you to stay inside, behind locked doors, until I tell you it's safe to go out. No sense taking chances, right?"

"Right. When do you think that'll be, Stan?"

Stan sighed. "I can't promise anything at the moment, but the wheels are in motion. I've got a meeting with Judge Strickland this morning to go over the new evidence."

"The footage you told me about?"

"That's right. But don't expect anything to happen overnight. These things take time. We both know you'll be cleared eventually, but it could take as long as a month or two. And don't forget, Mike— if the police apprehend you, they'll ship you right back to Oakdale."

"I'll stay in, Stan. I promise. But when can I see you?"

"Not for a while." Stan sighed. "Naturally, they'll

assume you'll try to contact me. And that means they'll watch me like a hawk. Let's set up a time for a daily call. How about nine o'clock every evening? That's not too late for you, is it?"

"No, that's fine. But won't they tap your phones?"

"Good thinking, Mikey." Stan had raised his eyebrows. He hadn't expected his brother to be reasoning that clearly. "I'll call from a different phone each night. But don't call me, whatever you do. Got it?"

"Okay, Stan. You're the boss."

"I've got to run, Mikey. Judge Strickland won't be very receptive if I'm late for the meeting. Now stay inside, and if you need anything at all, just tell me and I'll make arrangements to have it delivered. Check?"

"Check. Stan? The apartment's great, and the clothes all fit, and—well, thanks, Stan, for everything."

"Don't mention it, Mikey. I ordered a bunch of movies, so you can play catch-up. And if you want to read, there's a shelf in the bedroom with the latest novels. Now, I've got to run. You take it easy, and I'll talk to you again at nine tonight."

Stan hung up the phone and glanced around. No one seemed to be watching him. He thought about going to the men's room, but that could wait until he got to the office. Denny's facilities were undoubtedly adequate, but he preferred the luxurious surroundings of his own executive bathroom.

After his conversation with Stan had ended, Michael assessed his reflection in the mirror. He hadn't slept well without his medication, and the king-size bed had felt too large. Despite his lack of sleep, and his nerve-wracking escape from the hospital, he thought he looked better than he had in a long time. Freedom had visibly changed him. The slack, hangdog look of despair that had pulled down his features had disappeared. It was a brand new life, and he was ready to live it to the fullest. Stan had told him about the video, the man-on-the-street interview that had never been aired. He still didn't remember the details of the night, but now he understood his reaction at Oakdale when he'd pictured a man with a microphone shoved in his face. From what Stan had said, he was still a prisoner, in a sense, but his surroundings were palatial compared with his small hospital room at Oakdale. And as soon as Stan had positively identified him as the man on the tape, he'd truly be free.

Was it time for his shower? Michael laughed out loud as he realized that there was no longer a regulated time for his shower. And he could stay under the spray as long as he liked. None of the old get wet, soap up, rinse off, step out routine for the man who was now known as Mike Kruger from Cleveland. He was free to act just like a regular person.

Even though he knew that there was no one watching to see how long he took, Michael finished his shower in the allotted five minutes. Old habits die hard. He dried himself on a fluffy green towel, the first colored towel he'd seen in years, and put on the blue warm-up suit he'd found hanging in the closet. A pair of brand new Reeboks in his size were nestled in a shoebox on the shelf, and he found dozens of pairs of expensive athletic socks in the dresser drawer. It was a pity that no one could see him. Not only could he act like a regular person; now he looked just like a regular person.

Michael figured he could get used to this kind of
life. It would be a lazy day, no appointments with
his caseworker, and no interviews with the reality
therapist. His stomach growled, and Michael headed
for the kitchen. He was hungry, ravenously hungry.
He hadn't eaten since his dinner at Oakdale, and
when he'd arrived at the apartment last night, he'd
been too exhausted to even think about food.

His mouth began to water as he opened the door
and saw the array of food his brother had provided.
Sliced ham, roast beef, and turkey breast, all
wrapped in see-through plastic. A whole wheel of
Brie, his favorite cheese, plus cheddar, and Jarls-
burg, and Monterey Jack. There was a jar of
Gulden's brown mustard, the kind he loved, and
deli pickles. He'd make himself a triple-decker sandwich and go to the living room to eat it. Maybe he'd
catch the morning news or whatever daytime soaps
were popular now. Attention Ward B patients.
Michael Hart can eat while he's watching television!

There was a huge loaf of crusty rye on the counter,
and Michael put together a massive sandwich. Paper
plates were in the cupboard, right where he'd expected them, and there was a built-in microwave
over the stove. Michael cut his sandwich, covered it
with a piece of paper towel from the wooden holder
on the wall, and nuked it for forty-five seconds.
Perfect. Now all he needed was a pickle and something to drink. Stan had laid in a supply of root beer,
his favorite soda.

Ten minutes later, there was nothing left but
crumbs. Michael realized he'd forgotten to carry his
sandwich into the living room and sighed. Old
habits again. He put the plate in the garbage, wiped

off the counter, and poured the rest of his root beer into a glass, a real glass. Then he carried it to the living room, sat down on the couch, and clicked on the television set with the remote control.

Jeopardy was on and the host was still Alex Trebek. He didn't really look any older although Michael knew he must be. Perhaps this was a rerun. Michael wasn't sure. He hadn't seen it before and it was new to him.

Michael leaned forward as the program was interrupted by a news flash. This was what he'd been waiting for, the news of his escape. They'd probably flash his picture and warn everyone that he was considered dangerous.

A picture appeared on the screen, and Michael frowned. A fire in Santa Monica? This wasn't what he'd expected at all! He knew it was crazy, but he felt vaguely disappointed. He'd expected to be the center of attention, and his escape wasn't even important enough to interrupt *Jeopardy*!

Michael shut off the television and headed back to the kitchen to heat himself a cup of instant coffee. If he hadn't made the news by now, he probably wouldn't. But the sense of being an unimportant cog in a giant wheel stuck with him as he waited for his coffee to heat. In the confined world of Oakdale, events had seemed to revolve around him. There were Michael Hart's medications, Michael Hart's meals, and Michael Hart's time for therapy. But the real world was huge, and there were other, more important events. Out here, no one except Stan even knew or cared that Michael Hart existed. It was a sobering dose of reality.

* * *

Antonia Novak stood in the hallway, staring at the closed door to apartment 301. She was waiting for her best friend in the building. Doris Evans, so they could go for their morning jog.

The door to the stairwell opened, and Doris came barreling through. She was in her forties, with frizzy blond hair, and this morning she was dressed in a bright yellow warm-up suit that made her look like a very plump grapefruit. Doris had taken up jogging last year on her doctor's advice. She'd lost a few pounds, but it was an uphill battle. Doris claimed all the exercise just made her hungrier.

"Hi, Toni. Have you seen him yet?"

Toni laughed and shook her head. Doris was the unofficial information network for the building. She knew almost everything about everybody, and this morning she'd called to say that someone had moved into apartment 301, right across the hall from Toni.

"No one's come out, Doris, but I've only been here for a couple of minutes. How do you know he's a *he*?

"By the footsteps. They were too heavy for a woman." Doris bent over and started to do her stretching exercises. "I took some cookies down to Mrs. Ryskind in 201, and we both heard him. If we find out he's single, and he turns out to be nice, I think you should try to make friends."

"Forget it, Doris." Toni grinned as she took the rubber band off her wrist and pulled her long red hair back in a ponytail. "You're always trying to set me up, and it never works out. I'm perfectly content the way I am."

Doris nodded. "That's what you say now, but think about the future. You're not getting any younger, and you haven't even lived yet. It's not natural for you to stay cooped up in your apartment with only your computer for company. You've got to be lonely."

"Okay, maybe I am. End of lecture, Doris. Now let me stretch, and let's get started. I've got a lot of work to do today."

Doris raised her eyebrows as Toni began her exercises. This was the first time Toni had ever admitted that she was lonely, and it was a step in the right direction. Toni was an attractive woman, but she never dated. Doris had a theory about that. Since Toni's mother had died when she was quite young, no one had taught her feminine wiles. All Toni really needed was a couple of lessons on how to catch a man, and she'd be just fine. It was a good thing Doris was around to teach her.

As he sat at the table, enjoying his coffee, Michael decided that even instant tasted great. Caffeine had been restricted at Oakdale, and coffee and tea were forbidden fare for patients. He could understand that sort of restriction if there were medical reasons, but it was depressing to wake up to a gloomy day at the hospital without something hot and comforting to drink for breakfast. Cold juice or cold milk as the first beverage in the morning just wasn't right. Why hadn't they thought to serve decaffeinated coffee? Or even hot chocolate? He felt it would give the patients a lift.

The unfamiliar caffeine gave Michael's system a real jolt, and he decided to make himself useful. The paper from the pickles made the whole kitchen smell like the inside of a deli. It was a nice smell, but normal people carried out their garbage every day. If he remembered correctly, he'd passed an incinerator slot by the elevator door when he'd come in last night.

The metal door was there, right where he'd remembered it. Michael dropped his bag inside and listened to it slide down the tube and hit the hopper in the basement. He was about to close the door when someone shouted.

"Hello, there!"

Michael turned to see a plump blond woman dressed in a blinding yellow warm-up suit. She was smiling, and he smiled back. Then he noticed the woman who was with her, and his smile widened. The second woman was gorgeous. She was much younger, and she had long red hair. Not even the baggy grey sweatsuit she was wearing could hide her delectable shape.

"New tenant?"

Michael nodded. He didn't trust his voice. The older woman had asked the question, but Michael couldn't seem to stop staring at her companion, who was jogging in place.

Her whole body was jiggling, and it took an effort to tear his eyes away from certain parts of her anatomy. He guessed that was because he hadn't seen a woman in anything other than a white's nurse's uniform for years. Everyone wore uniforms at Oakdale, even the maintenance people. It was a convenient way to set the staff apart from the patients.

"You're in 301?"

Michael nodded again. The younger woman was wearing a perfume he thought he recognized. Channel No. 5? No, that wasn't right, but whatever it was, it certainly made him feel very short of breath. The women on the staff at Oakdale hadn't worn perfume. It was against the rules.

"You must be the strong silent type, Right?"

Michael nodded for the third time, and the older woman laughed.

"Well, you may not be much on conversation, but at least you jog. Good shoes, those Reeboks. And I like your warm-up suit. It's that new lightweight material isn't it? I like a man who's serious about his workouts. Most of the people in this building think that physical fitness mean driving to pick up their pizza instead of having it delivered. Were you looking for the track?"

Michael nodded again. He really couldn't force out a word with the younger woman so close.

"There's one two blocks from here, but they haven't resurfaced it in years. I'll show you our personal two-mile circuit instead. My name is Doris Evans, from 408. And this is Antonia Novak, apartment 305. You can call her Toni. Now, what do we call you?"

"Mike, My name is Mike Kruger." Michael gave the name on the phony identification Stan had provided.

"Nice. I like it. Michael means 'honorable' in Hebrew. Of course, you probably already knew that. Most people know what their name means. Mine means 'sea goddess' in Greek, but I haven't let it go to my head. Come on then, Mike Kruger, do your stretching and then we'll go."

Before Michael could think of an excuse. Doris had him going through a series of stretching exercises right there in the hallway. As she supervised his routine, she asked more questions.

"Are you married, Mike?"

"No. I'm single."

"So is Toni. I've been married for twenty years to the only man who'll put up with me. My husband is a man of infinite patience. Are you new to this area, Mike?"

Michael was about to shake his head, but he caught himself just in time. Mike Kruger had an Ohio driver's license.

"I just moved here from Cleveland."

"You'll love California, Mike. It's a paradise compared to the Midwest or the East. Of course, it always takes time to get used to a new area, so if you need to know where something is, just ask me. Or you can ask Toni. Isn't that right, Toni?"

Toni looked surprised, but she nodded. "Of course. I'd be glad to help."

Michael felt a pleasant jolt as he heard Toni's voice, for the first time. It was warm but slightly tentative. He could tell she wasn't as outgoing as Doris.

"Put your hands down a little lower, Mike." Doris gestured. "Now lean against the wall and extend. You have to get the kinks out before we start. So what do you do, Mike?"

Michael froze, what did he do? Luckily, Doris jumped in before he had time to think of an answer.

"No, don't tell me, let me guess. If you were a businessman, you'd be at work right now, so that's not it. And you don't have calluses on your hands. That rules out manual labor. You're not suntanned, so you work inside. And you watch people intently, especially Toni, but that's understandable. She's pretty, isn't she?"

Michael laughed and nodded. Doris didn't pull any punches. He glanced at Toni and noticed she was blushing, but she looked amused. Good. She had a sense of humor.

"Okay, Mike. Switch to the other leg. You're almost ready to run. Now, back to the subject of what you do. I get the feeling that not much escapes you, and that makes you a student of human behavior. You don't look like a school teacher, because you're not burned out. And I can't see you as a doctor or a dentist. I know! I bet you're either an artist or a writer."

Michael latched onto her suggestion. Not an artist. She might want to see some of his work.

"You're right. Doris. I'm working on a novel."

"I knew it! And you work at home?"

Michael nodded and Doris beamed. "That's wonderful! Toni and I work at home, too. I do custom sewing for a local designer. Toni? Tell Mike what you do."

"I'm a computer researcher."

Toni stepped a little closer, and Michael felt his heart beat faster. Since she didn't seem inclined to elaborate, he searched for something to say.

"I'm afraid I don't know much about computers, Toni. What kind do you have?"

Toni began to smile as she described a laptop with a second external hard drive with a graphics card that was on the cloud and hooked up to her hotspot. Mike didn't have the slightest idea what she was talking about, but he noticed that she didn't seem shy at all when she was describing the equipment she used for work.

As soon as Toni stopped speaking, Doris reached out to grab his hand. "Okay, Mike. Let's go get some exercise."

Then, before he even had time to catch his breath, Michael was jogging down the hallway between Doris and Toni, heading for the door to the stairs.

"Where do we go from here?" Michael slowed a little as they approached the door.

"Up one flight and past the four hundreds."

Doris led the way, running up the stairs backwards so she could continue to talk. Toni followed her, and Michael was treated to an even more enhanced view that thoroughly destroyed his breathing.

"In case you don't know, this building has seven floors. We don't bother with the first or the second. A couple of tenants down there have little dogs, and they always yap when somebody runs by. The hallways are six hundred and sixty feet long. We make a circuit, jog back to the starting point, and go up the stairs to the next floor. You're breathing heavy, Mike. Are you out of practice?"

Michael grunted his assent, and Doris gave him an encouraging smile.

"Don't worry about it. I'll have you back in shape in no time. Anyway, by the time we're back down on your floor, we've done exactly two miles. Not counting the stairs, of course. They're a bonus.

"That's nice."

"Nice? It's great!" Doris opened the door at the

top of the stairs and motioned him through. "That means we can jog every morning, rain or shine. And the hallways are heated in the winter and air-conditioned in the summer. It's an even seventy-six degrees, and we don't have to inhale the smog. It's a perfect surface for running, and no one's home after eight in the morning, so we don't disturb the tenants. I'm really glad you moved in, Mike. There are times when Toni and I feel like nuts doing this all by ourselves."

They were jogging past the four hundreds now. As they approached the end of the hall a door opened, and a uniformed policeman came out. Michael's heart jumped into his throat, and he turned his face away.

"Hi honey. Hello, Toni. Are you two girls ready to come down to the station and run my boys around the track?"

The two women stopped to jog in place, and Toni grabbed his hand, so he had to stop, too. Her fingers were firm yet soft. He'd forgotten what a real woman's hand felt like.

"Not unless you put us on the payroll." Doris laughed and kissed him. "Besides, your boys are so out of shape, they couldn't keep up with us."

"She always says that." The man winked at Michael. "This looks fairly serious with the hand-holding, Toni. Aren't you going to introduce me to your friend?"

"Oh!" Toni blushed and dropped Michael's hand. She looked thoroughly flustered. "I was only . . . never mind, Harry. Meet Mike Kruger. He just moved into 301, and he's from Cleveland. Mike, this is Captain Harry Evans, Doris's husband."

"Nice to meet you, Mike."

Harry held out his hand, and Michael could do nothing but shake it. It would have seemed strange if he'd turned tail and run.

"So fall in, Harry." Toni spoke up. "You haven't jogged with us in a long time."

Harry sighed. "I know, but I don't have the time right now. I've got to get down to the station. Some guy escaped from Oakdale last night, and there's a chance he might be headed our way."

Toni seemed interested. "What does he look like?"

"He's about Mike's height, and Doris thinks he looks like a young Robert DeNiro. Hold on, I've got his picture right here. They're going to run it on the evening news."

Harry handed Toni a picture, and she studied it carefully. Then she handed it to Michael.

Michael's hands were shaking as he took the photograph. There was no doubt that Harry was talking about him. But when he glanced down at the picture, he breathed an almost audible sigh of relief. It was his old mug shot, the one they'd taken when he was booked. And there was no comparison to the way he looked now, after all the surgery. The doctors had built him new cheekbones and changed the shape of his face when they'd reconstructed his nose. Michael had never thought he'd be grateful to the guys who'd smashed up his face in prison, but perhaps they'd done him a favor.

"Have you seen him, Mike?"

Harry was waiting for an answer, and Michael shook his head. He hadn't seen the face in the mug shot for almost ten years. Someone was definitely sleeping at the switch at the prison, at the hospital where the surgeries had been performed, or on the staff at Oakdale. Everyone was looking for the old Michael Hart, the man who had ceased to exist. If this picture was the only one the police had, he could walk right into the biggest precinct in Los Angeles and no one would give him a second glance.

CHAPTER 7

The rain had been coming down in sheets all afternoon and the gusty winds matched Margo Jantzen's mood perfectly. She was a hurricane looking for a place to destroy. It was already past six, and Lenny was over an hour late for their appointment.

The doorbell rang, and Margo got up to answer it, her high heels clicking against the tiles in an angry staccato rhythm. He'd better have a damn good excuse.

"What took you so long?" I told you it was urgent." There were high spots of color in Margo's cheeks as she confronted her ex-boss. How dare he treat her this way!

"So I'm here now."

Lenny brushed past her and tossed his navy blue coat on the couch. Margo winced as she noticed it was soaking wet. If the dye ran, her new white furniture would be ruined. She picked it up, holding it gingerly by the collar as she placed it in a less critical spot. With the money Lenny made, he ought to buy himself something decent. He still dressed like a street bum.

"Well? What did you want?"

Lenny stood there glaring at her, and Margo almost laughed. With his massive shoulders and his booming voice, he was glaringly out of place in the feminine room. A bull in a china shop, as her mother used to say. But she'd also used to warn Margo that you could catch more flies with honey than with vinegar.

Margo put on a smile as she led Lenny to the couch and tucked a pillow behind his back. "Sorry I was crabby, Lenny-bear. I guess I was worried about you. The traffic must be a mess with the rain and all."

"Okay, okay." Lenny didn't look like he was buying it, "Drop the phony stuff and get to the bottom line."

"I'm getting a little short of cash, Lenny-bear. It's time to make another deposit to my checking account."

Lenny shook his head. "The well's gone dry, Margo. Maybe you'd better go out and get yourself a job."

It was definitely time for Margo to go into her act. She knew the effect she had on Lenny when she pretended not to cry. He was a pushover, despite the bad reputation he had for being a tough guy. And Margo had learned just how to handle him. She'd been doing it for over five years now, ever since she discovered the evidence to expose his illegal sideline.

"Don't tease me, Lenny-bear." She pouted a bit, and her lower lip quivered. "If I took a regular job with regular hours, we couldn't have all those wonderful afternoons together."

Lenny's face was hard and set. "What wonderful afternoons? All you do is hit me up for more money. And don't be giving me that same old song and dance about those papers you got stashed away. I found a way to cut you off, and I'm doing it!"

Margo stared up into his unyielding face and felt the first stirrings of fear. What was he talking about? The papers she had could convict him!

"Come on, Lenny-bear. You know I love you. And I'd never use those papers. I promised you that."

"Sure you did. And pigs fly. But it's the end of the ride, babe. And if you're smart, you won't bother me again."

Margo began to panic as he got up and put on his coat. "Lenny! I don't understand!"

"Think about it real good, babe. And remember what I said. Nice girls, the kind that got plenty of smarts, don't get hurt."

Margo's mouth dropped open as the door slammed behind him. Then she jumped up and rushed to double-lock the door. He'd looked mean enough to kill her. Did he have an extra key? He'd bought this condominium for her, and she hadn't bothered to change the locks. She'd better call a locksmith immediately to put in a deadbolt. They'd charge her a fortune for working after hours, but it would be totally worth it. There was something terribly wrong. Lenny had never acted like this before.

After she'd called the locksmith, she hurried to the bedroom and pulled out the box of linens on the top shelf of the closet. Thank God, the papers were still there! Why hadn't she thought to put them in a safe deposit box? Anyone could break in and steal them.

Margo ran to the dresser and opened the top drawer. Maybe she was overreacting, but now she was glad she'd bought the gun.

It was already loaded and ready to use. The man at the store had showed her how. All she had to do was push the red button, point it in the right direction, and pull the trigger. If anyone tried to break in her door tonight, she'd shoot first and ask questions later.

Lenny let himself into his apartment and put the beer in the refrigerator. He'd bought a whole case. Eddie was coming over tonight, and they always went through a couple of six-packs talking about the old times when they were just starting out in Chicago. They were both respectable Southern California businessmen now. Eddie ran a big sports equipment outlet in the valley, and Lenny had his auto parts business. But you never got the streets of Chicago out of your blood. They both dabbled a little on the side.

Damn Margo! Lenny shrugged out of his coat and threw it over a chair. She was getting way out of hand. At least he'd scared the hell out of her, and that made him feel good. She didn't know it was all a bluff. He'd have to cough up some dough again in the end.

He grabbed a beer and turned on the television to catch the news. That Mexican guy was on with the weather, and there were loops and squiggles all over the map. He was saying it would rain tomorrow, so Lenny knew he could put away his umbrella. The weathermen were always wrong. You could make book on it.

The rain had been pouring down like a faucet this morning when Lenny had driven to work. Cars had been skidding and wiping out all over the freeway, but the weatherman on the radio had still been predicting a ten percent chance of showers. Lenny should have called the station and told that idiot to shut up and look out the damn window.

Lenny finished the beer and tossed the empty bottle in the case that was sitting by the couch. He felt like throwing it against the wall, but then he'd just have to clean up the broken glass before Eddie got here. Damn Margo for getting him in such a bad mood! She'd been real sweet when they'd started up, but lately she'd turned into a real liability. If she had her way, he'd be forking it over until the day he died. Or the day *she* died. Lenny sighed loudly. If he knew some muscle he could trust, he'd be tempted to have her hit.

A picture flashed on the screen, and Lenny leaned forward. It looked like Robert DeNiro in *The Godfather*, his favorite movie. The announcer said it was Michael Hart, a convicted murderer who'd escaped from Oakdale. They thought he might be in the L.A. area, and people were supposed to call in if they'd seen him. That name was familiar, Michael Hart.

It took a couple of minutes, but then Lenny remembered. The Hart trial, Margo had been working as his secretary then, and he'd had to excuse her for five weeks of jury duty. She hadn't developed all her fancy tastes back then, and she'd been real grateful to get an invite from the boss to have a beer and tell him all about the testimony she'd heard.

It had been like a puzzle with new pieces every day, and they'd worked it all out, all the evidence against the guy and how it had happened. Lenny had thought the story was better than a movie. The wife had gotten herself knocked up, and then she dumped on Hart. They'd had a big fight, so loud that the neighbors had heard it. Hart had slammed out and gone to a bar, where he'd had a few drinks to screw up his courage. Then he'd gone back home to murder his wife. Blam! One shot through the chest at close range. Hart's lawyer had tried to tell the jury that someone else had done it, but they hadn't swallowed it. Hart had no alibi, unless you counted that amnesia crap. And he'd been pretty stupid, too. He'd wiped the grip and the trigger before he'd ditched the gun in the dumpster behind his own apartment building, but his prints had been all over the cylinder.

Lenny had sort of hoped that Hart would get off. Wives dumped on their husbands every day, and they always got away with it. But he hadn't said that to Margo. She'd been hot for conviction. It was probably because the wife was pregnant. Women always reacted like crazy when there was a kid involved, even if the kid wasn't born yet.

He hoped Margo had heard the news. Lenny could see her now, sweating it out in the swanky condominium he'd bought her. The murderer she'd convicted was on the loose. Wouldn't it be something if Hart was carrying a grudge against the jury? Then Margo could be in big trouble. If Hart killed Margo, all Lenny's problems would be solved.

He needed another beer. Lenny went to the kitchen and came back with two bottles and the opener. Margo was driving him to drink. It was the only way he could forget about the way she was treating him. He'd made a big mistake right at the beginning, when he'd given her the first chunk of money. He should have laughed and said the papers were nothing important. Then she would have tossed them, and he wouldn't be jumping through hoops like a trained seal.

As Lenny sat down on the couch, again he had a startling thought. Hart was crazy. Oakdale was a maximum-security funny farm in Northern California. The poor stiff was probably wandering around out there in the rain, not knowing where he was or even who he was. What would happen if Lenny killed Margo himself? The way he felt about her right now, it would be a pleasure. Of course, he'd have to do it tonight, before Hart was caught. When Margo turned up dead in the morning, everybody would think Hart had done it. And to put the icing on the cake, Lenny could even hit a couple of the other jurors, just so everything pointed to Hart.

It was nine-thirty, and Michael was in bed, asleep. He'd tried to read for a while after Stan's call, but he'd dozed off twice before he'd finally given in and turned out the light. His bedtime at Oakdale had been eight o'clock, and it was difficult to stay awake past then.

Michael's eyelids began to twitch as his pupils moved. He was starting to dream. Long moments passed with no sound, only his slightly irregular breathing. Then a moan escaped his lips. His legs bent at the knees and then straightened. He was standing for the verdict. The juror's faces were huge and hard, like the sculptures of the presidents at Mount Rushmore. Their eyes were flat, gleaming stones that accused him. Guilty, Guilty, Guilty. Over and over. How could they say that? They were wrong! And then he was moving, hurtling over the rail in one soaring leap, right into the jury box, and . . .

He was awake now. Or was he? No, the dream was still playing, and the jurors had eluded him somehow.

The jury box was empty. He had to find them, but how?

The telephone book was on the table. He opened it and turned to the J's Jantzen. One woman's name was Jantzen; one woman's name was the same as the swimwear. And her first name was . . . Margo. There it was, Morningside Drive in Westwood.

His feet were moving, he could feel them. But everything was happening very slowly. He felt cold air on his face, and he wished he'd taken a jacket. Just as soon as he realized the cold air was only a part of his dream, he felt warm again. He was really in bed with the blankets around him, having another nightmare.

"Sounds good to me," Eddie leaned back and belched. "I never heard of a perfect murder before. Sometimes you got great ideas, Lenny."

"Yeah." Lenny sighed and opened another beer.

"But what good does that do me? I can't do it, Eddie. I don't have the killer kind of mentality."

Eddie laughed. "Sure you do, Lenny. Those guys are no different from you or me. The real pros look at it like it's a job that's gotta be done. And it's easy work. Digging a ditch is a lot harder than hitting somebody with a fancy rifle. But I can understand if you don't wanna get your hands dirty. You want me to put you in touch with a guy I know?"

Lenny hesitated, and Eddie could tell he was tempted, but then he shook his head.

"That's okay, Eddie. I don't wanna get involved with that element. But thanks, and—hey, I almost forgot. I got a little present for you on the table. Two tickets to the championship fight tomorrow night."

"You're a real pal, Lenny." Eddie grinned and picked up the tickets. Then he reached for his wallet. "Now, what do I owe you? I hear you can't touch these babies for less than a hundred on the street."

Lenny waved him away. "Forget it, Eddie. I got some connections that owe me favors. They didn't cost me a dime."

"But that ain't right! You got me the Super Bowl tickets last year, and you didn't let me pay. And how about that big Dodger game that was all sold out? You make me feel like a mooch, Lenny. I'm taking advantage of your good nature."

"We're friends, right? Friends do things for each other. And I told you, they cost me nothing."

Eddie sighed deeply and stuck his wallet back into his pocket. "Okay, Lenny, if you won't take cash maybe I can do you a favor sometime. Would that square us?"

"Sure. But I don't keep books, Eddie. As far as I'm concerned, you don't owe me a thing."

There was a worried expression on Eddie's face, but then he smiled and jumped up so suddenly, he almost knocked over his beer. "I'll be right back, Lenny. I just remembered a phone call I gotta make."

"You can use my phone. Go ahead."

"Yeah, I would but, well, I left the number at home. When I come back, what d'ya say we turn on the tube? If you don't have no other plans, that is."

"Sure, Eddie. I'll turn it on right now. What channel?"

Eddie shrugged. "It's up to you, but since you got cable, I was kind of hoping to watch the Knicks knock the crap out of Boston. I got two big ones riding on it, and I like to keep an eye on my investments."

There was a patter of something on the roof, and Margo Jantzen roused herself from the late movie to glance out the window. It was raining, and the top was down on her new convertible. She hadn't bothered to pull it in the garage when she came home, and it was still sitting in the driveway. The weather had cleared while the locksmith was working, and she'd dashed out for cigarettes. When she'd come back her phone had been ringing, and she hadn't taken the time to pull the car inside.

Margo grabbed her car keys and raced to the bathroom to find a big towel. Then she hurried out the kitchen door to the connecting garage and hit the switch on the electric garage door opener. Her expensive leather upholstery would be ruined if she didn't do something quick!

The driver's seat was soaked, and Margo cursed as she hopped behind the wheel and pulled the car into the garage. Then she closed the garage door with her dashboard control and got out to wipe down the seats. The towel was soaked by the time she finished, and Margo tossed it into the laundry basket that sat on top of her washer. As she was inching past the bumper of the car toward the kitchen door, the interior of the garage went dark.

Margo swore as her expensive silk pants caught on the corner of the license plate and tore. The garage was pitch black, and it was her own fault. She'd forgotten to turn on the garage lights when she'd rushed out the front door to get the car. The garage door opener had an automatic light, but it clicked off after a couple of minutes. Now she'd have to feel her way to the connecting door.

Margo's heart was racing as she reached out and felt her way past the back of the car. It was frightening to be out here alone in the dark. She almost screamed as something repulsive and sticky brushed her arm. A cobweb. She'd have the cleaning service give her garage a thorough cleaning tomorrow.

As her eyes began to adjust to the blackness, Margo could see a sliver of light in the distance. It was the crack under the kitchen door. At least she could see her destination.

There was a huge black shadow looming in front of her, and Margo stopped. What was it? She couldn't remember storing anything that big in her garage. At least it wasn't moving, but she'd be damned if she'd touch it until she knew what it was.

Margo held her breath as she inched past the shape, and then she sighed in relief. It was only the box from her new refrigerator. She'd told the delivery men to put it in here.

There were more shadows, but she recognized them. Her exercise bicycle was draped with a sheet to keep off the dust. She really ought to have someone carry it in. Her thighs could use a little work. And just beyond the bicycle were the bags of leaves and cuttings that the gardener had stored for mulch. They made the garage smell as musty as an old basement. She'd catch him on Friday and tell him to move them to the patio.

She was almost there when she heard a small noise. What was it? Bugs? Or something bigger? Something more dangerous?

Margo froze, only inches from the light and comfort of her kitchen. Had some animal dashed into the garage when the door was open? They had opossums in this area, ugly gray animals with beady little eyes and pink, fleshy tails. And squirrels. And all kinds of rodents, but she didn't want to think about it now. Not while she was still out in the dark.

Deliberately, Margo forced herself to concentrate on finding the doorknob. She was almost there now. Only a few steps to go. All she had to do was keep her hand on the wall and follow it to the door.

Her hand grasped the knob and turned it. There! She'd made it! There was a relieved smile on her face when something heavy and sharp punctured the top of her skull, resulting in her death with one well-placed blow.

CHAPTER 8

It was 10 a.m. and Toni was sitting at the table in Doris's kitchen. A mouth-watering aroma was coming from the oven. Doris was baking.

"How much longer, Doris?"

"Just a couple of minutes. Relax, Toni. Munch on one of those cookies while you're waiting."

Toni took a cookie from the jar and chewed thoughtfully. "I think I know why you can't lose weight, Doris. There's got to be a pound of chocolate chips in these."

"Twelve ounces. And six ounces of chopped macadamia nuts. Harry likes them better than walnuts. And a half pound of butter."

"Stop! No wonder you can't lose weight. Maybe you should try eating my cooking for a change. I can't even make instant soup without something going wrong."

Doris sighted. "Look, Toni. Anyone can cook. You're a bright woman, and you can follow directions. You just have a block that's all."

"Some block! I tried to make your never-fail biscuit recipe, and they turned out like paperweights."

The stove timer buzzed, and Doris tossed Toni a pair of kitchen mitts. "Take those out for me, will you?"

"Sure." Toni got up and took the pan of cinnamon rolls out of the oven. "Where do I put them?"

Doris gestured toward the cooling rack on the kitchen counter. "Now see that plate? Put six rolls on it, and cover it with aluminum foil. It's the third drawer down to the right of the sink."

Toni put six rolls on the plate and covered it with foil. "Now what?"

Now march up to Mike's apartment and tell him you just took these out of the oven and you wanted to share them with him."

"But he's going to think I baked them!"

Doris laughed. "That's the general idea. But remember, Toni, you're not lying. You did take them out of the oven. He'll offer to make you some coffee, and you say fine, that would be lovely. And after you're all finished socializing, you come back here and tell me everything he said. That's step one."

Toni frowned. "What's step two?"

"I'll tell you later. Now get out of here before those rolls get cold."

"You're positive the way to a man's heart is through his stomach?"

"I'm positive."

Toni swallowed hard and picked up the plate of rolls. "Okay, I'll do it. But I'm warning you, Doris . . . if this whole thing backfires, I'm going to tell Harry exactly how much you spent on his birthday present."

* * *

Michael groaned as he stepped out of the shower. He'd turned up the water as hot as he could stand it, but it hadn't done any good. Every muscle in his body still ached. This was his second shower of the morning. He'd taken the first when he'd crawled out of bed at eight, hobbling into the bathroom in an attempt to look presentable before he met Toni and Doris for their morning run.

It had been bad enough yesterday, trying to keep up with the pace, but this morning it had been pure agony. He must be in much worse condition than he'd thought. But all his aches and pains hadn't been as painful as his loss of pride. Doris had noticed his discomfort and suggested they skip the stairs and take the elevator.

He stopped to sneeze twice as he was dressing. Somehow, he'd caught a cold. That wasn't surprising. Now that he thought about it, he'd lived in a protected environment for ten years; and he hadn't been exposed to viruses outside Oakdale's locked doors. He would probably come down with every bug in town before his immune system caught up with the times.

It wasn't a pleasant thought, and Michael frowned as he went to the kitchen to scare up some breakfast. He was in the process of reading the directions on a box of Instant Cream of Wheat that didn't seem to be so instant after all, when the doorbell rang.

Should he answer it? Michael hesitated, his fingers on the knob. It couldn't be a salesman. The outside door was kept locked and door-to-door salesmen couldn't get in. And it certainly wasn't

Stan. When Stan had called last night, he'd stressed again that they couldn't meet face-to-face until things calmed down. It had to be either Toni or Doris. They were the only people he knew inside the building.

"Just a second," Michael released the chain and started to open the door, but he stopped abruptly as he realized that there was one other person he knew. Captain Harry Evans. What if someone had come up with a new picture, a photo that had been taken after the surgeries?

"Who is it?" Michael felt like a fool shouting through the door, but what else could he do? Actually, he might as well go ahead and open it. There was no way to back out now, and no place to run. If Doris's husband had come to arrest him, there was no other option but to go along quietly.

"It's me! Toni! If you're busy, I can come back later!"

Michael pulled open the door and gave her a broad smile. Now she probably thought he was crazy. "Sorry Toni, come in. I . . . uh . . . I wanted to make sure who it was."

Toni smiled, but she seemed nervous as she handed him a plate covered with aluminum foil. "Why didn't you just peek through the fisheye?"

Michael felt like an idiot as he noticed the peephole in the door. There were no peepholes at Oakdale, just grates with mesh over them so the nurses could keep eyes on the patients. He'd forgotten that fisheyes existed.

"To tell the truth, I forgot it was there. My last place didn't have one. Come in, Toni. I don't bite."

Toni walked in and perched gingerly on the arm

of the couch. "Those are cinnamon rolls that I just took out of the oven. I figured they'd get your mind off your sore muscles. You haven't eaten breakfast yet, have you?"

"Not yet." Michael lifted up the foil and inhaled deeply. They smelled delicious. Toni was sitting there expectantly, and suddenly he remembered his manners.

"Why don't you join me? I can make some coffee, but it'll have to be instant."

"Decaf?"

"No, it's the regular kind."

"Oh good." Toni sighed. "I could use the caffeine." Michael knew he looked surprised. "But, Toni, I thought you were big on physical fitness with the jogging and all."

"Oh, I am." Toni nodded. "But I don't believe in going overboard. I jog because I sit behind a desk all day, and it's the only exercise I get. As far as the rest of it goes, I'm certainly not one of those health food fanatics with all the fiber and gluten-free things. My favorite ingredients are cream, butter, and sugar."

"But don't you believe in watching your diet? You are what you eat? That kind of thing?"

"Heavens no! I eat exactly what I want, anytime I want it. And if my clothes get too tight, I just eat less for a couple of weeks. I know they say you can add ten years to your life by watching what you eat, but they don't mention it's the last ten years of your life they're talking about. I'm not sure that I want to stick around just so I can drool on myself."

"I see what you mean." Michael bit back a smile and nodded. "Maybe these all-natural foods aren't good for you. After all, people die of natural causes all the time."

Toni blinked and then she laughed, a rich, full-bodied sound that made Michael feel he'd said something wonderful. She was beginning to relax around him, and that was good.

"Can I use your phone for a minute, Mike? I finished a report last night, and I wanted to tell my client it's ready."

"Sure. It's right there by the couch. And the book's around here someplace. I'll go start the coffee."

An expression of surprise crossed Michael's face as he spotted the phone book. It was lying open on the coffee table. That was strange. He hadn't made any calls. He was frowning as he went into the kitchen. There was something about the nightmare, something that had been different last night. The jury box had been empty, so he'd looked up the name of a juror in the phone book. Had he actually done it? Gotten out of bed and opened the phone book? He must have.

There was something else, too. It had been raining, and he had forgotten to take his jacket. Had he really gone outside in the rain? He wasn't sure.

Michael sighed and filled two cups with water. It really didn't matter. After all, it was only a dream. But he was still frowning as he put the cups in the microwave and watched them go around on the carousel. When Toni left, he'd check the clothes in his closet to see if anything was damp. The sensation of cold rain hitting his face had been very real. He sure hoped he hadn't been sleepwalking again.

* * *

Lenny closed the door to his tiny office and poured himself a cup of coffee. Ten o'clock. Time for his mid-morning break. The bozos out there could handle the customers while he read his morning paper.

Trouble with the Arabs again. And the Israelis. Too bad we didn't have a president with muscle enough to straighten them out. If JFK were alive, he could do it. He was the only president Lenny could remember who hadn't taken lip from anybody.

Lenny blinked hard as he thought about Kennedy. It was the first time and only time he'd cried. All those years ago, and he still remembered where he'd been and exactly what he'd been doing when he'd heard the news.

He had been five years old, riding in a truck with his father. His father was a pickup man back then, running loads from Miami to Chicago. The boss had told his father to drive straight through, so they'd been on the road all night with the radio on for company. They'd been on a clear stretch of highway just outside of Atlanta when the announcer had said the president was dead. Lenny's father had pulled over to the side of the road and bawled like a baby, and Lenny had cried, too. He wasn't sure what was going on, but he hadn't liked seeing his father cry. His father was a tough guy, a careful guy who'd never been in trouble, but that morning he hadn't even cared that the Georgia cops might stop to ask what was wrong and search the truck.

Lenny sighed as he turned to the sports section and flipped to the scores. He added up his winnings and losses and shrugged. He'd broken even today and he guessed that was better than losing. He didn't bet that much anyway, never more than he could afford. He just did it to make the games more interesting. It was like going to the track and betting on a horse because you like the color the jockey was wearing. Sometimes you won and sometimes you lost, but it all evened out in the end.

The comics were next, but they weren't very funny today. Lenny read them all, but he didn't find anything to make him laugh out loud. They used to be better. He was sure of that. This political correctness thing was ruining everybody's sense of humor.

Lenny flipped to the obituaries, and he read each one carefully. Then he gave a relieved sigh. No one he knew had died. That was great. And almost everyone who'd died, with the exception of a kid on a motorcycle who was probably high on something or other, had been older than he was. That made Lenny feel good.

One quick glance at the weather and he was through. The weather guys in the paper were the worst of the lot. Lenny wasn't even sure why he bothered to look. He shoved the paper to the back of his desk and got up to go back to work when an article in the Metro section caught his eye. Some woman had been murdered last night in Westwood. That was where Margo lived. Too bad it wasn't her.

Lenny's mouth dropped open as he read the name of the victim. It *was* Margo! There it was in black and white. Margo Jantzen on Morningside Drive. And he'd been talking about killing her just last night. He was sure glad he hadn't mentioned it to anyone but Eddie!

It took a second to sink in, but then Lenny began to sweat. He'd laid out the whole thing, and Eddie'd said he knew the right guy for the job. And when Lenny had given him those tickets, Eddie had promised to do him a favor. They'd been sitting there talking when Eddie had jumped up to make a phone call, one he didn't want to make from Lenny's apartment. It didn't take a lot of brains to figure it out. That stupid little scum had put out a hit on Margo!

Michael unlocked his apartment door and ducked inside. His heart was racing, although he was almost certain no one had seen him dash out to get a newspaper from the dispenser in front of the apartment building.

The paper listed a number on the front for people who wanted to subscribe. Michael dialed it and made arrangements to have the paper delivered to Mike Kruger's apartment every morning. Even though Stan had told him to ask for anything he wanted. Michael didn't see anything wrong with taking a little initiative. Then he hung up and stared down at today's newspaper, almost afraid to open it and find out what was inside.

After Toni had left, he'd discovered a damp pair of jeans and shirt in his closet. It was clear he'd been sleepwalking in the rain last night, just as he had feared. Now he wanted to find out where he'd gone and what he'd done.

Michael's hands were trembling as he paged through the paper. The world news could wait, and so could the sports and the business section. If he'd actually done what he feared, it would be in the Metro.

There was an article about a woman who'd been murdered in Westwood, and Michael shuddered. As he read the name of the victim, his face turned white.

The phone book was still open on the coffee table, and Michael forced himself to look at it. Margo Jantzen's name and address were right there in the middle of the page.

It was like the nightmare was happening again, except this time it was real. Michael sank down on the couch and held his head in his hands. The psychiatrist had told him that his nightmare was caused by the hatred he felt for the jurors who'd convicted him. The whole idea had seemed ridiculous, but he'd promised the doctor he'd think about it.

At his next session Michael had told the psychiatrist he was wrong. He didn't hate the jurors. It was true they'd made a mistake, but people weren't infallible, and you couldn't blame them for an honest error. After all, the body of evidence against him had been overwhelming.

The psychiatrist had made one of those non-judgmental comments like, "I see," or, "Oh," and Michael had gone on to explain. It was true that he'd shouted at Carole. And he'd told the bartender at Barney's Beanery that she'd be sorry that she ever left him.

Of course, he hadn't meant that he was going to go back and kill her, but how were the jurors supposed to know that? And the gun, Michael's gun with his fingerprints on the cylinder, had been in the dumpster outside his apartment building. Didn't the doctor agree that all these facts were

pretty incriminating? And to make it worse, he had
no alibi, none at all. He still couldn't remember
where he'd gone after he left the bar. All he knew
was that he hadn't killed Carole, but it sure as hell
looked as if he had. It wasn't the jurors fault he'd
been convicted. It was reasonable for them to reach
that conclusion even though it wasn't true.

The psychiatrist had smiled and nodded. They
always smiled and nodded when they were about to
knock your props out from under you. And then
he'd asked a question. What was the dream if not
tangible proof of the animosity Michael was harbor-
ing toward the jurors?

Michael had sighed and given in. It did no good
to argue. But he hadn't believed it. He hadn't believed it at all until now.

"I don't believe it!" Doris reached across the table
to pour Toni another cup of coffee. "That's three cinnamon rolls you've eaten in less than five minutes.
Didn't you have any with Mike?"

Toni shook her head. "Mike ate. I was too nervous."

"You were too nervous to eat? This is serious,
Toni. I think you're in love."

"Really?" Toni raised her eyebrows. "I don't know
about the love part, but I *do* like him, Doris. He's got
a good sense of humor. Did I tell you what he said
about natural foods?"

Doris nodded. "You also told me that his favorite
color is blue, he enjoys old movies, his favorite musical is *West Side Story*, and his hobby is reading
Shakespeare. It sounds like a line in a high school

yearbook. Did he say anything personal at all? Or ask you for a date?"

"No. But he seemed glad to see me. And he asked me in right away."

"Okay, that's something." Doris sighed. "Did you wear your cute little yellow sundress?"

Toni put her fourth roll down with a thump. "I'm sorry, Doris. I knew I forgot to do something."

"You wore that?" Doris pointed to Toni's jeans and T-shirt, and she groaned when Toni nodded. "Well, that explains it. I think it's definitely time for step two, if you remembered to get his phone number."

"I remembered that. I asked to use his phone and I memorized the number. "What's step two?"

"Dinner at your place. Honey-cured ham, sweet potatoes, spinach soufflé. And lemon meringue pie for desert. He won't be able to resist."

"It sounds wonderful." Toni sighed. "But, Doris, you know I can't cook a meal like that."

"You won't have to. I'll make the dinner and bring it down to your place. All you have to do is look gorgeous and accept compliments."

"But that's cheating, Doris. And I've never cheated in my life!"

"It's not really cheating if you come up here and help me make it. Now go and call him and invite him to dinner. And then run down to your place and bring back an apron. We've got cooking to do."

It was a long time before Michael moved. The phone had rung twice before; ten rings each time, but he hadn't felt composed enough to answer. Now it was ringing again, and he roused himself enough to pick it up. It was probably Stan, calling to tell him that he had to go back to Oakdale now that he'd seen the article in the paper, and decided that Michael should be locked up after all.

"Mikey? It's Stan. I'm glad I caught you."

Michael was so nervous he almost laughed out loud. Why wouldn't Stan catch him? He was supposed to stay right here, behind locked doors.

"Where were you, Mike? I called twice and no one answered. Were you sleeping?"

"No." Michael thought fast. "But I took a long shower, Stan. That must have been when you called. The cord's not long enough to reach in the bathroom."

"That's okay. Don't worry about it, Mikey. Normally, I wouldn't call in the middle of the day, but I wanted to get to you first, before you saw the news on the television. One of the jurors who served at your trial was murdered last night. Her name was Margo Jantzen. But the police don't suspect you, so relax. There's no cause for alarm."

"They—they don't suspect me?"

"No. Two things happened, Mike. Good things for you. A couple of nurses from Oakdale swear they spotted you at the Oakland Airport last night."

"They do?"

"That's right. Of course, you and I both know they're wrong, but we're the only ones who know that."

"I've got a double?"

"Apparently. The ticket agent remembers selling you a one-way ticket to New York, and the police in

California have called off their search. Isn't that good news?"

Michael swallowed hard. "Yes, Yes, it's very good news. Does that mean I can see you now?"

"Not yet, Mike. They'll still figure you'll try to contact me, so we'd better lay low for a while longer, just until we're sure."

"Whatever you say Stan, You said there were two good things?"

"That's right, Michael." My contact at the police station told me there's an important development in the Jantzen murder. She's the juror, remember?"

"Yes, Stan. I remember."

"Well, they've discovered evidence that she was blackmailing her former employer. They're concentrating on that aspect now, to the exclusion of anything else. They haven't even discovered that she was a juror at your trial."

"That's wonderful, Stan. Thanks for telling me."

"What's wrong, Mikey? You sound worried. Are you all right?"

"Yes, I'm fine, Stan. It's just . . ." Michael paused for a second. Should he tell Stan about the sleepwalking?

"Come on, Mikey. Spit it out. Whatever it is, I can fix it."

Michael took a deep breath. "I think I might be sleepwalking, Stan."

"Is that all?" Stan chuckled. "Look, Mike. Don't worry about it. You used to sleepwalk as a kid, right after we moved into Aunt Alice's place. She was worried that you might hurt yourself, but you never did.

And it stopped after a couple of months, when you got used to your new surroundings."

Michael tried to remember the first few months at Aunt Alice's, but the memories were too vague. "I don't think I remember that, Stan."

"Of course you don't. You couldn't have been more than three years old. Anyway, you shouldn't let it upset you. It's probably just a reaction to your new environment. Have a brandy or something right before you go to bed, and you'll sleep like a baby."

"You don't think it's dangerous?"

"I seriously doubt it. If you're still sleepwalking after a couple of weeks, we'll figure something out. Okay?"

"Okay, Stan."

"I've got to dash off, Mikey. I've a briefcase full of papers to file for your appeal. I'll talk to you at nine o'clock tonight, right?"

"Right."

Michael had no sooner hung up the phone than it rang again. Was it Stan calling back to say he'd reconsidered? That he thought sleepwalking was dangerous after all, and Michael should go back to Oakdale? His fingers were shaking as he picked up the receiver.

"Hi, Mike. It's Toni. I am calling to invite you to my place for dinner."

Michael was so surprised it wasn't Stan, his mind went completely blank. Finally, he forced out an answer. "Thanks, Toni. I'd really like to, but—" his mind raced, trying to think of an excuse, "I'm having a problem with work."

"You mean with your writing?"

"Yes," Michael answered, remembering he'd told Toni and Doris that he was a writer. "It's my main character. Something just isn't working right."

"That's too bad, Mike." Toni's voice was sympathetic. "Maybe you need to relax and get away from it for a while. After all, you need to eat dinner somewhere and it might as well be at my place."

Michael began to smile. It was true he needed to relax and get away from it, but Toni didn't know that *it* was his anxiety about his sleepwalking. But talking to Toni seemed to make him feel better. It was also true that he had to eat dinner. "You're right, Toni. I'd like to come if you're sure I won't be intruding."

"Intruding? Don't be silly. We're having ham, sweet potatoes, and spinach soufflé. With coffee and Lemon meringue pie for dessert. We'll eat at six, if that's all right with you."

Michael's mouth was watering as he accepted her invitation and hung up the phone. If the cinnamon rolls were any indication, Toni was a terrific cook, and he hadn't had a good home-cooked meal in more than ten years.

Just thinking about the meal Toni had described was making him hungry. Michael found a box of crackers in the cupboard and made himself a snack of Brie and crackers. After he'd eaten he felt much better. Stan hadn't been a bit worried about his sleepwalking. And Stan was usually right. He'd go over it one more time to try to see things objectively.

Michael sat down on the couch and went through the whole thing again. The phone book had been open to Margo Jantzen's name. He'd gone out into the rain last night. Those were the facts, but they didn't add up to murder. He'd never done anything the least bit violent while he was sleepwalking as a kid, and he'd checked his damp clothing carefully and found no evidence of bloodstains. It was possible, even probable, that'd he'd walked a few blocks in the rain and then retraced his steps and gone back to bed.

A glance at the clock, and Michael was on his feet. He had to hurry. It was already five-thirty, and Toni had said to come at six. He felt so relieved, he found himself singing an old Beatles refrain while he was dressing in tan slacks, a wine-colored sweater, and a pair of brown loafers. They were bound to be acceptable, even though he had no concept of the current styles. He'd have to remember to check the ads in the paper to see what the well dressed man was wearing.

Michael was about to go out the door when he remembered the dinner parities he'd gone to with Carole. Everyone had arrived with a gift for the hostess. It didn't have to be much. You could arrive with a box of candy, a bouquet of flowers, or a bottle of wine. Almost anything was acceptable, but no one had arrived empty-handed. He couldn't go out to buy candy or flowers, but there might be some wine in the apartment. All he had to do was find it.

There was a shelf of white wine in the refrigerator, but Toni was serving ham. Wasn't there some rule about red wine with meat? If Stan had bought white wine, he'd probably picked up some red at the same time. But where had he stored it?

After a five-minute search, Michael was ready to give up until he remembered Stan's advice about drinking brandy before he went to bed. If he had

brandy, there was a liquor cabinet. Was it behind the
stained glass doors he'd noticed in the living room?

Michael hurried to the living room, pulled open
the doors, and smiled as he saw vodka, gin, brandy,
Scotch, and every brand of liquor conceivable. And
there were twelve bottles of something called Lafite
Rothschild nestled in the built-in wine rack. He
grabbed one and headed out the door. He knew
nothing about wines. He'd always served beer
because it was all he could afford. He'd just have to
trust that his brother's taste would please Toni.

CHAPTER 9

Neal Wallace was scowling as he unlocked his mailbox and pulled up on the metal door. The rusty hinges were stuck again. How the hell was he supposed to get his mail when the damn door wouldn't open? Somebody ought to drag Hennessy out of his fancy beach house in Malibu and force him to move into his own rotten building. Then things would be fixed in a hurry! A couple of years ago some judge had actually sentenced a slum landlord to six weeks of living in one of his units. Neal had read all about it in the paper. If he could only remember the judge's name, he'd sic him on Hennessy.

There were plenty of things wrong with Hennessy's building. The pipes leaked, the toilets flushed erratically, and there were hunks of plaster missing from the walls. It was clear the place was falling apart, but Hennessy refused to make repairs. Unless he was openly breaking some law, he didn't have to. When Neal had complained about his toilet, Hennessy had told him to fix it himself or move out.

There were people on the waiting list to get his loft. Artists were willing to put up with massive inconvenience as their lofts were big with plenty of light. Good work space was tough to find.

Neal's face was like a thundercloud as he struggled with the mailbox door. The morning had begun very badly. There had been a late-night party for a friend who was leaving town, with plenty of food and drinks. And when he'd crawled out of bed this morning with a pounding head and the terrible thirst of a man who'd munched on salted peanuts all night, he'd discovered that he was out of orange juice.

There had been no choice but to go out and buy some. The water was terrible, and he refused to drink it. It tasted every bit as vile as it looked, with particles of sludge from the decrepit pipes. For all Neal knew, it could be toxic. Maybe he ought to sic the Hazardous Waste Commission on Hennessy.

There was a convenience store three blocks down, and Neal had thrown on an old pair of jeans and a Cal Arts sweatshirt to make the trek. And while he was standing in line behind some construction workers who were getting refills on their plastic cups of coffee, some little queer had tried to pick him up! Why did everyone assume that all artists were gay?

On the way home, Neal had studied his reflection in every window he passed. He didn't look gay. Sure, he pulled his long brown hair back in a ponytail, but long hair was coming back. And he didn't walk gay. No mincing little steps or a swish of the butt. Of course, he wore an earring, but that shouldn't matter. Pirates had worn gold studs in their ears.

And now the mailbox wouldn't open. Neal felt

like ripping the whole bunch right off the wall. He'd be doing the rest of the tenants a favor. Hennessy would have to replace them to comply with postal regulations.

It took another few tugs and a good whack with his fist, but at last the door opened with a squeal of protest. Neal stared at the contents of his narrow metal cubicle with shock. There was a whole pile of letters inside, all addressed to him. Not circulars, not bills or advertising offers, but real, personal letters. Neon by Neal was finally getting some public notice. And it was all because he'd landed that commission from the City of Los Angeles.

A pale blue envelope with the *Avant Garde* insignia caught Neal's attention, and he ripped it open eagerly. There was a questionnaire inside with a handwritten note from the editor. Could he please be so kind as to fill out the enclosed? *Avant Garde* was interested in his formal training, his current work, and his future goals. Neal knew exactly what the questionnaire meant. An acquaintance of his had gotten one once. *Avant Garde* was sounding him out about a feature!

Neal picked up the bag with his orange juice and dropped the letters inside. Then he held it under one arm while he unlocked his door. The moment he was inside, he plopped down on the awful green and white flowered couch his mother had given him when she'd redecorated her living room, and propped his feet up on the coffee table. The couch was white wicker, one of Neal's least favorite materials, with a thin cushion on top. Definitely uncomfortable. And the chair that matched it wasn't any better.

He reached for the orange juice and took a swig straight from the bottle, a habit he'd developed in his teenage years that had driven his mother crazy. Who should he call to share his good news? He'd better wait until *Avant Garde* had made a firm commitment before he told his mother. She'd call all the ladies in her bridge club to brag, and if the article failed to appear, she'd take it out on him. His mother's wrath was something Neal went out of his way to avoid.

Neal reached for the phone and dialed the Cal Arts switchboard. The only person he really wanted to tell was Tom. Tom had landed a teaching position after they'd graduated, and he was still doing some decent work on the side. One of his pieces had hung in the County Art Museum. It wasn't his best work. Those pieces were a little wild for the general public. but it was still a real achievement. Because this was Tom's conference hour, he'd probably be in his office on campus.

After a moment's thought, Neal hung up the phone before the call could go through. Tom would be so excited at the news that he'd rush right over with a bottle of champagne. Then they'd sit around and get stoned all night, and two nights in a row were more than Neal's system could take. He had to be in good shape to start work on the city mural tomorrow. It was the most ambitious project he'd ever attempted. As far as he knew, no one had ever done a neon mural on a freeway overpass before. His scaffolding was already in place, and the electrical cables were in. He'd provided the workers with a diagram of the wiring, and everything had been done to his specifications. Tomorrow Neal would personally connect the tubes so that the mayor could throw the switch at the public unveiling this weekend.

Neal shivered a little as he thought about the scaffolding. Whenever he made signs, he hired someone else to climb up on the roof to bolt them in place. Heights scared him. He got dizzy just climbing up on a step stool to get something out of the cupboard. The thought of lowering himself on the scaffolding with nothing but the freeway beneath him was a real white-knuckle proposition. He'd been planning on hiring a crew to connect the tubes while he directed them by walkie-talkie from the nice safe ground below. But then the hostess of *On the Town*, a local television program, had called to ask if she could do on-the-spot coverage.

The request from *On the Town* had changed Neal's whole outlook. His fear of heights had seemed insignificant in light of the publicity he'd get. It had always been his dream to be featured on the cover of a national magazine, and now he had a good shot at it, especially if *On the Town* got some good footage of the fearless artist at work, his ass hanging out in the breeze.

Neal looked through the rest of his mail and sorted it into piles. A letter from a lady who'd been to MONA, the Museum of Neon Art, and had seen his display. She wanted to buy Blue Flamingo, the piece he'd donated to the museum. Everyone loved that damn thing. He could make a fortune if he mass produced it, but that wouldn't be fair to MONA. He'd call and try to sell her one of his other works.

Two people wanted estimates on business signs, a restaurant on Pico and a real estate office in the valley. Neal hated to do signs, but they were his bread and butter. It was boring work, and they never wanted anything creative or different, but he always got his money up front, and it paid the rent. After *On the Town* made him famous, maybe he could turn down the sign work.

Another letter, on cream-colored monogrammed stationery, sounded promising. A lady in Beverly Hills wanted to commission a large neon sculpture for her husband's office. Beause he owned a film production company, Neal knew that it meant plenty of people going in and out to admire his creation. This could lead the way to a goldmine in private commissions.

The rest of the mail was stuff he could answer later. There was a student who wanted to work as his apprentice for the summer, and a request for him to teach a class in neon technique. They couldn't pay much, just a small stipend. He'd call to find out how small their stipend was.

The last letter, written in ballpoint pen on tablet paper, was a real gem. It was a plea for help from a couple in Minnesota named Deke and Sally Torgesen. Neal had no idea how they'd gotten his address. The Torgesens had inherited her grandfather's farm, and they were turning the old barn into a neon museum. They'd resurrected over a hundred antique neon signs. That was very nice, but the last few sentences were the ones that had captured Neal's interest.

Deke and Sally were doing the outside wall of their museum, the one that faced the highway, in neon. They were using an original quilt pattern that had been designed by Sally's great-grandmother.

Because the pattern called for a rainbow of colors, they were desperate to know the mixture of gases that would make up a good strong purple.

Neal laid Deke and Sally's letter on top of his pile. It was the one he'd answer first, right after he'd filled out the *Avant Garde* questionnaire. A barn draped with a neon quilt. The concept fired his imagination. When he got the money for the city mural, he might just fly out to see it.

Michael watched through the peephole as the delivery man walked away. It was a bit like Christmas, and Stan had played Santa again. When they'd talked last night, Michael had mentioned he wanted a computer. Was there some way he could rent one? Since Stan had told him to stay in behind locked doors, he might as well put the time to good use by learning something about the new technology. Then he'd be better equipped to find a regular job after Stan had won his appeal.

Stan had seemed pleased at his interest, especially when Michael had confessed that he was going a little stir crazy, and that he was really tempted to go out. But if he had something productive to do, he was sure he wouldn't even think about leaving the apartment. Stan had told him to sit tight, and he'd promised to see what he could do. And less than fourteen hours later, the delivery man had rung his bell.

Michael had stripped off his shirt and opened the door with the chain on. He'd told the delivery man that he was just out of the shower, and he'd asked the man to leave it in the hallway. Michael would take it in himself just as soon as he put on some clothes. The only part of Michael Hart's anatomy the delivery man had seen was his right arm poking through the crack in the door to sign the receipt. Not even a borderline paranoid like Stan would be worried that the delivery man could recognize his bare arm!

When Michael was sure the hallway was empty, he opened the door and lugged the heavy box inside. He'd call Toni right away. She was the one who'd told him what to order so his system would be compatible with hers. Now that he thought about it, he'd really put his foot in his mouth when he'd told her he was a writer. That first night at dinner she'd seemed so uncomfortable, he'd asked more questions about her computer. And after she'd demonstrated a couple of functions her system could perform, he'd commented that it seemed like a useful tool for a writer to have. That one little comment had opened the floodgates.

The next night she'd told him about software. There was a wonderful thesaurus program that came with Microsoft Word. And their user-friendly dictionary contained more than a hundred and thirty thousand words.

Later that evening, after a delicious roast pork stuffed with apricots and apples, she'd zeroed in like a preacher saving a sinner's soul. They'd been sipping a glass of Stan's Lafite Rothschild when she asked if he remembered the spelling program she'd mentioned. Michael had nodded, and Toni had continued to tell him about it. Had she told him that it was interactive? That meant he could run it and correct his misspelled words right in the document itself. Wouldn't that save him time if he didn't have to worry about checking his spelling?

The next night they'd covered printers. Toni had served five-alarm chili with big hunks of meat and no beans. After dinner, she'd started to talk about computer things again. It seemed the new laser printer could give him camera-ready documents, and since it had to down-loadable fonts, he could call up any typeface he wanted. And if Michael bought a system that was compatible with hers, he could bring her a memory stick and use her printer to print his work.

The next night was turkey with oyster stuffing and creamy mashed potatoes. As soon as they'd eaten and gone into the living room, they'd discussed training. So what if he knew nothing about computers? The training was simple as long as he didn't try to download and read the manuals. Toni swore they'd been translated into English by someone in a third world country. And she'd promised that she could teach him everything he needed to know to write his novel. He'd be computer literate in just a couple of days.

The next afternoon she'd called him to come over and look at her modem. It connected her computer with data banks all over the country, and it made her research a snap. He would have no need to buy expensive reference books or go to the library. If he had a computer and a modem, everything would be right there at his fingertips.

Michael was aware that Toni was wearing down his resistance. He'd given her the argument he'd been saving for this moment. Computers were expensive.

Not really, Toni had countered. Michael should

realize that he wouldn't have to buy any of the extras. She could provide practically any program he needed. She'd simply give him a link to the software she'd stuck on the cloud and he could use everything she had.

Michael had hesitated and finally agreed that it sounded like a computer was something he could use. But he wasn't sure he was quite ready. It was true that it would be much less expensive if he bought a stripped-down model and relied on Toni for the software, but it was still a lot of money to spend, especially since he was living off a limited family inheritance.

Toni played her trump card. If Michael could lay out the cash to buy those marvelous bottles of Lafite Rothschild, he could certainly afford to invest some money in a system that would make his work easier. Besides, business expenses were deductible on his income tax. And speaking of that, she had a great program to figure out taxes. Just follow her to the office, she'd show him how it worked. Once she'd done that, they'd have dinner. She had a beef roast in the oven with those little browned potatoes he'd mentioned last night. He was staying for dinner, wasn't he?

Michael grinned as he thought about Toni. She had more energy than anyone he'd ever met. She threw herself into projects with such wild abandon that Michael was amazed just watching her. He'd never realized how contemplative he'd become during his time at Oakdale. Being with a spontaneous person like Toni was doing him a world of good, and it had certainly cured his depression.

The first full day of his freedom had been rough. During his escape and the long drive to Los Angeles he'd been running on pure nervous energy. Manic excitement was what the psychiatrists would call it. The run with Toni and Doris the next morning and the encounter with Captain Evans had prolonged his exhilaration. When he'd come back to his apartment and settled down, alone with no stimulus, he'd crashed. And his fears about his nightmares had driven him into the depths of depression. He'd been completely unable to make even a simple choice like whether or not to answer the phone. Small decisions like what to eat or which clothes to wear had taken on the same magnitude as critical decisions. He'd no longer trusted his own judgment, and he'd been crippled by his fear of making a mistake.

Looking back on those moments, Michael realized that he had lost all sense of perspective and now he knew when that had happened. At Oakdale he'd been under constant scrutiny. Everything he'd said had been written down and analyzed by psychiatrists. Every move he'd made had been chronicled in the nurse's daily report. He'd never been paranoid—at least he didn't think he had—but the whole system at Oakdale had encouraged paranoia. And even worse had been the loss of his sense of humor. How many times had he asked himself whether something was really funny or whether the nurse would decide it was his craziness that had made him laugh?

He was doing it again. He had to learn to be less analytical and more spontaneous. Michael picked up the phone and called Toni to tell her that his computer had arrived. As he opened the box and stared at the contents, he realized that he'd committed himself to a project. If he didn't write something to print out on her fancy printer, Toni would be suspicious. And that meant he had to write something. But what should he write?

Write what you know. The phrase came back to him from one of his college professors. Since he'd told Toni that he was working on a novel, perhaps he'd write his memories of Oakdale and disguise them as a work of fiction. He certainly had the background for that!

CHAPTER 10

Toni let out a very unladylike whoop as she hung up the phone. Mike had a computer. Now they had a common interest, and she could spend hours teaching him how to use it. Even more important, this was the very first time he'd called her. With Doris's coaching, she'd been making all the overtures, inviting him over for dinner almost every night and dropping by his apartment during the day.

With one quick motion, Toni saved her file and shut off her computer. She certainly couldn't go over to Mike's looking like this. Her hair was a mess. She'd pulled it all back in a plastic clasp while she was working. She'd have to style it before she went to Mike's apartment. What should she wear? She couldn't ask Doris. Doris had gone to Santa Monica to visit her mother, and she wouldn't be back until it was time to fix their dinner.

Toni sighed. She didn't like to be deceitful about the meals she'd served, but she was learning how to cook. The last batch of never-fail biscuits she'd made had been almost good enough to eat. She supposed she was making a fool of herself, but she couldn't help being interested in Mike. First of all, Mike was the only bachelor she knew in the building, unless you counted George Schilling down on two, who had to be at least sixty. There was a stockbroker who was separated on eight, but Toni was positive his wardrobe contained nothing but identical gray three-piece suits, a clean one for every day of the week. She'd never seen him in anything else, and there was no way she could be interested in a man who wore a suit and tie to empty the garbage.

Mike was different. He was a handsome man in a brooding sort of way, and he was definitely intelligent. When she'd first met him, he'd been much too serious. And the way he'd watched her every move had made her a bit uncomfortable. It was almost as if he were noticing things for the first time, things other people took for granted, and then mulling them over and memorizing them. She could almost hear his mind clicking, storing information for future reference just like the hard disk on her computer. If she really let her imagination run wild, Mike could be an alien from another planet, adopting a human form to observe the culture and fit in without attracting undue attention.

Toni laughed out loud. She didn't believe in alien life forms for a minute, but there really was something hidden and secretive about Mike. That made her all the more determined to crack through his reserve and find out what it was. He was just a little too careful about what he said and what he did. There was a lot more there than met the eye.

Her uncomfortable feeling of being observed and evaluated had disappeared when Doris pointed out that he was a writer. Then it had all made sense. Talented writers saw things through fresh eyes. She'd heard that in an interview once, and it seemed perfectly reasonable. And some writers were so busy observing that they didn't take time to enjoy life. She'd make sure that didn't happen to Mike.

He was good for her, no doubt about that. Toni knew she was compulsively spontaneous. She was on the go every minute, no time to sit around in solitary reflection. But since she'd been spending time with Mike she'd leveled off a little. His questions had forced her to think about what she was doing and why.

Mike hadn't made a pass at her yet, even though she'd given him a couple of opportunities. Doris had told her not to worry, that it was bound to happen eventually. He certainly liked her, he made that perfectly clear. Perhaps he'd had a bad experience in the past and was reluctant to get involved again.

Toni peeled off her clothes and put on a shower cap. Then she turned on the water and jumped under the spray. There wasn't much time. She'd use the scented soap that Doris guaranteed would drive Mike wild and hope for the best.

A quick once-over with the washcloth and a final rinse, and she was finished. Toni toweled off and rushed to the closet. None of her dresses seemed right for the occasion, but there was a bright red silk lounging outfit hanging in the back of her closet, and Toni pulled it out. It was the first thing she'd bought for herself after she'd moved into this apartment. Back then, the idea of wearing a bright red outfit had seemed terribly wild and exciting. Now she slipped it on and smiled in satisfaction. It was six years old, but it still fit perfectly. She was lucky she had an active metabolism. Most women would blow up like the Goodyear blimp if they ate the way she did.

Toni studied her reflection in the mirror. The silk clung to her body, and the neckline was cut in a daring V with a tiny gold zipper that ran all the way down the front. She'd never had the nerve to wear it before. She opened her dresser drawer and found the matching red-and-gold-patterned scarf that she had bought to go with the outfit. Time for a decision. To fill in the neckline or not'?

If Doris were here, she'd say to forget the scarf. Toni tossed it back inside the drawer. The neckline wasn't low enough to be indecent, and she wanted to be provocative.

One last glance in the mirror, a quick spray of perfume, and she was ready. Toni picked up her keys and the tiny screwdriver she'd need to attach the cords to Mike's computer. What else did she need? A word processing program, of course. And an operating system, just in case his computer had come without one. While she was at it, she grabbed a couple of games from her shelf of software. Mike had really enjoyed playing Flight Simulator. She'd zip the games on his hard disk right away. It was important for him to have a positive experience the first time he used his new computer. They could get to the harder stuff tomorrow. And when she got a free minute, she'd alter the programs so they could both play at the same time.

Toni was humming a catchy little tune as she went out the door. What was it? Her father had come home singing it one night when he'd had one too many. Some of the words began to come back to her as she walked down the hall and hummed in rhythm. It was something about bride and groom, and . . . another season and another reason for . . . for what? Toni got to Mike's door just as she reached the refrain, and she was laughing when she rang his doorbell. She'd been humming the tune to "Making Whoopie."

It took several minutes of deep breathing before Stan was able to control himself. Damn this new computer system! Since Joyce had already left for the day, he'd tried to locate a client's file himself. And the damn machine kept telling him that Raymond Schwartz didn't exist. Stan knew damn well he existed in there somewhere. He'd seen Joyce enter the data yesterday.

Carefully, gritting his teeth all the while, Stan typed in the name again R..A..Y..M..O..N..D, and then S..C..H..W..A..R..T..Z, the question mark Joyce said would locate the file, and the enter button to start what Joyce called the global search. The machine made a noise like a dryer spinning, and its little red light flickered. It was doing something in there.

The red light stopped flickering, and an answer flashed on the screen. FILENAME RAYMOND SCHWARTZ DOES NOT EXIST. This new system certainly wasn't reliable if it lost information overnight.

Stan stared at the screen for a moment, and then he shook his head in disgust. He'd better try it once more, just to make sure. It was always possible he'd hit the wrong letter and misspelled the name. He'd never been a very good typist.

When Stan pressed the key that was supposed to clear the screen, the computer gave an irritating beep, and another message flashed. It was blinking on and off demandingly. ARE YOU SURE? ARE YOU SURE? ARE YOU SURE? Of course he was sure! He wouldn't have pressed the damned button if he hadn't been sure!

It seemed to be waiting for an answer, so Stan pecked out A ... F ... F ... I ... R ... M ... A ... T ... I ... V ... E and hit the enter button. The machine beeped again and another message replaced the first. Enter "Y" FOR YES OR "N" FOR NO. Stan snorted. The damned computer was cracked up to be so intelligent. He'd read a report that said they were developing new models that could diagnose and repair themselves when something went wrong. And this one wasn't even smart enough to know what affirmative meant?

"What's the matter with you? Affirmative means yes!"

"Mr. Gerhardt? Is everything all right?"

One of his junior law clerks was standing in the doorway, looking at him with a worried expression. Stan's face turned red, and he felt like crawling under the rug. What was her name? Oh, yes . . . Wilber. Catherine Wilber.

"I'm fine, Catherine. I was just taking out my frustration, that's all. This new computer system isn't working."

Catherine nodded and looked very serious. "Maybe I can help, Mr. Gerhardt. I went to all the training sessions. What were you trying to do?"

"The Raymond Schwartz file. I need a copy."

"Sure, that's easy." Catherine stepped over to the machine with a confident smile. "You just type in the name, Mr. Gerhardt. See?"

Catherine started to type, and Stan tapped her on the shoulder. "Raymond starts with an R, Catherine. You made a mistake."

"No, Mr. Gerhardt." Catherine beamed up at him. "You have to enter the surname first. Schwartz, Raymond, with a comma separating the fields. If you reverse the order, it won't work at all."

Catherine finished typing the name and smiled up at him again. "That must be what you did wrong, Mr. Gerhardt, but it's simple if you remember that it's just like a real file cabinet. The computer searches for the first three characters you enter, and if it locates more than one filename that matches, it goes back to compare them to the rest of the name. When you typed in Raymond, it searched for R-A-Y. And naturally, it didn't find anything that matched."

He felt like an idiot, and her attitude certainly wasn't helping. He didn't want instruction on how to use the computer from a junior law clerk. He wanted the Schwartz file so he could go home.

"Now watch, Mr. Gerhardt. When you've typed in the name, you hit a question mark. That tells the computer to locate the file. And then you press the enter button. That starts the global search. See? The light's flickering. That means it's searching right . . . there you go!"

"Thank you, Catherine." Stan drew a deep breath. I'll take it from here."

Catherine looked concerned. "Are you sure, Mr. Gerhardt? The print program's a little tricky.

It's easy to get confused. I'd better run the hard copy for you. Did you need one copy or two?"

"Just one. I'm going to get a drink of water, Catherine. Just leave the file on the desk when you're through."

Stan shut the door to his executive washroom and locked it behind him. Then he walked toward the mirror and peered at his reflection. He didn't look well at all. His heart was pounding hard, and he was sure his blood pressure had risen to a dangerous level. When he'd gone in for his annual physical the doctor had said his blood pressure was normal, but doctors made mistakes. At times like this, when his heart pounded alarmingly, Stan knew he had to be careful.

Deep breathing should help, coupled with the technique he'd learned in that seminar on stress. Breathe in, breathe out. Breathe in, breathe out. At least he wasn't a smoker. If he'd smoked, he might have had a coronary right there in front of that damn computer.

Stan closed his eyes and concentrated on his personal stress-relieving image. The other lawyers in the group had used the ones that had been described in the lecture. There were waves breaking on a sandy beach, sunlight glistening on the surface of a clear blue lake, and a field of tall grasses waving gently in the breeze. They were nice, but Stan's image worked better. He pictured the decisions that his law firm had lost and fed the papers into a shredder. The Alden decision, confetti. The Chandler decision, confetti. The Donelley decision, confetti. It never took more than five to relax him.

In a moment or two Stan decided his color was better. His hands had stopped shaking, and his breathing was deep and even. Computers might be the wave of the future, but they had to build them better than the one in his office. The salesman had promised that the new, sophisticated models could process thousands of bits of information in nano-seconds. Lists, figures, calculations, permutations, and extrapolations, It did them all with lightning speed and efficiency. But it shut down cold if you failed to type the last name first.

Stan waited until he was sure that Catherine had left before he went back into his office again. She'd known exactly what he'd done wrong. Would she mention it to anyone else in the office? Just to be on the safe side, he'd call Joyce at home and tell her to assign Catherine to that case they were handling in Sacramento. Roger Merrill could use a hand up there, and Catherine was a bright young woman. She'd understand that her plum assignment was a trade-off for keeping her mouth shut. And if she didn't, he could always fire her later. Their comple-ment of junior law clerks was much too large anyway.

The Schwartz file was on his desk. Stan picked it up and tucked it in his briefcase. Working with the computer was a frustrating experience he didn't care to repeat. It could drive one completely crazy. Was it possible he'd made a terrible error when he'd sent that computer to Mike? If Mike got frustrated, he might go out and do something stupid. And if the police arrested Michael, it would put a real crimp in his plans.

CHAPTER 11

Neal Wallace woke up with a groan and reached for the button on his snooze alarm. He needed another ten minutes of sleep. Then he remembered why he'd set the damn thing in the first place. He had to get ready to start on the city mural. Since *On the Town* would be filming him, he had to take a shower and look his best. There was a little orange juice in the bottle from yesterday, and Neal slurped it down in one gulp.

Then he headed for the shower, hoping there'd be hot water. That was another thing wrong with Hennessy's building. You never knew if the water heater would work or not. Maybe when he got rich and famous he'd take this place off Hennessy's money-grubbing hands and fix it all up. He could make It into an artists' sanctuary, no rent required. All you needed to do to get your loft was demonstrate you had talent.

Neal turned on the water and stuck his arm into the old metal shower stall. The water was icy cold, but that was always the case when he first turned it on. Only time would tell. After a couple of minutes, he thought he felt it warming slightly but he wasn't sure. It was also possible the cold water pelting against his arm had numbed it. As he stood there on the cracked linoleum floor, naked and shivering, the pipes gave a rumble and a moan. Neal jerked back his arm. He knew what that meant. And a scant second later, steam hissed out of the nozzle. At least the day was starting with a good omen. He adjusted the taps so he wouldn't scald himself and stepped into the cubicle.

After he'd lathered himself thoroughly with the expensive soap his mother had given him for Christmas, Neal decided he wouldn't buy Hennessy's building after all. Why give that scumbag a break? He'd make a deal on one of those huge hotels on Western Avenue and invite all his friends to move in. The lobby would be filled with potters' wheels, and he'd make a giant kiln out of one of the fireplaces. There'd be easels by the windows and daises in the corners for the sculptors, and everybody could work together and have a wonderful time. They'd hire a French chef for the dining room and take their meals together, some fabulous entree every night, and no one would have to worry about money for food.

What about his musician friends, especially Trista, the wonderfully tall, leggy blonde who was into Appalachian folk music? He'd have to convert one floor into a sound studio and soundproof the whole thing so the neighbors couldn't complain. And since a couple of people he knew were doing experimental films, he'd build their setup right below—screening rooms, editing rooms, the whole ball of wax. Then he'd take the top floor and knock out all the walls so he could create his dream studio, the biggest work space an artist had ever owned. He'd call the place the Neal Wallace Hotel of the Arts, and talented students would come from all over the world to gather at the feet of the masters. If they turned it into a school, with Tom and his colleagues as teachers, he might even be able to get a government grant to help with the financing. Of course, he'd be so rich he wouldn't need it, and it would be a real pleasure to tell Uncle Sam to shove all that paperwork.

With a deafening squeal from the ancient pipes the water turned icy cold, and Neal jumped out of the shower like a shot. Somebody always dumped cold water on his dreams. Damn Hennessy to hell!

It didn't take long to dress. Neal had planned his outfit carefully. Because *On the Town* would be there, he'd sprung for new jeans. A black turtleneck sweater went under his denim work shirt. It would probably be breezy up there. And he had a pair of practically new black leather boots his mother had given him for his birthday.

The finishing touch was a long yellow silk scarf with a fringe. Trista had left it in his loft one memorable night, and Neal had kept it for a souvenir. He'd tell her he'd worn it for good luck. As Neal gazed at his wavy reflection in the old mirror he'd propped up against the wall, he thought he looked very dashing, a bit like the ace pilots in the newsreel footage from World War Two.

There was a honk outside the window, and Neal looked out to see Tom's old VW bus pulling up in front. Tom had taken the day off to watch Neal's debut. The door opened, and Tom got out the passenger's side because the driver's door didn't work. As he walked toward the door, he waved in the direction of Neal's window.

Neal hurried to the hot plate that served as his stove. He'd better put on water for coffee. Tom drank it by the gallon, and he swore his students wouldn't recognize him without a mug of coffee in his fist and a Marlboro hanging from the corner of his mouth.

"How's it hanging, Neal?" Tom came through the door, puffing a little. The three-floor climb always winded him. "I hope you put on the coffee."

"It'll be ready in a minute. Take a look at the foam packing I designed last night. I think we could carry raw eggs in those boxes, and they wouldn't even jiggle."

While Tom admired the packing materials, Neal admired Tom. He'd really dressed up for the occasion. Tom was wearing a new leather jacket that Neal had never seen before, and he'd definitely trimmed his beard. He had a brand new blue beret, too. The old one had been mint green with a stain on the side. Tom always wore a beret. He'd told Neal that a person lost eighty percent of his body heat through the top of his head, and he got cold in the winter without it. And in the summer, Tom claimed he was susceptible to sunstroke. Neal wished Tom would just come out and say that he wore the beret to cover up his premature baldness.

It took only twenty minutes to pack up the boxes. They lined cardboard packing crates with the foam that Neal had cut and placed the tubes carefully inside. The city had offered to transport his equipment, but Neal had declined. City employees who were used to carrying heavy metal desks and sewer pipes wouldn't be cautious enough with his precious cargo.

"All set?" Tom opened the passenger door and slid over behind the wheel. "You're quiet this morning. Nervous?"

"A little. Or maybe it's just too early to talk." Tom took the hint and was silent as he started the bus and pulled out into the heavy morning traffic. He didn't say a word until they were turning left on Melrose Avenue.

"Do you think *On the Town* will do any live interviews?"

"I don't know. Maybe." Neal grinned as he realized why Tom had worn new clothes. "I suppose they might talk to some of the spectators, if there are any."

"Oh, there will be. I told my students to come out and watch. They're going to carry a big sign that says NEON BY NEAL FAN CLUB. The fan club part was Suzanne Dickson's idea, and I couldn't talk her out of it. Arrested adolescence. How do I look?"

"Great, Tom. You look like everyone's conception of an artist, except you're a little too clean. You ought to smear some paint on that jacket so the folks out there in La La Land will know you're serious about your work."

"But I just got this jacket! There's no way I'm going to caulk up a hundred and fifty bucks' worth of leather with . . ." Tom glanced at Neal, and his voice trailed off. "You were kidding, right?"

"I was kidding. If I get a chance to talk to the producer, I'll point you out. That way you can get in a plug for the college. They'll be so impressed, they might even raise your salary."

"Oh, sure!"

The engine on Tom's old bus was laboring hard, but it made it up the steep grade. Tom pulled over to the shoulder at the top of the freeway overpass and parked as close to the scaffolding as he could. Then he turned to Neal with a serious expression on his face.

"I went to see my father last night, and he's going to watch *On the Town* every night until they run It. Do you think it'll be soon?"

"I'll find out. Hey . . . maybe I should do a Carol Burnett and tug on my earlobe to send him a signal."

"He'd really like that. Come on, Neal. We'd better get this show on the road before the camera trucks get here."

Neal sighed as he got out of the van. Tom's father was in the hospital with terminal leukemia, and he wasn't expected to last much longer. It must be a real bummer to know you were going to die, especially if there wasn't a damn thing you could do about it. When he hit the big one, he hoped it would be fast and painless.

Cars whizzed past them in the fast lane as they began to unload the boxes. The roar was deafening and every time a big rig passed, Neal and Tom were buffeted by the wind. Everyone who drove past stared at them, and a few drivers honked their horns. One driver actually pulled over to the shoulder and asked Tom if he should call Triple A. Tom explained the situation, and the man decided he'd stay and watch. He said it must take real balls to climb out on that scaffolding and hang over the freeway below. He didn't know if he could do it, but he sure wished Neal luck. Neal smiled and said it was no big deal, but his hands started to sweat just thinking about it, and he had to wipe them off on his shirt before he could go on with the unloading.

Then three carloads of Tom's students pulled up, and Neal had to shake hands all around and admire their signs. They all wanted to help, and he let them carry some of the boxes after they'd promised to be very careful. Neal noticed that Suzanne Dickson, the one who'd come up with the fan club idea, stuck so close to Tom that she almost tripped him up a couple of times. She was a design major, and she certainly had designs on Tom.

They had just finished unloading when an *On the Town* mobile unit drove up. One of the students shouted out that there was another mobile unit parked on the shoulder of the freeway that crossed beneath the overpass. Neal didn't look down to check. It was best if he didn't think about the distance from the top of the scaffolding to the freeway below.

The producer got out of the mobile unit. He had a big clipboard tucked under his arm, and he looked so young that Neal wondered whether this was his first assignment. He had to shout to make himself heard over the blasting horns and the traffic noise as he explained to Neal about double coverage. He was in charge of the first unit, and they'd be shooting from up here. The second unit was the truck below. They'd intercut so the folks at home would have some concept of the height involved. What they were after was exciting coverage.

The producer took time to answer a couple of Tom's questions. No, the hostess of *On the Town* wouldn't arrive for a couple of hours. They'd do her spots with Neal later in a quieter setting. This traffic noise was driving the sound man crazy. And yes, he thought an interview with Tom would be a nice touch. They'd been roommates in college? That was good. A little human interest was always a plus. Why didn't Tom walk over to the scaffolding with Neal and steady it while he climbed on? He could pull on the cables and look a little worried about the rigging. Then the audience would wonder whether something was wrong, and it would punch up the drama.

The cameraman finally got what he said was primo footage of Neal strapping on his specially designed backpack with the long padded pockets that held the fragile glass tubes. It took five takes before he was satisfied. Then the producer shouted that Neal should get on the scaffolding. They'd wing it from there. Neal should just forget about them and start his work.

Neal's legs were shaking a little as he walked toward the scaffolding with Tom. He was glad his back was toward the camera. Tom was the one who was supposed to look worried, not him.

Tom said something, but Neal couldn't hear him with all the noise. He was probably reminding him to tug on his earlobe. Then Tom held the platform, and Neal climbed up over the rail. Good thing he'd bought new jeans. The old ones were getting a little thin in the crotch.

The camera was on him now, and Neal put a big smile on his face. Then he gave the thumbs-up signal and Tom released his hold on the platform. The scaffolding gave a sickening lurch, and it was all Neal could do not to scream in terror. Why hadn't he hired a crew to do this part? The publicity wasn't worth it.

Neal slid off his backpack and bent down over it, hiding his face from the camera as he fumbled in one of the pockets. He needed a little time to compose himself before he lowered the scaffolding with the pulley system they'd rigged. Thank God he'd ordered waist-high walls on the sides of the scaffolding. He'd told the producer it was a special safety factor to protect the motorists below. If he dropped a neon tube, it could cause a terrible accident as cars swerved to avoid the glass. That wasn't the only reason of course. The walls kept him from looking down and they made it easier for him to pretend that he was standing in a little room with no ceiling. Of course, this particular little room would be swinging out over the freeway, but he wouldn't think about that or he'd puke right here on camera.

Neal took a deep breath. It was time to stand up and release the lever on the pulley to begin his descent. If he fiddled around much longer, somebody would come over and ask what was wrong. And when they did, he'd probably break down and beg to get out.

With legs that were trembling a little, Neal stood up. Courage. He had to look courageous as he reached for the lever. He knew the system worked perfectly because he'd watched the workmen test it. The cage would lower three feet for every pull of the lever. And once he was down to the level he wanted, a safety latch would hold it in place.

With a tug on his earlobe for Tom's father, and the most heroic expression he could muster, Neal grabbed the lever and pulled it. His heart was in his throat, and he held his breath as the cables creaked and the scaffolding began to lower. One foot, two feet, three feet, and the cage stopped moving. He let out his breath with a whoosh of relief and grinned widely. That hadn't been so bad. He could handle a smooth elevator ride like this, no sweat.

Neal was still grinning up at the camera as he tugged on his earlobe a second time and pulled the lever again. People might think he had a problem with his hearing, but he didn't care. Naturally, they'd edit the footage before they ran it, and Neal wanted to make sure at least one tug stayed in for Tom's father.

As his safe little room started to lower the second yard he remembered the other mobile unit below and turned slightly so they'd get a good shot. Maybe he'd call his mother tonight and tell her the tug on his earlobe was meant for her. She didn't know Tom's father, so she'd never find out the truth. The ladies in her bridge club would be green with envy.

Another pull of the lever, and Neal was down to the first connection. This was fun in a crazy kind of way. He could learn to like being a media star. He reached in his backpack with a flourish and pulled out the long U-shaped tube that would light up with a strong, vivid purple. He'd written to the Torgesens last night with instructions on how to mix the gases. If they ran *On the Town* in Minnesota, Deke and Sally would be thrilled that such an important artist had taken the time to answer their letter.

As Neal reached up to connect the tube he realized that his hands were dry and steady. No sweating, no trembling at all. Was it possible he'd conquered his fear of heights through some sort of aversion therapy? He sure as hell didn't want to lean over the sides and look down to check.

Neal made the second connection, a bright green. And then the third. It was childishly simple. Every socket was perfect. The electricians had done their work well.

The fourth connection was a foot to his right, but that was no problem. Neal leaned against the side of the scaffolding and reached out to slip the fourth tube—a double-humped fuchsia—into place. He could feel his fellow scarf fluttering in the breeze, and he gave a cavalier wave to the camera below. Then there was a sound like a gunshot high above his head, and the scaffolding lurched, throwing him hard against the far wall. Another shot—oh, God! The cable had snapped and then he was falling, clutching at the empty air where the platform had been, the freeway hurtling up to meet his horrified face.

Several cars swerved and crashed as motorists attempted to avoid the human obstacle that had dropped from the sky. Brakes squealed and locked in all five lanes and there was a series of sickening crunches as fast-approaching cars rammed into an impenetrable barricade of twisted steel. The effect of the massive pileup would be felt for miles in both directions.

The cameraman from the second unit swore loudly Christ! It was bedlam out there! But he was a professional, and he kept his camera steady and rolling. It was a cinch he'd win an award for this footage, but he felt for that poor guy who'd fallen off the scaffolding.

The award winning live footage of the "Disaster

on the Interchange," as the announcer would call it, would run barely an hour later. And the editor of *Avant Garde* would see it as he ducked into Winchell's to pick up a jelly doughnut for his midmorning break. When he rushed back to his office, his secretary would bring in the morning mail with Neal's questionnaire on the top of the pile. And there would be an emergency staff meeting where everyone would agree to change their layout to feature the tragic artist on the cover. Neal Wallace's fondest dream would be realized. But right now he was much too dead to care.

CHAPTER 12

Michael pressed the escape button and then the letter R for replace. The program asked him which word he wanted to replace, and he typed M ... I ... C ... H ... A ... E ... L. When it queried WITH WHAT? He typed in B ... O ... B. Then he hit the enter button and watched as thirty-seven MICHAELs were replaced with BOBs. A message flashed on the screen, "37 REPLACEMENTS MADE." Michael nodded. Using the search and replace program was easy, once Toni had coached him. In just a few seconds he'd turned his true story about Oakdale into what everyone would think was fiction. Now what should he call Oakdale? Elmwood sounded good. The Elmwood Facility for the Criminally Insane.

It took only moments to make that replacement. Michael pressed the proper sequence of keys to save his file and leaned back in his chair as the computer did the work. Toni was an excellent teacher, and he'd gotten the hang of it right away. Stan had been worried for no reason at all when he'd called last night.

Michael shut off the computer and leaned back in his chair. Why had Stan thought that using a computer would be frustrating? It was easy if you followed the prompts that appeared on the screen. Stan had even asked Michael to promise to quit if he ran into a snag. Naturally, he'd promised, but now it seemed rather silly. He'd finished his run with Toni, taken a quick shower, and sat right down to work. And everything had gone perfectly. Of course, Stan might find it frustrating. He'd never been good at things that were mechanical.

Michael thought back to Stan's college days. He'd needed a lamp for his living room, and they'd found a beauty in a thrift shop. It hadn't worked, but Michael had convinced Stan that lamps were simple to fix. There were only a couple of things that could go wrong, and it was easy to spot them. Poor Stan had almost come unglued that night, trying to rewire the lamp. He'd been ready to throw it against the wall, and Michael had come in just in time to rescue it. Michael had found the loose wire and connected it, and the lamp had worked just fine. It was probably still working unless Stan had tried to fix it again.

Now that he thought about it, Michael realized that Stan had a terrible temper when he got frustrated. He always got flustered when things didn't go exactly the way he'd planned. That was probably why he was so worried about the computer. Since it would be a frustrating experience for him, he was afraid it would be frustrating for Michael. And since Stan blew his top when he got rattled, he assumed that Michael would react in the same way. Michael chuckled a little. Stan was projecting, and that was a defense mechanism. He heard a psychiatrist at Oakdale explain it to one of the nurses. Defense mechanisms were a normal part of human behavior, but when they become exaggerated they could cause all sorts of havoc. Were Stan's defense mechanisms exaggerated? It made Michael feel better to think that his seemingly perfect brother might have a quirk or two.

Stan had always regarded Michael as the flighty one, the baby brother he had to keep in line for fear he'd do something impulsively stupid. In all honesty, Michael had to admit he'd pulled some stupid stunts to warrant Stan's concern. Perhaps part of the reason he'd done them was that Stan had expected him to. Then Stan could play his role as the stable older brother.

Michael stretched and got up. He was hungry now, although he hadn't felt like eating breakfast. He guessed he'd still been a little upset about the dream. It had started the same as all the others, with the courtroom and the jurors' faces as the judge read the verdict. Then he'd found himself on a city bus, riding through the dark streets to a destination that filled him with fearful exhilaration.

Had he actually done it? He still wasn't sure. He'd been taping a string across his bedroom doorway every night and checking in the morning to see if it was still in place, but that certainly wasn't a definitive test. He'd done some pretty complicated things in his sleep. One night at Oakdale, he'd dressed and gone into the nurses' lounge without being noticed. He'd put on a fresh pot of coffee and had been in the process of drinking his second cup when they'd discovered him. For all he knew, he could have taken down the string, gone out the door to do whatever it was he did in his sleep, and then replaced it again before he climbed back into bed.

For some strange reason, the dreams didn't upset him as much anymore. He was still worried about what he'd done, but that was normal. The first night he'd had the dream in this apartment, he'd spent the next day in a state of anxiety, attempting to recall every little detail. Now he accepted the dreams as something he'd have to cope with, and he refused to spend too much time dwelling on them. The morning jog with Toni and Doris helped, he was sure of it. They really ought to use jogging at Oakdale to exorcise the demons of the night.

There was some leftover roast that Toni had given him, and Michael used it to make a sandwich on whole wheat bread slathered with plenty of Gulden's mustard. The mustard jar was almost empty, and Michael checked the list by the phone to make sure he'd ordered more.

The day after Michael moved in, Stan gave him the number of a grocery store that delivered and told him that he'd opened an account in Mike Kruger's name. All Michael had to do was call in an order, and Stan would pay the bill at the end of the month. There was also some cash in the billfold, in case Michael hadn't noticed. A couple hundred bucks in small bills. That was for later, when it was safe for Michael to go out.

Since the refrigerator had been so well stocked, Michael hadn't called in an order until today. They promised to deliver by noon, so his groceries should come any minute. He'd ordered everything he craved plus a big leg of lamb as a gift for Toni. She'd asked him if he liked lamb last night, and they'd both decided it was one of their favorites. Of course she'd have to cook it. Michael knew nothing about preparing lamb. But it was a way for him to help out on her food bill. He'd been enjoying those fabulous meats at her apartment every night, and he wanted to contribute something.

The doorbell rang just as he was about to bite into his sandwich. Michael covered it with a paper towel and started to take off his shirt. Stan had told him not to open the door, just to tell the delivery boy to leave the groceries in the hall. But Michael figured he'd pull the same stunt he'd used when they'd delivered the computer. He'd be remembered if he didn't give the boy a tip.

"Just a second!" Michael hesitated and then rebuttoned his shirt. The whole sham seemed ridiculous. He was more than a hundred and fifty miles away from Oakdale, the Los Angeles police had a mug shot that didn't even resemble him, and the delivery boy would have no reason to be suspicious. Stan's paranoia was just as exaggerated as his projection with the computer.

Michael glanced through the peephole. That wasn't paranoia, it was just good sense: A delivery boy was standing in front of his door with a cart piled with groceries. He hadn't ordered that much, had he? He opened the door, and the boy gave a friendly smile.

"Hi. I'm Rick from Culbertson's Market. I've got an order here for Mr. Kruger?"

"That's me." Michael smiled back and gestured toward the table by the door. "Just put it down over there."

Michael watched as the boy carried in four bags with Kruger written on the side. Then he handed the kid a couple of ones for a tip.

"Thank you, Mr. Kruger." The kid seemed pleased as he tucked the money in his pocket. "I hope you'll call Culbertson's again. By the way, is there a holiday or something this week?"

"I don't think so." Michael was puzzled. "Why?"

"I was just wondering, that's all. I've never delivered two legs of lamb to one building before except at Easter. Well thanks again, Mr. Kruger. I've got to get this other order over to Mrs. Evans. She told me she needed her lamb by noon so she could serve it for dinner tonight."

"Mrs. Doris Evans?"

"That's right. I've delivered an order to her every day this week, and she says our meat is the best in town."

Michael smiled. "That's what Miss Novak says, too."

"Miss Novak? In 305?"

Michael nodded, and the delivery boy shrugged. "That's funny. Miss Novak never orders anything but junk food and frozen pizza. She told me she's a terrible cook."

After the delivery boy had left, Michael went right to the phone. It took only a moment to find out what he needed to know. Toni had already ordered the lamb for their dinner tonight. From Culbertson's.

Michael was chuckling as he stuffed his lamb in

the freezer. Toni didn't know how to cook, so she'd hatched a plot with Doris. And all those nights he'd raved about Toni's delicious meals, he'd really been eating Doris's cooking. His first instinct was to go right over and tell Toni that he didn't care if she could cook or not. But the fact that he'd caught on to her little ruse might embarrass her terribly. Perhaps it would be better to wait until she trusted him enough to admit the truth.

It was almost noon by the time Michael had everything put away. He carried his sandwich to the living room and switched on the television. At least he no longer had hang-ups about his eating only in the kitchen. He was much less rigid than he'd been a couple of days ago. And he was beginning to trust his own judgment about things, except for women.

Michael flipped through the channels to catch the news, but it didn't seem to be on anymore. NBC had *Days of Our Lives* opposite ABC's *All My Children*. Michael turned to CBS and was relieved to see that they hadn't climbed on the soap wagon.

There was a news team Michael didn't recognize, sitting behind a U-shaped table. The station officials must be saving their big-name anchormen for the evening ratings. Michael fiddled with the volume. The sound was so low, he couldn't hear it, and the button on the remote control didn't seem to be working right. He took another bite of his sandwich and got to his feet. He'd turn up the volume manually and fix the control later.

Michael was just crossing the room when the night anchorman came on. This must be a special report if they were bringing in their "A" team. Michael moved closer and as he watched, the anchorman's face disappeared and was replaced by some footage of a man on a scaffold. The platform tilted, and he fell to a freeway below. At first Michael assumed it was some daredevil stunt for a movie, but the man actually hit the pavement. The result was horrible, and Michael felt a little sick to his stomach. As motorists on the freeway crashed into each other right and left, the telephone rang.

Michael reached for it without a second's hesitation. If it was anyone other than Toni or Stan, he could hang up.

"Mike? Stan here. I wanted to catch you before you saw the news."

"I'm watching the news right now. Did you see the guy who fell from the scaffolding?"

"I saw it, and that's why I'm calling. I didn't want you to get nervous."

"I'm not nervous. I mean, it was a horrible thing, but—"

Stan broke in before he could finish. "Then you didn't catch the man's name?"

"No. The sound was off."

"Thank God for that! Now listen carefully, Mikey. That fall was an accident, got it? I checked to make sure. A tragic accident, got it?"

Michael was thoroughly puzzled. "Okay, Stan. It was an accident. But why did you think I'd—?"

"The man's name was Neal Wallace. He was a—"

This time Michael broke in. "I know, Stan. He was one of the jurors at my trial."

"That's right. You're not too upset, are you?"

"No Stan" Michael sighed. "I'm not too upset. It's a tragedy, though. Neal Wallace seemed like a pretty nice guy."

"He was. I ran into him a couple of years ago at a Cal Arts fundraiser. He was talented, too. Are you sure you really are all right?"

"I'm fine, Stan." Michael paused a second. "I'm really glad you called me to tell me it was an accident. Neal Wallace is the second juror who's died since you helped me break out."

"The third, Mike. Remember that older woman? The one with the blue hair?"

"I think so. Wasn't her name Sotherby?"

"That's right. Helen Sotherby. She died in a hospital the day before yesterday. Bone cancer."

"Then only nine jurors are left?"

"Fewer than that, Mike. Do you remember the heavyset man with the beard dozing off during the medical examiner's testimony?"

"Yes. His name was Cassinger, wasn't it?

"That's right." Stan sounded pleased. Oscar Cassinger. You've got a good memory for names, Mikey."

Michael wasn't sure what he should say. Of course he remembered the jurors' names. They were the people who had condemned him to a life without hope. But Stan went on before he had time to think of a response.

"Oscar Cassinger had a fatal heart attack seven years ago. That brings it down to eight. And then there's Sylvia Weintrob. She was killed in an auto accident last March. The others are out of the country. Gayle Hochsdorf—you remember her, don't you, Mike? She sat in the front row next to the nun."

"I remember."

"She married a man from England, and she's

living in Northumberland, on his family estate. And Chong Lee?"

"Yes. The Chinese intern."

"He finished his residency and went back to China. There are only five jurors left, not counting the two who've moved out of the country."

Michael frowned. Stan certainly knew a lot about the jurors. "It sounds like you kept tabs on them, Stan. Why?"

There was a moment of silence, and then Stan laughed.

"That's part of my job, Mike. You never know when something might come up, and once in a while it helps to contact a former juror."

"That sounds like a lot of work. You've kept track of every juror you've ever had?"

"Of course not." Stan laughed again. "Only the jurors from the trials I've lost. There haven't been that many of those. Mike. I'm very effective in the courtroom. I've only lost two cases in the entire time I've been practicing. Plus yours, of course."

Michael's frown deepened. Was he just another case to Stan? A file in a drawer that irked him because it didn't have the proper notation at the end? It certainly wasn't Stan's fault that he'd lost Michael's case, but he didn't have to be so offhand about it. Stan hadn't gone to prison, he had. And Stan hadn't been locked up in Oakdale for all those years.

Stan cleared his throat. "I've got to get back to work, Mikey. I'm taking a deposition for your appeal at one. Are you sure you're all right?"

"Yes, Stan."

"Okay. I'll call at the regular time tonight. The police still think you'll try to contact me, so it pays to be careful. And if working with that computer frustrates you, you're going to shut it off and watch a movie or something, right?"

"Right, Stan."

Michael was still frowning when he hung up the phone. He was growing tired of being treated like an incompetent by Stan. Was Mikey all right? Was Mikey upset? Would Mikey promise to be a good boy and not get frustrated? For Christ's sake! Michael knew for a fact that he took frustration better than Stan did.

The television was still on, but the news was over. Now the channel he'd chosen was running a talk show with five loud women. Perhaps it was a good thing that the volume control didn't work. He had no desire to watch the favorite show of nurses at Oakdale.

Michael got a screwdriver from the toolbox in the utility closet and took apart the remote control. He cleaned the corrosion from the contact strip and made sure the connections were tight. Then he replaced the batteries and tested it. One of the female panelists was agonizing over failed marriage. Michael could hear her perfectly now, but he didn't want to. He clicked off the television. There wasn't much to watch in the afternoon, and he wasn't due at Toni's until five.

Thinking about Toni made him uncomfortable in the most pleasant sort of way. She'd been gorgeous in the red silk outfit she'd worn yesterday. And when she'd leaned over to hook up the cables on his computer, Michael had experienced an almost overwhelming desire to reach out and touch the smooth warmth inside her low-cut neckline. He hadn't, but he'd come very close.

In his college days Michael wouldn't have shown

such restraint, but now he was much more cautious. Toni gave him the impression that she'd be receptive, but it was possible he'd been totally misreading her actions. The outfit she'd worn couldn't be taken as a strong indication. The styles were more revealing these days. Michael studied the paper every day for clues to the world he had rejoined. And he'd seen one model in a bodysuit that would have earned her a citation for soliciting ten years ago.

How did men make their moves now? Had behaviors changed? Michael was years out of touch, and he didn't want to jeopardize his friendship with Toni by making a mistake. Oakdale had destroyed his conception of how men should act. At Oakdale, he'd been case number fifteen sixty-three, a mindless eunuch to feed, and to medicate, and to observe. Jack had been the only one to mention sex at all, and that was only to joke about it. Michael hadn't had the opportunity to act like a man for so long, he was more than a little unsure of himself.

Even now, when he was supposedly free to act like a responsible adult, his brother had stepped in to fill Oakdale's role. Michael was supposed to stay behind locked doors, eat right, sleep for eight hours every night, and not get upset for any reason. It didn't help Michael's self-confidence at all to know that Stan was afraid that his younger brother would do something thoroughly inappropriate.

Michael jumped up and hurried to his office. He had more than three hours until dinner, and that would be plenty of time to do his revision. He'd just decided to make his main character into a man who'd been dominated by a loving but overprotective older brother.

CHAPTER 13

Lester Robinson was puffing hard as he climbed up the inside staircase and opened the door at the top. For the past three years, when he'd gone in for his annual physical, his doctor had told him to lose weight. He was a heavyset man in his middle forties. He combed his sparse blond hair to cover his growing bald spot and used his wife's hair spray to hold it in place. Appearance was everything in his profession, and he dressed very carefully in a white shirt and a dark suit every day. He kept a clip-on tie in his office downstairs, all ready to snap on in case it was needed.

"Sarah? Is the coffee on?"

His wife appeared in the kitchen doorway. Quite the opposite of Lester, she was very thin, and she moved with quick, birdlike motions that were surprisingly graceful. Her energy and drive was a real asset to Lester's profession. She helped him with things that would bother most women, and Lester was very glad he'd possessed the foresight to marry her. She was ten years older than he was, and both families had been against it at first, but Lester knew he'd made the right decision.

"I just made a fresh pot, dear." Sarah Robinson wiped her hands on a blue checkered towel and sighed as she noticed Lester's sweating face. "Why didn't you use the elevator, Lester? All those stairs can't be good for you."

"You worry too much, Sarah. I need the exercise and every time I try to go out and walk like the doctor said I should, the telephone rings. Where's Dad?"

"He's gone for a little drive, dear. With Mr. Reese. They're going out to have a piece of strawberry pie."

"They went out for pie? When you make the best pie in the world right here at home?"

"Thank you, Lester."

Sarah smiled, and her thin face took on a little color. She looked almost pretty, and that made Lester feel good. He complimented her every chance he got and she was always pathetically grateful. Poor Sarah had been shortchanged in the looks department, but she made up for it in a million other ways.

"It's good for him to get out, dear. And Mr. Reese came all the way over here to invite him. He said they need a fourth for bridge at the senior citizens' center, and your dad seemed interested."

"That would be good for him, as long as he doesn't forget how to bid in the middle of a game. It's a good day, then?"

Sarah nodded, and her tightly permed curls bobbed up and down. "He spent an hour this morning telling me all about his first service at Emerald Hills. And he didn't get confused once."

"That's one of Dad's favorite stories." Lester grinned and poured himself a cup of coffee. "He's got hundreds of them, Sarah, a whole lifetime of funny anecdotes. If he ever wrote them down, he'd have a guaranteed bestseller.

"Maybe." Sarah looked dubious as she sat down at the table with her husband. "I don't know about that, dear. Some people might think they were in questionable taste."

"But, Sarah, they're funny. You've got to have a sense of humor in this profession. Did I ever tell you about the time Dad climbed into the top-of-the-line bronze with Mom and had a photographer take their picture?"

"I saw the picture, dear." Sarah couldn't help but smile. "My father thought it was the funniest thing he'd ever seen. He had a marvelous sense of humor, too. He used to say you had to have the tact of a diplomat, the disposition of a saint, and the humor of Groucho Marx just to survive in the business."

"That's true. I've got a rough one down there right now, Sarah. It's a lot easier for me to handle things if I don't know them, but I knew this guy pretty well."

"The artist." Sarah nodded. "It's a strange coincidence, Lester. You don't get many you know personally in a city this large."

"That's right, but his mother's a member of Grace Presbyterian. I'm on the inside track over there. That reminds me, we really ought to drop in at the Saint Agnes fundraiser on Saturday, spend a little money, and shake a few hands. So much depends on public relations. When grief strikes a family, they call the first place they think of."

"Saint Agnes has always been Kingman's territory. Do you think we could make a dent?"

"I don't know, but now's the time to try. I heard a lot of people say they don't like the way he redecorated."

Sarah laughed. "1 know, dear. Diane Adams was telling me about it just the other day. Kingman's had an open house. Can you believe that? An open house at the mortuary! Diane went, naturally. You know what a busybody she is. And she said they had lavender flocked wallpaper in their display room. Belinda Kingman's never had any sense about what's proper. That's what happens when you marry someone from outside."

"Do I detect a note of sarcasm, Sarah? Maybe a little nudge from the green-eyed monster?"

"Of course not! I know you dated her back in high school, but that was long before you knew me."

"Well, I'm lucky I had sense enough not to marry her." Lester reached out and took her hand. "You've helped me a lot, Sarah. You're wonderful with the bereaved, and you always know exactly the right thing to say. You're the best wife a man could have."

"Thank you, Lester." Sarah looked down at her coffee cup and blushed. "Well, I'd better order those remembrance cards for the Wallace family. It takes two days to get them printed."

"And I'd better get back down there and go to work. At least you don't have to worry about me falling off my diet today. I don't think I'll be able to eat a bite when I'm finished."

"It's that bad?"

Lester nodded. "There's not much to work with, Sarah, but I don't want to go into details. And Mrs. Wallace insists on an open casket. It's going to be tough."

"Do you think you can do it, dear?"?

Sarah looked worried, and Lester stood up to give

her a kiss on the cheek. "Of course I can do it. I'll just have to pull out all the tricks I know. Do you think you'd have time to come down and help me with the makeup in an hour or so? You do the best flesh tone in town."

"Oh, Lester!" Sarah smiled again. "You know I love to help you. I'll call down in an hour to see if you're ready."

Lester kissed her again and headed for the door. He stopped with his hand on the knob. "If Dad comes back, try to keep him up here, will you? He's always saying he wants to keep his hand in, but this wouldn't be a good one. We'll let him comb the hair or something when we're all through."

Michael put down his glass of wine and sighed. It was almost time to go back to his apartment for the call from Stan. Why did his brother feel it was necessary to check up on him every night?

"Toni? I'm sorry, but I have to go now. I'm expecting a call."

Toni stretched, and the material of her lacy sweater clearly outlined her breasts. Michael could tell she wasn't wearing a bra.

"You always have to leave in time for a nine o'clock call. Very mysterious."

"Not really. Those calls are from my brother. He likes to keep in touch."

"Your brother?" Toni laughed. "And all this time I thought you were getting calls from brokenhearted women you left behind in Cleveland."

"Your imagination is working overtime, Toni. I'm not the heartbreaker type."

"Oh, I don't know about that. You're handsome

enough. And those dark brown eyes of yours are definitely intriguing."

"Anything else?" Michael was grinning.

"Well, your body's good. Muscles in all the right places. And . . ." Toni stopped as she noticed his grin. "You're just fishing for compliments, Mike Kruger!"

Michael stood up. "Of course I am. It makes me feel good to get compliments from a beautiful woman who's also a gourmet cook and a computer expert."

Toni blushed and looked embarrassed. "But I'm not really an expert at anything! And I even forgot to print out your disk. I'll do it while you're on the phone, and you can come back and get it. Who knows what might develop if you're here past nine o'clock? If I were you, I'd come prepared."

Michael stared at her. Her words were bold but she was blushing beet red. She was so embarrassed, she had trouble meeting his eyes. There was a line from Shakespeare floating around in his head. Did it apply to the strange inconsistencies he'd noticed in Toni's behavior? He was willing to bet it did.

"You're on, Toni. I'll be back. And I'll bring a bottle of cognac. Remember what Dorothy Parker wrote about liquor?"

Toni's face turned even redder. She remembered that quote very well. It was, *Candy's dandy but liquor's quicker.* Did that mean Mike was actually going to try to seduce her?

Michael turned at the door and took one last look. She was still blushing, and she looked a little dazed by his sudden response to her advances.

"I suppose I could suggest that you slip into

something more comfortable, but you look pretty comfortable already."

Michael chucked as he closed the door. He smiled all the way down the hall, and he was still smiling as he entered his apartment and flicked on the lights. The discovery he'd made about Toni was a real revelation.

He'd thought about Toni a lot during the past few days, but nothing had emerged from all that analysis. It was clear that Toni wanted him to make love to her, but there was something that had made him hesitate.

Naturally, his own uncertainties had played a part, but some stronger instinct had warned him to wait and watch for a while longer. And then, just a few moments ago, that quote had popped into his head. Hamlet had said, *The lady doth protest too much, methinks.* It was a reversal, the one thing he hadn't expected, but now he was positive he was right.

Michael got out the cognac and nodded. Everything made sense. The way she'd worn provocative outfits and then blushed when he'd stared. The suggestive remarks she'd made that had sounded forced and unnatural. All Toni's flirtatious overtures had contained a concealed anxiety that had thoroughly confused him. But tonight he'd finally figured it out, thanks to the Bard.

When the phone rang, Michael picked it up immediately. He'd try to cut Stan short tonight—reassure his brother that everything was fine and that he wouldn't crack up before tomorrow's call. And then he'd get right back to Toni's apartment for the evening they'd barely begun.

* * *

Toni slipped the disk into her computer and brought up the print option program. Mike had certainly thrown her for a loop right before he'd left. Of course, she'd been teasing him by wearing that lacy sweater. It had been another of Doris's suggestions. They'd decided this morning to pull out all the stops. But Toni hadn't actually thought it would work!

Was Mike serious when he quoted that line of Dorothy Parker's? Was he really planning on coming back to make love to her? Her hands were trembling a bit as she stacked paper in the printer tray. Naturally she wanted him to. She'd set out with that objective in mind. She'd encouraged him and urged him and practically flaunted herself in front of him to encourage this very reaction.

When it came to the number of copies, Toni hesitated, and then she typed in the number two. She wanted to read Mike's work, but he might have reservations about showing it to her. If it was terrible, she'd never mention she'd read it. But if it was good, she might be able to help him find a publisher.

The laser printer activated, and sheets of hard copy began to drop in the tray. Ten pages. That was a wonderful start. Toni took the first batch and stacked them on her desk. As the duplicate began to print, she thought about what Mike had said. Cognac. He was bringing cognac. Did that mean what she thought it meant? She had to stop thinking about it right now or she'd drive herself into a tizzy.

Toni turned on her desk lamp and started to read. She supposed she was doing something she shouldn't, but there was no way she could turn away from an opportunity like this. She wanted to know more about Mike, much more. Perhaps what he'd written would give her some insight into his character.

Luckily, she was a fast reader. It took Toni less than five minutes to finish. It was good. More than good. What she'd read was captivating and sensitive. It didn't really give her any insight into the man, Mike Kruger, but she could hardly wait for the next batch of work. It was fiction, naturally—the story of a man in a mental institution—but Mike was a very talented writer. She was absolutely amazed by the glow of reality he'd brought to an environment he knew nothing about.

He would be back any moment now. Toni shivered a little as she put her copy in a drawer. That crack he'd made about slipping into something more comfortable was certainly a change for him. He'd never said anything like that before! If she had just an ounce more nerve, she'd actually wear that erotic peignoir set Doris had given her from Frederick of Hollywood.

CHAPTER 14

Stan was still frowning as he mixed his nightly protein drink and poured it into a glass. Mike had seemed anxious to cut their conversation short tonight. He'd claimed he was tired and said he planned to unplug the phone and go right to bed.

Unplug the phone? Stan had thought that was crazy until Mike had explained what had happened. Three wrong numbers in the early hours of the morning, and Mike hadn't been able to get back to sleep. That had put a different light on things. Mikey needed his sleep.

There was something happening with Mike, and it made Stan nervous. His brother had changed in the past few days. He wasn't as pliable as he'd been before and he didn't seem to need Stan's advice. Even more frightening, Mike didn't require the long chatty conversations they'd held in the first few days after his escape. That wasn't a good sign, according to the psychiatrists. Everybody needed someone to talk to, and Mike had seen no one but him. Stan could only conclude that his brother was becoming introverted and secretive, one of the first signs of a deteriorating personality. What if Mike broke down completely before he'd brought this whole thing to a satisfactory conclusion?

The protein drink was far from tasty, but Stan finished it and left the glass on the counter. Maria could wash it when she came in tomorrow. She'd told him that he was throwing away money, that there wasn't enough work to justify hiring her on a daily basis. But Maria took only full-time positions, and Stan didn't want to take a chance on hiring someone new. He could trust Maria. She was scrupulously honest, and she didn't snoop through his things. He knew that for a fact. He'd tested her several times, and she'd passed with flying colors.

Stan went into his office and switched on the light. There was work to do. This problem with Mike had cut into his time for his clients, and now he had to play catch-up.

The first file he pulled out of his briefcase was the Goldstein case. A new will. Old Hal had married again, and he was making quite a few changes. His daughter was out—she hadn't approved of the marriage—but his son was back in again. It was fairly routine, and it took Stan only a few minutes to pencil in the new material. He'd have Joyce make the changes on the computer tomorrow, and Goldstein could come in to sign it.

The next file was marked with a red tab, which meant it was due to reach the court calendar this month. Stan sighed as he paged through it. An unnecessary lawsuit at best, but they were earning a hefty fee for handling it. Because there were complicated statutes involved, it would be too difficult for a paralegal to handle. He'd give it to one of his junior partners at the staff meeting tomorrow.

Mrs. Burke's file took a little longer. It was never a picnic when you sued the city. But everything was tied up very nicely by the time he'd put in a half hour's work. He'd plead this one himself. It was a sure winner. As Aunt Alice had been so fond of saying, it would be another scalp to add to his belt.

The last file was Richard O'Connell's. Stan sighed as he flipped through it. Richard was Joyce's problem son, and last month he'd been picked up for possession. An ounce and a half of pot. How stupid could the kid be? Everyone knew they slapped your wrist for under an ounce, but one gram over was intent to sell.

When Joyce had first approached him, Stan had told her he didn't handle narcotics cases. But Joyce was a really good secretary, the best he'd ever had, and he'd given in.

Stan began to smile as he thought of a perfect solution. He'd have a heart-to-heart with Joyce in the morning, tell her that he wanted to do the best for her son but he felt like a fish out of water. He would refer it to an expert at handling this type of case, and offer to pay the fee because of the valuable contribution she was making to the firm. That would impress her, and he would be off the hook. And even if the expert lost the case, which he was sure to do, Joyce couldn't blame him.

He was all through with his work for the evening. Stan leaned back and sighed. Just a few more things to do and he could get some badly needed sleep.

He opened his file drawer and pulled out Professor Zimmer's file. Stan had recorded their meeting. He recorded all his conferences and kept the ones that were important. Now he listened to it again, all the way through, and came to the same conclusion he'd drawn earlier. With the professor's tape for evidence, there was an excellent chance that Mikey would be acquitted. He'd been absolutely correct to proceed with the plan he'd formulated.

Toni opened her eyes and blinked twice. She was dizzy, and she stared up at Mike in amazement. She'd done some kissing in the past, but she'd never had this kind of reaction before. Every cell in her body was crying out for more, but before things went any further, she had to tell him the truth. She couldn't go on deceiving him and living a lie.

"Mike? I have to make a confession. You see, I really don't—"

"I know, Toni. That doesn't matter."

Toni sat up straighter. "What doesn't matter?"

"That you don't know how to cook."

"But how did you—"

And then, before she could finish her question, he was kissing her again. How could he have this effect on her? She wanted to kiss him for the rest of her life, maybe longer. When he stopped at last, she had trouble catching her breath. She should say something now. Tell him she liked the way he kissed her. But she more than liked it. Before she could think of an appropriate adjective to describe something that defied description, he was lifting her up off the couch.

Toni held on with both arms, but there didn't seem to be any danger of falling. He was breathing hard, but so was she. What would he do now? The bed, of course. He was putting her down on the bed.

He proceeded to undress her. He didn't have a bit of difficulty with snaps and buttons. She'd dressed very carefully tonight for exactly that reason. Everything she'd put on was easy to take off.

He had already taken off his clothes, and she peeked, then shut her eyes quickly again. He was beautiful, strong and masculine and . . she'd better not think about that part.

And then he was touching her. Her heart was beating so hard she wondered if she'd have a heart attack and die before . . .

"Do you like this, Toni?"

"Oh yes!" Toni's cry was a prayer for more. His mouth was so hot, liquid fire on her naked skin. But what if he didn't understand?

"Mike? I have to tell you that I've—"

"I know. Just leave it up to me. Please, Toni?"

Toni made a supreme effort to sit up. He obviously thought he knew what she was going to say, but he didn't.

"But Mike, you have no idea what I'm talking about!"

"Yes, I do." He bent to kiss her again, and Toni found herself falling back on the bed, hugging him tightly. So this was what it was supposed to be like, this feeling of total lethargy and abandon. But she had to tell him before it was too late and he was shocked and upset with her.

"Please, Mike. You really have to let me say this."

He brushed back her hair, and she shivered. What she had to tell him could ruin everything. Maybe he wouldn't want to, if he knew the truth. And then he laughed, throwing her completely off guard.

"Don't be so serious, Toni. It's not the end of the world. I don't need to know your life history or the reasons why. It's none of my business. You had me pretty confused for a while with those sexy remarks and the seductive clothes. And you've been coming on to me like there was no tomorrow, but I know you're—"

Toni cut in before he could finish. Her words came out rapid-fire, like bullets in a machine gun, and every bit as lethal.

"You think I'm a whore?"

This time he laughed so hard, she was afraid they were going to fall off the bed. And the last place she wanted to be right now was in bed with a man who thought she was a whore. Toni struggled to get free, but he held her tightly. If she could move her arm, she'd slap him. She'd never been so mad in her life!

Just as quickly as her temper had risen, it cooled with terrible suspicion. Could she really blame him for thinking that? She might have acted like a whore, for all she knew. She couldn't very well fault him for reaching a reasonable conclusion.

Tears came to her eyes, and she blinked them back. Everything was turning out wrong, and now she could see that it was all her fault. She'd played a seductress, and she'd done it so well that she'd fooled Mike. She'd done everything wrong, and now it was too late to explain. He'd never believe her.

He was kissing her neck and the corner of her eyes, holding her so tightly she was even more confused. When he stopped, she couldn't think of a single thing to say. Did he want to make love to a whore? Maybe that was what had turned him on. And when he found out it was all an act, he'd probably despise her.

"Mike?"

"Oh, Toni. You really are a nut."

At least he'd finally stopped laughing. Toni guessed it was impossible to kiss and laugh at the same time. And his voice was soft and tender. Was there hope, after all?

"You're a terrible tease, and you drove me up the wall with all those conflicting signals, but I never thought you were a whore. I'm just damned grateful you picked me to be the first."

"You know?"

She'd never been so embarrassed in her life. It was a good thing the lights were off, or he'd be sure to notice that her face was red. Probably her whole body was red. She felt like she was blushing all over.

"It took me a while, but I finally figured it out." He brushed back her hair again, and she trembled. "Have you changed your mind about me?" "

"Changed my mind?' Toni shook her head. "Oh no, Mike. As long as you still want to. I never change my mind when it comes to something important. And this is very important to me."

"It's important to me, too."

He was serious. She could hear it in his voice. He really cared about her. That made her feel warm. and wonderful, and very, very secure.

"Mike? If we're going to—well—may I ask a favor?"

"Yes, Toni. Anything you want."

"Oh, good! Could you do that again? The exact same thing you were doing before I stuck my foot in my big mouth?"

"And what was that, Toni?"

"The boneless chicken thing, Mike."

Oh, God! She'd done it again. Open mouth,

insert foot. People weren't supposed to joke around at a time like this, were they?

"What was that about a boneless chicken, Toni?"

Toni knew she had to explain. He was waiting. There was nothing to do but blurt it out.

"That's what I felt like. A boneless chicken. I was trying to think of the right word to describe how I felt when you kissed me, but it eluded me before. A boneless chicken is exactly right."

"Is that a compliment?"

"Oh, yes! Very few things in the world could make me feel like a boneless chicken. As a matter of fact, I can't think of anything else that would do it."

"Okay. If you say so." Mike sounded dubious, but then he laughed. "I'm almost afraid to ask what you feel like after we make love."

There were no more words, only sensations that were so heavenly, they were timeless. Toni didn't know how much time had passed, but finally she roused herself. She propped up her head on one elbow and smiled at Mike. "Go ahead, Mike. Ask me."

There was a long silence. Mike was taking a long time to ask her. He cleared his throat and turned to face her. "All right. I can't stand the suspense any longer. Tell me, Toni . . . what did you feel like when we were making love? But I'm warning you that if you say chopped liver, I'm going home for a loaf of rye."

Toni laughed. "It's a deal! I love chopped liver on rye. But really, Mike, I felt like the most beautiful woman in the world."

CHAPTER 15

"Lester? Wake up, Lester!"

Lester woke up with a start when Sarah shook his arm. He glanced at the luminous face on the alarm clock and groaned. It was two in the morning. Why did people always die in the middle of the night?

"Okay, Sarah. I'm up." He rolled out of bed and snapped on the light. "I didn't even hear the telephone ring."

"It didn't. Somebody's downstairs, Lester. I heard a noise."

"Oh." Lester blinked hard to clear the sleep from his eyes. Sarah wasn't the type to get alarmed over nothing. And she didn't imagine noises in the middle of the night. She had grown up living over a mortuary, and she was comfortable with the concept.

"What did it sound like?"

Sarah frowned. "I'm not sure. There was a crash that woke me up. And then a thump."

Lester nodded and slid his feet into his slippers.

He'd figured it would happen again, sooner or later. He'd gone down the other morning to find a cat in the preparation room. The poor thing had crawled in somehow and was frantic to get back out. He'd scooped it up and released it in the back yard. Then he'd inspected every window and vent, but everything had been locked up tight.

"Relax, Sarah, I'll check it out. It's probably that same cat again. I never did figure out how it got in."

"It sounded bigger than a cat, but I suppose you're right. Be careful, dear."

Lester smiled. He couldn't resist teasing her a little. "Maybe one of our guests is breaking out, Sarah. Lavender was Mrs. Radzinski's favorite color. She's probably walking over to Kingman's right now to lie in state in his purple room."

"Don't joke, Lester. I really did hear something."

"I know you did. If it's that cat again, I've got half a notion to keep it. Dad used to always have a stray downstairs to take care of the mice."

Sarah looked thoughtful. "That's not a bad idea, Lester. Why don't you take some milk with you? If you feed it once, it'll stay forever. Do you want me to come along? I'm good with animals."

"No, I can handle it. There's no reason for you to get up. Go back to sleep so you can deal with Mrs. Wallace tomorrow. She's got some plans for the service that are just plain crazy, and I can't get through to her."

"The music?"

"Not only that. Now she wants to charter a boat and hold the interment at sea. And she's determined to videotape the whole thing so she can give copies to all her friends."

"Lord!" Sarah pulled the covers up to her chin."
All right, Lester. I'll do my best to talk some sense
into her. Just be careful with that cat, will you? You
don't know what diseases it might be carrying, and
animal scratches can cause infections."

"I'll be careful." Lester put on his robe and slippers, and then padded off to the kitchen to get some
milk. He decided to warm it a little in the microwave,
so he went back to the bedroom to ask Sarah how
many seconds he should give it.

"Sarah?" Lester peeked in, but his wife was snor-
ing softly. He admired Sarah's ability to get right
back to sleep. He wished he could do it, but once he
was up, he was awake for a couple of hours. He
wouldn't disturb her with his silly question about
the microwave. If the cat turned up its nose at cold
milk, that was just too bad.

Lester juggled the bowl and the carton in one
hand as he opened the door. The stairs were dark,
but he didn't want to turn on the light. It might
scare the cat and he'd never find it if it hid in a
corner somewhere.

He knew these stairs like the back of his hand.
After all he'd grown up right here at Robinson's
Mortuary. The proudest moment of his life had
been when Dad had changed the name to Robinson
and Son.

He turned right at the bottom of the stairs and
went into the preparation room. The familiar odor
assailed his nose as he opened the door. It was a
combination of embalming fluid and the ammonia
he used to swab the floor and the table.

Lester flicked on the lights, and the room shim-
mered under the harsh fluorescent glare. It was

every bit as immaculate as an operating room in a hospital. The metal embalming table gleamed in the light. It was level now, but there was a lever to tilt it when he drained the fluids. The top had a removable neck rest that snapped in place to hold the deceased's head. The neck rest was made out of hard rubber, and it was shaped like a diagram of a concave lens.

In Mortuary Science 103, Lester had learned that the Japanese frequently used similar neck rests for sleeping. Pillows were thought to be bad for the back, while neck rests cleared the air passages and forced the sleeper into a proper position. Since Lester had always been plagued with lower back pain, he'd gone right home to try it. He'd appropriated his father's neck rest from the preparation room and taken it to bed with him that night. All he'd received in return for a sleepless night was a very sore neck.

Lester looked under the table and in the closets. Nothing there. He even checked the rack of gleaming instruments, but the cat wasn't hiding among them. He flicked off the lights and tried the display room next.

The room was long and narrow with caskets lined up like sentinels on both sides of the aisle. In Mortuary Marketing 217, Lester had learned that their placement was critical. His father had always lined them up at random, but Lester had changed all that when he came home from college. As a result, Dad's profits had risen almost immediately.

The bereaved tended to shy away from inspecting every casket in the room. They wanted to make their choice quickly and walk away from the reality of

death. They generally stopped midway, deciding on
one of the first few models. Naturally, that was where
Lester had placed the expensive caskets.

"Here, kitty, kitty." Lester walked down the aisle
and called out softly, but there was no answering
meow. He was standing by the middle-range models
now the ones most folks almost picked. Lester had
devised a way to bring them up a notch by deliberately stocking the two middle-range models in homely
colors. The one on the left was orchid, and its opposite number was puce. It had almost backfired on
him for the very first time with Mrs. Radzinski. But
the family had decided to place a special order after
he'd pointed out that their dear mother's skin tones
wouldn't be all that good on an orchid-colored satin
pillow.

Lester called the cat again, and a moment later,
he heard a scratching noise that seemed to be
coming from the front of the building. The cat was
in one of the viewing rooms and he sure hoped it
hadn't taken a notion to climb in with one of the deceased. Cats might do that, for all he knew. They
probably wouldn't have scruples about lying down
next to something that was dead. Lester switched off
the lights and hurried down the hallway to see. He'd
have to redo all the makeup if it was smudged.

There were three viewing rooms. They used the
small one for family-only services. The second was
larger, with couches and end tables to make it
comfortable for the bereaved. The large viewing
room had a conversational grouping at one end,
and they brought out folding chairs if they had a
crowd. Not the cheap metal kind for Robinson and
Son. Sarah had shopped all over the area to find

padded folding chairs with arms that looked like something you'd find in someone's den. If it weren't for the caskets, you'd never know you were in a mortuary.

The caskets sat on collapsible metal stands, light-weight and sturdy. Sarah draped the stands with velvet to hide the struts and the wheels. The loved ones were surrounded by a grove of artificial palm trees, the expensive kind that looked natural even though they were made out of washable plastic.

Lester reached the doorway of the medium-sized room and clicked on the lights. The room was illuminated with a soft bank of rose-colored bulbs. That had been Sarah's idea. It made the bodies look almost alive, as if they really were only sleeping.

Mrs. Kaczynski was fine. No little cat tracks anywhere on her or on the metal casket her family had chosen. He flicked off the lights and went to the second viewing room.

Baby Boy Thompson was undisturbed in his tiny white casket with the needlepoint of praying hands on the inside cover. No feline intruders here. Sarah had done wonders with the Thompson's stillborn child. The little tyke looked so real, Lester had the impulse to pick him up and rock him.

They'd put Neal Wallace in the largest viewing room. He was resting in the most expensive bronze Lester had in stock. Now he wished that he'd picked up that gold-leaf beauty he'd seen at the last casket show. If Mrs. Wallace had spied it in his display room, she would have forked out another four grand.

Neal Wallace's funeral promised to be an extravaganza, if his mother had her way. He hadn't told Sarah yet, but there was even a possibility of television coverage. They'd scheduled the first visitation, and Mrs. Wallace had told him to expect more than four hundred between the hours of eight and ten. Lester just hoped they'd come in shifts. The room would be stifling with all those people, and Neal's preparation had been a bit iffy. He'd have to remember to turn the air conditioner on full blast. Neal wouldn't last long if he heated up too much.

Lester turned on the overheads and walked toward the casket. He was only halfway across the room when he stopped in his tracks. The milk carton fell from his nerveless fingers, covering the new gray carpet with a large, irregular splotch of white. Lester was staring, his eyes focused on the deceased with horror. They'd never be able to put Neal back together again, not in a million years. Some weirdo had broken in to desecrate the body.

He backed away and opened his mouth to yell for Sarah, but the sound died on his lips before he could force it out into the silent, flower-scented air. A final stab with the long embalming syringe and Lester was the second dearly departed in the large viewing room.

Sarah awoke at six in the morning. It was still fairly dark, but she didn't bother to turn on the light. She wouldn't wake Lester until seven, providing the telephone didn't ring. He'd probably had trouble getting back to sleep after he'd chased down that cat.

In less than ten minutes, Sarah was dressed and ready to start her day. This was her favorite time. The coffee sang a cheerful tune as it perked in her old-fashioned perculator—no modern drip machines for her, thank you very much!—and Sarah smiled in enjoyment. It had been difficult to find a new percolator when she had gotten married. It seemed everyone used drip coffee makers now. Sarah had finally found the percolator in a thrift shop, and she'd shopped around in other secondhand stores until she'd found three more percolators to use for spares. Perked coffee was much better than drip coffee. She could testify to the truth of that!

Sarah opened the kitchen window and inhaled the crisp air of the morning. It was too early for smog. The commuters weren't even out of their beds. It was wonderful to breathe in air that hadn't been polluted by exhaust fumes and faulty catalytic converters. This was the clean morning smell she remembered from her childhood.

The coffee was done. Sarah took a Guardian Casket Company insulated mug from the shelf and poured herself a cup. Then she sat down at the kitchen table and thought about how lucky she was to be Lester's wife. Several years before Lester had asked her, she'd already resigned herself to being single. The face that confronted her in the mirror every morning was far from pretty. Even though her mother had always claimed that beauty was only skin deep, Sarah knew her looks would never attract a husband. The few men she'd met had shied away when they'd found out where she lived, and even though she'd lied and said she'd never had anything to do with what happened downstairs, they hadn't asked her out again.

Lester had come along as an answer to her prayers. He was intelligent, and industrious, and very good

looking. When he'd asked her to marry him, she'd
been so happy she'd broken down and cried. Her
life would have been so predictably dull without him.
She would have kept house for her father, gone out
to an occasional movie with a friend, and grown
older and uglier with each passing year. There had
been no options for her. Even if she'd left home
and gone out on her own, she had no skills to
speak of. She knew she could easily have earned a
degree in mortuary science, but that would have
been a terrible waste of time and money. No one
would have patronized a mortuary run by a woman.
Yes, Lester was a godsend, and she did her utmost to
be an asset to him.

There was ironing to do. Sarah got the bag of
shirts she'd sprinkled last night and started to work.
Lester changed shirts at least twice a day, and she
wanted to have some hanging in the closet for emer-
gencies. Sarah and Lester both agreed that white
shirts were required in this profession. Belinda
Kingman had started buying pastels for her husband, but Sarah didn't think that was right. Mint
green and baby blue were much too casual, and
pink was totally inappropriate. If Belinda had been
a friend, Sarah might have warned her, but she'd
decided to let the Kingmans make their own mistakes. If people didn't like the way Harvey Kingman
dressed, they might just switch over to Robinson
and Son.

Sarah glanced at the clock. It was almost seven.
She'd hang these shirts in Lester's closet, and
then she'd wake him. She rattled the hangers a bit
as she arranged them in the closet, but Lester
didn't wake up to ask her what time it was. When she

was through she walked over to the bed and spoke to him softly.

"Lester, dear? It's time to get up."

The covers were mounded on his side of the bed. He had a habit of pulling the blankets over his head when it got light outside and he didn't want to wake up. She lifted them gently and leaned over to kiss him on the cheek, but the bed was empty.

Sarah frowned as she went back to the kitchen to fix him a hot cup of coffee. She knew exactly where he was. He'd been so tired after chasing that cat, he'd stretched out on a couch in one of the viewing rooms, rather than make the climb up the stairs to bed. That meant he'd be sure to wake up with a stiff neck.

She carried the coffee down the stairs, along with the three aspirin she'd tucked in her apron pocket. Now which viewing room would he have chosen? Not the little one, certainly. It held two love seats, and they'd be much too small for Lester's six-foot frame. And the couches in the middle one had scratchy material. He'd pick the largest, no doubt about it. He was probably sleeping like a baby right now on their new eight-foot crushed-velvet couch.

CHAPTER 16

Michael rolled over on his back and smiled in pure satisfaction. Early morning sunlight streamed into his bedroom and was apportioned into slivers of gold by the mini-blinds on his window. He felt marvelous after the best night's sleep he'd had in as long as he could remember.

He stretched and got out of bed, then walked barefooted, to the window. It was the most perfect day he'd ever seen. The grass in the courtyard was lush and green, a thick carpet of vivid emerald spread out below him, and above him the sky was a clear, unsullied blue. It was a picture-postcard morning. He wished he had a camera so he could send a snapshot to all those unfortunate people who didn't live in Southern California.

Michael slipped on a robe and went to the kitchen to make his coffee. While he was heating the water, he glanced at the clock on the microwave. Twenty past seven. He was up early this morning. He usually crawled out of bed just in time for his nine o'clock run with Toni.

Toni. Michael stopped short as he recalled what had happened last night. No wonder he felt so good! He remembered how contented he'd felt as they'd fallen asleep in each other's arms. But why was he here, in his own apartment? He didn't remember getting up and coming home.

Michael rushed back to the bedroom and checked the chair where he usually tossed his clothes. The pants and the shirt he'd worn last night were there. At least he hadn't sleepwalked through the hallway to his door buck-naked!

Would she think it was strange when she woke up and found he'd left? Of course, she would. He'd have to think of some excuse fast. Then he remembered hearing his telephone ring. Was it true? Had it really rung? No, that was impossible. But he could always tell her he'd dashed out to get something for their breakfast.

Michael opened the freezer and found something that would substantiate his claim. Six frozen Danish would do. While the Danish was defrosting inside the microwave, he rushed back to the bedroom and dressed in the same clothes he'd worn last night. Then he hurried back to the kitchen to get the Danish and raced down the hallway to knock at Toni's door. No time to think about what he'd done last night after he'd dressed in a dream and left Toni's apartment. He could try to remember later, when he was alone.

"Mike!" Toni opened the door and smiled as she saw the Danish. "I was wondering where you'd gone."

"Did you just wake up?" Michael made an effort to keep his voice steady. If she'd missed him in the middle of the night, he'd have to make some other explanation.

Toni nodded. "I put on the coffee right away, but it isn't quite ready yet. "Those Danish look wonderful. I'm starving to death. What time did you leave?"

"I'm really not sure. I didn't look at the clock. But I was very quiet."

"You didn't have to be quiet on my account. A brass band could march into my bedroom playing 'The Stars and Stripes Forever,' and I'd sleep right through it. I absolutely never wake up before seven-thirty."

"You must sleep like a rock."

"A boulder."

"How did you ever manage to get up for that seven o'clock computer class you told me about?"

"Oh, Doris came up with a sure-fire system to get me out of bed. Are you sure you want to hear all this? I think the coffee's ready by now."

"I want to hear it."

"Okay. Harry was working the graveyard shift back then, eleven to seven. Doris told me to put the telephone right next to my bed, and Harry called me at six every morning."

"The telephone woke you when the alarm clock didn't?"

Toni nodded emphatically. "Oh, yes. There's something about a ringing telephone I just can't ignore. My curiosity gets the best of me, and I have to find out who's calling."

"So you answered?"

"That's right. And to keep me from hanging up and going back to sleep, Harry made me sing 'The Star Spangled Banner' all the way through."

"It worked?"

Toni nodded. "Like a charm. By the time I got to 'and the rocket's red glare' I was awake. I always have trouble with those high notes. Come on in the kitchen, Mike. The coffee must be ready by now, and we can start in on those Danish."

"After we eat maybe we could climb back in bed. I think I'd better take advantage of the fact that you're awake."

"Good idea." Toni blushed just a little. "When I woke up this morning I was going to ask you if you wanted to shower together. I read something about that once and it sounded like a whole lot of . . . on second thought, the Danish can wait. I m not very hungry after all. Unless you are."

Michael's stomach rumbled, but he shook his head. There were some things more important than food.

Lenny carried his coffee into his office and picked up the phone to try Eddie's number again. He was at work early, after a sleepless night. It seemed Margo was even more trouble dead than alive. The cops had put him through the wringer with all their questions, but he thought he'd convinced them that he knew nothing about Margo's murder. He'd come clean and admitted that she was blackmailing him, and he'd probably get a slap on the wrist and a fine from the IRS for those papers she'd kept, but they really weren't all that incriminating. The dizzy little broad had ditched the ones that could have gotten him indicted, and the only things she'd hung on to concerned a little bit of perfectly legal revenue he hadn't reported to the government. If he'd known that was all she'd had on him, he would have cut her off right at the beginning.

Ten rings and Eddie still hadn't answered. Lenny hung up the phone and took a big gulp of coffee. Where the hell was that little creep? He'd called Eddie's apartment a dozen times a day, but he was never home. Lenny had to get him to call off his hit man. Two jurors had been killed already and if Eddie had fingered the whole damn jury, the cops would wise up sooner or later.

Was there any way to weasel out of it? Lenny sighed deeply. He could claim they'd just been joking around, and he'd never expected Eddie to do something that dumb, but that was really lame. This could turn into some serious business. If Eddie opened his mouth to the wrong person, he'd be up the river for the big one. Or the big two. Or however many people got hit before that crazy little bastard came home.

Lenny opened the paper and glanced at the front page. What he saw made his face turn white and pasty. Holy Crap! There was number three!

There was a picture of Lester Robinson and his wife in front of their mortuary. Margo had liked Lester when they'd served on the jury together, and she'd gotten all romantic and mushy when she'd received an invitation to his wedding eight years ago.

Lenny groaned as he read about Lester's murder. The hit man had been pretty smart, carving up that artist's body to make it look like some weirdo had done it, but the police were bound to catch on pretty quick. First they'd go after Michael Hart. He was the logical suspect. But what if the officials couldn't find him? Or what if Hart had an alibi? Or what if Eddie's guy hit the next one after Hart had already been picked up? This could turn into a real mess and there wasn't a thing he could do to fix it.

"Mike? Stan here. Did you catch the news?" Michael saved his file and leaned back in is chair.

"No, Stan. Another juror's dead?"

"How did you know? You just told me you hadn't seen the news."

"I didn't watch the news. But that's the only reason you ever call me in the middle of the day. Are you serious, Stan?"

"I'm serious. Remember Lester Robinson the mortician?

"Sure." Michael sighed. "He sat in the back. Thinning blond hair, moon-shaped face, and he perspired a lot."

"That's uncanny, Mikey. Your memory for detail is amazing. I don't remember that much about him."

"I was an actor, Stan. We were trained to look for character types in class. How did he die?"

"It's not a pretty picture, Mike. I'd rather not upset you by going into details. But suffice it to say he was found dead in his mortuary this morning."

"Heart attack?"

"No, Mikey. Murder."

Michael began to feel real panic. He knew he'd had the dream again last night. He vaguely remembered it. And he'd certainly sleepwalked. There was a wide gap in his memory between the time he'd fallen asleep in Toni's apartment and when he'd opened his eyes this morning to find himself in his own bed.

There had been something about a taxi in his dream, a ride through the darkness. Was that just his imagination, or had it really happened?

"Mikey? Are you there?"

"Uh . . . yes, Stan. It's just a shock, that's all. Do the police know who did it?"

"They've already pulled in a suspect for questioning, and my contact at the precinct says the odds are he did it. The guy's a real nut case. Same M.O., although he hasn't resorted to murder before."

"How did it happen?"

"It's pretty clear that Robinson surprised an intruder, someone who'd broken in to"—Stan stopped and cleared his throat—"well, that part of it's irrelevant. I just wanted to reassure you that there's no way they could possibly connect you to this one. I hope I didn't upset you too much, Mikey."

"No, you didn't."

Michael felt the relief wash over him in waves. If the police had already picked up the killer, there was no reason to suspect he'd done anything in his sleep except walk through the hallway to his own apartment. "Thanks for telling me about it, Stan. Will you be calling again tonight?"

"Of course I will, Mikey. Don't you worry about that for a minute."

Michael began to smile. He hadn't been worried about it. He'd been hoping to get out of their nightly call so he could spend an uninterrupted evening with Toni.

"Do you suppose you could do something for me, Stan?"

"Anything you want, Mikey. All you have to do is ask."

"I was just thinking about Aunt Alice's house, the

one she had when we first moved in, and I was wondering if there were any pictures."

"Pictures?" Stan sounded surprised. "I don't have any. Why do you want them?"

Michael thought fast. He couldn't very well say that he was writing the true story of his life and needed them for a setting. Stan would insist on reading the finished product, and he wouldn't be at all pleased by the character representing him. .

"It just bothered me, Stan. I know we slept in separate rooms, but I can't visualize more than two bedrooms. Aunt Alice's was downstairs. I remember that. And so was mine. But where was your room?"

"Are you sure dredging up old memories is good for you, Mikey? You have to be careful to keep on an even keel."

"Don't worry about that. I'm doing just fine now that you got me out of Oakdale. I happened to remember the house last night, and I'd like to get a clear picture, that's all."

"Oh, that's different." Stan sounded relieved. "A little reality check, right?"

"That's right."

"Well I can help you out on this one. I'll never forget the layout of that house. Aunt Alice converted the dining room into a bedroom for you. That's why we always ate in the kitchen, even when we had company. I slept upstairs."

"Why didn't she put me upstairs with you? The room was big enough, wasn't it?"

"It was enormous—the whole length of the house. It was more like an attic than a bedroom. But don't forget you sleepwalked, Mikey. Aunt Alice was afraid you'd tumble down those stairs. And there was another reason, too."

"What was it?"

"It was too scary for a little kid up there. All those rafters and empty spaces by the chimney. She thought you'd have nightmares, and she'd have to climb the stairs every night. I was older, and she must have figured it wouldn't bother me."

"So she gave up her dining room for me?"

"For two years. Then we moved into an apartment building. Aunt Alice and I had the rooms in the back, and you had the big master bedroom."

"I remember that place. Do you have any idea why she gave me the big bedroom, Stan?"

"That's easy. You had such a large collection of stuffed animals that they wouldn't all fit in one of the smaller rooms. Aunt Alice used to buy you a different one every week. I remember I counted them once, and there were over three hundred."

Michael nodded. He remembered the toys. "Aunt Alice must have had some money back then."

"No not really. But you were the baby, and she said babies' shouldn't grow up without toys. Don't you remember the stuffed lion you got for Christmas, Mike? It must have been at least five feet tall. She had your picture taken with that lion, and it was bigger than you were."

Michael frowned as he began to remember the elaborate presents Aunt Alice had given him. "What did you get that Christmas, Stan?"

"Oh, I don't know. Probably a book. Aunt Alice always gave me books. She said she wanted me to be a good student. And she was never satisfied unless I was at the top of the class."

"But you always got excellent grades, Stan. I remember your report cards. Aunt Alice must have been very proud of you."

"She never said so. Not once." There was bitterness to Stan's voice that made Michael wince. "If I did well, she claimed all the credit because she'd made me study so hard. And if I dropped a few points on a test, she blamed me. It was my entire fault because I hadn't applied myself."

Michael sighed. "She must have been disappointed in me, then. I never made the honor roll once."

"No, Mike. If you got a bad grade, it was the teacher's fault, not yours. You could do no wrong as far as Aunt Alice was concerned."

"I'm surprised you didn't grow up hating me, Stan. It sounds like you had good reason."

"Don't be silly, Mike. You're my brother. I figured out Aunt Alice's reasons before long anyway. You looked like Mom, and she was Aunt Alice's favorite sister. It was almost like having her back again. And I looked like Dad. Aunt Alice always blamed him for that accident, you know. She was nice enough when he came to see us, but there was no love lost there."

Michael was silent. He'd never understood the whole thing before. Of course, he'd known that his aunt had been partial to him, but it sounded as if Stan had really gotten a raw deal. If the shoe had been on the other foot, he wasn't sure he could have been so forgiving.

"Well, I've got to run, Mike. Things are moving right along on your appeal, but there's still a lot of work to do. Joyce is taking an extra hour for lunch today but just as soon as she gets back I'll have her print out the file she typed in yesterday. Then I can start tying up the loose ends."

"The file is on your computer?"

"That's right."

"What kind do you have, Stan?"

"IBM. I bought the whole system through them. They installed it and trained the girls."

"What's your operating system?"

There was a moment of silence, and when Stan answered, his voice was tentative. "I'm not sure, Mikey. Something that starts with a D, I think. They told me, but it was one of those computer terms, and I didn't pay much attention."

"Do you know if you're using Microsoft Word?"

"That sounds familiar. Why?"

"If you need that file right away, I think I can tell you how to print it out. Got a pen?"

"Sure, just a second." Michael heard his brother snap open his briefcase. "I'm ready, Mike. Shoot."

"You have to call up the file. Do you know how to do that?"

Stan sighed. "I do now. One of my junior law clerks had to show me how the other day."

There was a note of chagrin in Stan's voice, and Michael decided not to comment on how simple the task was. His brother was obviously embarrassed he'd been forced to ask for help.

"First turn on your printer, if it's not already on. There should be an on–off switch on it somewhere. And then do whatever you have to do to bring up your file. When you see it on the screen, hit the escape button on your keyboard. It's the one marked ESC. In a second or so, you'll see a menu on the bottom with all kinds of stuff you don't have to worry about. Just hit P for print and press the Enter button. That should make your file print out."

"Okay. I got it written down. How did you know all that, anyway?"

"That's easy. They sent an instruction book with

the computer you ordered. It's sitting right here in front of me, and I've been reading it out loud to you."

"Oh, no wonder!" Stan sounded relieved. "Now, you're sure this'll work on my machine?"

"I'm not sure of anything, but it's worth a try."

"Thanks, Mikey I'll do it. That computer I sent, it's not too frustrating for you, is it?"

"No, not at all."

"So you think it's easy, then?"

There was an edge to Stan's voice, and Michael backed off. "No, Stan. It's certainly not easy, but remember, I'm just playing around. If an operation's too difficult for me, I just skip it and go on to something that's simpler."

"Yes, that makes sense." Stan sighed deeply. "I guess computers are only frustrating when you're working on a project. Okay, Mikey. I'll go back to the office and try those instructions you read to me. And I'll call you at nine. Check?"

"Check."

When Michael hung up the phone he was smiling. He didn't have the instruction book in front of him, but it had been wise to claim he did. Stan would feel good if he managed to print out that file. He'd attribute it to his superior intelligence. But if something backfired, he could blame it on Michael's faulty instructions.

As he went back to work on his writing, Michael realized that Stan was a lot like Aunt Alice. She claimed it was all to her credit when Stan had aced a test. But if he'd received a mark that was less than perfect, it was all Stan's fault for not studying hard enough. Now Stan was treating Michael exactly the way Aunt Alice had treated him.

CHAPTER 17

Michael and Toni were in the bedroom that he'd used as his office. She'd just installed a thesaurus program on his computer, and now she was in the process of teaching him how to use it.

"It's all set, Mike. All you have to remember is to select the word then press Control 7 to access the program."

Michael bent down to kiss the back of her neck. She looked very cute with her hair pulled up on the top of her head.

"Cut that out, Mike. You're not concentrating."

"Oh, yes I am. You said to select the word and press Control 7."

"All right, then." Toni stood up and gestured for Mike to take her place in front of the keyboard. "Type a word, any word, and try it."

Mike was trying to think of a good word to type when she bent over and kissed the back of his neck. He grinned and typed the word KISS.

"Good word, Mike. Now use the thesaurus program."

They watched as the screen divided into two

parts. A message flashed on. LOOKING UP KISS After a surprisingly short time, part of the screen filled with synonyms.

"Look at that, Toni. It's listing my favorite words. There's caress, embrace, fondle, hug, squeeze, and touch."

Toni laughed and picked up her keys. "I think I'd better leave before that list gives you ideas. Dinner at six? I've got a couple of frozen pizzas I can attempt to incinerate."

"Sounds great to me." Michael walked her to the door. "I haven't had a pizza in years."

"In years?"

Toni looked at him sharply, and Michael winced. "I guess it just seems like years. I really love pizza. I think I could eat it every night."

"Don't say that. If you stick with me, you may have to."

Toni opened the door and ran straight into Harry Evans. He was holding a plate in one hand and reaching for the doorbell with the other.

"Hi, Harry." Toni reached for the plate and uncovered it. "Doris's molasses cookies!"

Before Harry had time to react, Toni grabbed a handful and ran down the hall to her own apartment. Harry looked at Michael and shrugged. "This whole plateful was for you, but I guess it's a little late to tell you that. I sure hope Toni doesn't decide to try purse-snatching. My boys could never catch her."

"At least she left me a couple." Michael took the plate Harry handed him. "Would you like to come in?

Harry nodded. "Sure, Mike."

Michael opened the door, and Harry headed

straight for the couch. "Nice place, Mike. Did you decorate it yourself?"

"No, I rented it furnished. Would you like a cup of coffee?"

Harry shook his head. "I've got to get back down to the precinct, but I wanted to talk to you first. Did Doris tell you we picked up a suspect in the Robinson murder?"

Michael nodded. "Yes, she mentioned it this morning."

"Well, we had to let him go. Turned out he had an airtight alibi, and now we have to start over from scratch."

"That's too bad. Do you have any other suspects?"

"A few. You don't mind answering a couple of questions, do you, Mike?"

"No, Captain Evans. Of course not." Michael's heart began pounding, and he fought to keep his apprehension from showing. Had someone uncovered a current picture of Michael Hart? Or told the police about the surgery?

"Call me Harry. I'm only Captain Evans at work, and we're friends, right, Mike?"

"Sure, Harry." Michael braced himself. Harry was trying to throw him off balance by acting friendly.

"Doris tells me you're writing a book. Who's your publisher, Mike?"

"I don't have one yet."

"No publisher?" Harry frowned. "That means you don't have a contract. Or an advance."

"That's right, Harry."

"It must be tough to do all that writing without knowing if it's going to sell or not. What do you do for money, Mike?"

Michael thought fast. Harry was probing into his background, and it was best to stick to the story he'd given Toni and Doris. "There's some family money. If I'm careful, it should last until the book's finished."

"Well, that's good to hear, Mike. You moved here from Iowa, right?"

"No, Harry. I'm from Cleveland, Ohio." Michael took a deep breath. Harry was trying to trip him up, playing with him like a cat with a mouse.

"That's a good place to be from," Harry laughed. "You're not married, are you, Mike?"

"No, I'm single."

Harry nodded. "That's what Doris said. She thinks you're a real nice guy, Mike. It's a lot harder for me to take people at face value. I guess I've been a cop too long."

Michael couldn't stand it anymore. If Harry had figured out who he was, why didn't he just arrest him and get it over with? "Why all these questions, Harry? What do you really want to know?"

Harry cleared his throat. "You see, Mike, Toni's a good friend of ours, and I can see she's really interested in you. I wouldn't like to see her hurt, if you catch my drift."

It took a moment for Harry's words to sink in. When they did, Michael breathed a big sigh of relief. Harry was probing into his background, his finances, and his marital status because he was concerned for Toni. "You can relax, Harry. I'd never hurt Toni. She's very important to me."

Harry grinned and slapped him on the back so hard that Michael winced. "That's what I like to hear. I guess I can stop worrying about Toni and concentrate on the Robinson case. You want a quick rundown, Mike? It'd make one hell of a book!"

"Sure, Harry."

"Okay, but don't mention it to Toni. It's not for a lady's ears, if you know what I mean. I've been on the force for twenty years, and this was the worst one I've ever seen."

"The paper said Robinson was stabbed."

"Oh, he was, Mike. I'm talking about the stiff. That even made the photographer puke and those guys have seen everything."

"The stiff?"

"Yeah, remember the artist who fell off that scaffolding on the interchange?" Harry waited until Michael nodded. "Well, he was in the casket, and the perp hacked him up into little pieces. The police shrink says some wackos get their kicks that way. Can you imagine?"

Michael felt sick. "Not really."

"We get necrophiliacs once in a while, but they usually don't do any damage. Just love 'em and leave 'em. You know what a necrophiliac is, don't you, Mike?"

"Not from personal experience, but I've heard about it."

Harry laughed and slapped him on the back again. Michael figured he'd probably have bruises in the morning.

"That's a good one, Mike. Anyway, there were pieces of this stiff all over the place. Took us almost an hour to find them all."

Michael swallowed hard. "Did he cut up Robinson, too?"

"Nope. And it's a good thing. The lab boys would

have gone crazy trying to separate the pieces. I figure Robinson came down to check out the noise. And the perp got scared and stabbed him in the back with his own embalming needle."

"That's—uh—very interesting, Harry."

"It was no picnic, I can tell you that! Took me an hour before I could eat my breakfast. Say, Mike, you're not going to get sick on me, are you? You look kind of green around the gills."

Michael swallowed again. "I'll be all right. I just never realized that police work was so hard on the stomach."

"Sometimes. But it can be fun, too. Some of those stories the old-timers tell are a riot. You want to join me for a beer sometime? I can take you to a cop bar and introduce you around."

When was the last time someone had asked him to go out for a beer? At least ten years, that much was certain. The opportunities for social contacts at Oakdale had been nonexistent. There had been Jack—Michael counted him as a friend—and one nurse he'd liked, but that was about it. Carrying on a conversation with a catatonic was a lot like talking to the wall. Patients weren't encouraged to interact with other patients. Each one was a separate island of pain and misery, and no one attempted to build a bridge with words.

Harry was still speaking, and Michael hoped he hadn't noticed his momentary lapse of attention.

". . . promise you, Mike. You'd hear lots of stories for your books. So how about it?"

Michael started to agree. A cop bar would be a great setting for a book. But then he remembered his current situation.

"That sounds like fun, but can I call you, Harry? I'm pretty tied up for the next couple of weeks."

"Anytime, Mike. Just let me know." Harry stood up. "Well, I've got to run. Doris is fixing me some dinner, and all this talking's made me hungry."

An hour later, Michael still hadn't tasted Doris's cookies. Harry's story had taken away his appetite, but at least he had a wonderful setting for his second book. It would be about a group of old-time policemen who traded stories in a cop bar. He couldn't start writing it yet—not until he'd finished his current work—but it was never too early to start gathering information.

Michael made a glossary of police slang and entered the word "perp." Then he selected it and tried out the thesaurus program. "Perp" wasn't listed, but "perpetrator" was. He got a list of eighteen synonyms, including convict, felon, and scofflaw, a word he'd never seen before.

The perp who'd killed Lester Robinson had been a real wacko, to use Harry's word. Michael didn't bother looking that up in the thesaurus. He knew what it meant from personal experience.

Michael leaned back in his chair and sighed. It was clear Harry thought the mutilation of Neal Wallace's body had been the random act of a madman. But what if it wasn't? What if the perp had known Neal and hated him enough to want to wipe out any trace of his existence?

There was a frown on Michael's face as he thought about the juror. It was a good thing Harry didn't know that Neal had been the foreman of the jury that had convicted him. If the police ever made that connection, Michael Hart would be the number one suspect. He was a wacko, after all. At least Harry would think so. They didn't lock people up at Oakdale for no reason. And if Harry ever interviewed the Oakdale psychiatrist, he'd claim that Michael hated Neal Wallace enough to do such a bizarre thing, especially if Michael had been sleepwalking and in the grip of his nightmare about killing the jurors. But he hadn't done it. Michael was sure of that. Nightmare or no nightmare, sleepwalking or no sleepwalking, he just couldn't believe he was capable of that kind of insanity. But someone had done it. And the perp had to be a wacko who was even sicker than Michael had been at his sickest.

Slightly relieved, Michael brought up the file for his current book. He worked for an hour before another piece of the puzzle clicked into place. The moment it occurred to him, he saved his file and reached for the phone. "Toni? It's Mike. I really hate to disturb you, but Harry gave me an idea for a murder mystery, and I'm trying it on for size. Do you have a program for statistics that I could borrow?"

Michael frowned as Toni answered. "Thanks, Toni. Of course it would be great if you ran it for me, but how about your work? You're sure? Okay, I'll hold on while you load it, no problem."

Michael drummed his fingers on the desk as he waited. He'd have to think in terms of plot points now, and hide his real reason for needing the statistics. Toni was bright. And she put things together in a flash. He didn't want her to guess who he really was before Stan had cleared him. Then he could tell her the whole story.

Toni's voice came back on the line and Michael smiled. "You're ready? Okay. I'd better give you the whole story, because I'm not sure which numbers you'll have to use. Let's say there are seven people left out of an original group of . . . I'm not sure. Let's make it seven out of a dozen. What kind of group? Let me think . . ."

Michael took a moment to think of something that would be close to a jury. "A panel, Toni. An important panel where they had to give their opinion on an issue. And they were chosen at random from the community. They didn't know each other before they appeared on the panel."

Toni asked another question, and Michael frowned. This was more difficult than he'd thought. "Yes, let's put them in roughly the same geographical area—a large city the size of Los Angeles. Then three of them are murdered only days apart. You've got it? Good. Can your program tell me the probability that the crimes are related?"

Toni asked a question, and Michael nodded, even though he knew she couldn't see him. "Seven left out of twelve, that's right. The other five? Let's say they all died of natural causes. Or accidentally."

There was a moment of silence, and then Toni asked another question. "No. The panel's disbanded now. It has been for, say, ten years. Let's assume they haven't stayed in touch. Age group? From early thirties to sixties. That should cover it. Sex? Make it half and half for the original panel. You've got it? Thanks, Toni. I'll wait."

Michael held his breath as Toni's program ran. He wasn't sure he wanted to hear the results. When she came back on the line, much sooner than he'd expected, his hands were shaking. And they were shaking even harder when she'd told him the results.

"Are you sure?" Michael fought to keep his voice steady. "Okay. Thanks a lot, Toni. I really appreciate it. What? Yes, it'll work out just fine. One other question, if you have time. Is there any way you can give me the probability that the other four will be murdered?"

In only a few seconds, Toni was back on the line. Michael swallowed hard as she gave him the answer.

"All right, Toni. I've got it all written down. What? Oh, sure. I'm looking forward to it, too." That was when Toni said something else that made Michael wince. His acting skills were rusty if she'd picked up that easily on his anxiety. "Wrong? No, Toni. There's nothing wrong. I'm just a little preoccupied with this story, but I promise to leave it all behind when I see you at six. And thanks, Toni. You've really helped. I honestly don't know what I would have done without you."

Michael hung up the phone. His hands were sweating, and he could feel the hair rising on the back of his neck. His stomach had turned into a painful knot of tension, and he actually felt sick. After the numbers Toni had given him, there was no longer any question that the jurors' deaths were related. Someone was killing them off one by one. But who? And why?

Had he done it? Was he slipping out in the dark hours of the night to weave reality into the fabric of his nightmare? Michael refused to believe it. But someone was killing the jurors. That was frighteningly clear. And Michael knew he'd better figure out some way to warn them before it was too late.

CHAPTER 18

"Papa? Wake up, Papa. Mama says to tell you that dinner's ready."

Jose Sanchez rolled over in bed. It seemed as if he'd just gone to sleep, although Marguerita always made sure he had at least two hours. He yawned and stretched while the little boy watched, and then he reached out and pretended to grab his son's nose.

"Look what I have, Berto."

Jose held his thumb between his fingers, and the little boy laughed in delight. It was a game Jose had played with all of his children, and it made him sad that soon Roberto would be too old to play.

"Tell Mama I will have Berto's nose for dinner. It is much more delicious than her very best cookies. But perhaps I should put it back. The other boys will laugh if the youngest son of Jose and Marguerita has no nose on his face."

"That's your thumb, Papa. It's not my nose." Roberto ran to the mirror and pointed to his nose. "See? My nose is still here. You can't fool me anymore.

"My son is too smart for me." Jose sighed in mock

grief. "Soon he will go out into the world and forget all about his poor father and mother."

"No I won't!"

"Yes. It is true. Soon Roberto Felipe Luis Sanchez will be rich and he will live in a big white mansion with a high white wall around it. And he will have a long white limousine with a driver in a bright red uniform to take him past the home of his poor old father and mother. But will he stop?"

"Yes, I will!" Roberto was giggling now. He knew what was coming.

"No, he will not. For he will be on his way to the inauguration of the President of the United States. The election has been a grand victory, the first and only time in history that all electoral votes have been cast for a single man. And that great man will be—" He paused and smiled at his son. "Roberto Felipe Luis Sanchez"

Roberto jumped on the bed and threw his arms around his father. Even though moments before, Jose had been tired and exhausted, he now felt happy and eager to complete the eight hours of work that still awaited him. If he earned enough money to pay for his children's education, it would give them an advantage Jose had never had. Not that Roberto was likely to become president. That was a game Jose had created to teach his children to reach for the sky in their dreams. But all six of Jose's children were intelligent and hard-working, and there was no reason why they could not reach those goals that had proved unattainable for their parents.

"Are you filling my baby's head with wishes again, Jose?" Marguerita stood in the doorway watching

them. Her voice was solemn, but there was laughter
in her eyes. "His head will grow so large, it will no
longer fit his body. Which is it this time? President?
Or king of the world?"

"President, Mama." Roberto giggled. "With the
mansion and the long white limousine."

"What became of the swimming pool with flowers
that float on the water?" Marguerita broke into a
smile. "Or the famous chef who prepares dishes
from each country in the world?"

"The chef's you, Mama. You know how to make
Italian chicken."

"Pollo alla cacciatore, Berto." Marguerita corrected him. "And I am finished with Italy. Tomorrow
morning I will begin in France."

"What will we have then, Mama? French chicken?"

Marguerita laughed. "No, Berto. I will make
boeuf bourguignon. You will like it, I know. Now
hurry in the kitchen and help your sister set the
table."

When Roberto had left, she turned to Jose with a
smile. "I have decided to wait with the German
book. The food has much starch, and I am twenty
pounds greater than when we were married."

"You look even more beautiful to me, Marguerita."

"Ah! That is good to hear. You will like the food
from France, Jose. The recipes are very different."

"I know I will." Jose stood up and hugged her.
The whole family had pooled their money and
given her a set of cookbooks for Christmas. Seven
cookbooks from seven countries. Marguerita had
been delighted. She was already an excellent cook,

and she welcomed the challenge of preparing food she had never before tasted.

"Jose? I have a sad thing to tell you. Lester Robinson is dead."

"The man with whom I served on the jury? You are right, Marguerita. It is sad. How did he die?"

"He was murdered, Jose. In the night. The man on the television said the police are searching, but they have not yet caught the one to blame. Shall I send his family a card?"

"Yes, in English. And tell the children to sign it also, even Roberto. It would be right."

"You will light a candle?"

Jose nodded. "Tonight. On my way to work. Our Lady will intercede for Lester. He was a worthy man."

"That is three, Jose. Three on the jury with you who have died in such a small time. Is it a sign?"

"No, Marguerita." Jose hugged her again. "It is a tragedy, but do not worry. In English they call such a thing coincidence."

Michael leaned back in Toni's kitchen chair and stared at her in utter amazement as she reached for the last piece of pizza. Where was she putting it? The top of her head came up to his chin when they were facing each other. That meant she couldn't be taller than five-five or five-six at the most. And he was willing to swear she didn't weigh over one hundred and ten pounds stripped down. Picturing her that way was a delightful thought, and he sighed in contentment.

"You look happy, Mike."

"I am. Between the pizza and the company, I feel great, Toni."

They had just finished two huge pizzas with everything on them, washed down with two cokes apiece. He'd brought another bottle of good red wine, but Toni had told him it was a crime against nature to have expensive wine with pizza.

"Do you want me to run off your hard copy, Mike?" Toni asked, finishing the last bite of pizza and wiping her lips on a paper napkin. "I'm done with my job for the cable company, so the decks are clear."

Michael frowned. "I knew I forgot to bring something. I'll get it when I go back to take my call, and you can print it later if you feel like it. I didn't do all that well today, Toni. Only eight pages."

"But that's good, Mike." Toni sounded pleased. "Besides, you spent a lot of time working out that idea for your new book."

"My new book? You're right, Toni. I completely forgot about the time I spent on that. That reminds me, is there any way to locate a person in those data banks you told me about?"

"There are lots of ways. Do you want me to show you? We've got some time before your call, and we'd better not start . . . uh . . ."

Toni blushed, and Michael laughed.

"I mean, we'd better not get involved in anything that . . . Stop laughing, Mike. You know what I mean. Follow me and don't make any wisecracks."

Michael followed her into her office and pulled another chair up to her computer console. When the system had warmed up, she turned to him with a smile. "First I have to connect to the proper data bank. Who do you want to locate, Mike? Just pick a name, and I'll plug it in."

He grinned at her. She looked adorable with her hair pulled up in that silly plastic clip. "My cleaning lady in Cleveland asked me to look up her cousin. His name is Sanchez. Jose Sanchez."

"Sanchez, Jose." Toni began to make a file on her computer. "Do you know how old he is?"

"In his late thirties, I think".

"Do you have his last known address?"

"No. I've got it written down somewhere, but it would take a while to find.

Toni sighed, "Okay let's go at it from another angle. Is there anything distinctive about him, Mike? Something that might set him apart from other people?

"Let me think." Michael concentrated on remembering the biographical sketches Stan had prepared on the jurors. "There's one thing, but I don't know if it'll help. He's married to a woman named Marguerita. She's not a U.S. citizen. My cleaning lady said she was glad that the children were born here so they got their citizenship automatically."

"Wife's name, Marguerita. That's good, Mike. I'll check immigration for Marguerita's green card, and we can find Jose through the address she gave. She's legal, isn't she?

"I think so. Yes. I'm sure she is, Toni."

"Okay, we'll try it. I'm going to access the INS data bank."

Michael watched, and a message came up on the screen. AUTHORIZED ACCESS ONLY. ENTER KEY CODE NOW.

"What does that mean?"

Toni sighed. "It means I'm attempting to access a guarded data bank. I'll try once and show you what happens. Of course, I won't have the proper code. The chances of hitting one at random aren't even worth mentioning. "

Toni entered a code, and another message flashed on the screen. INVALID CODE. ENTER KEY CODE NOW.

"Okay, let's try another one."

Toni typed in a second code, different from the first one she'd tried. Then she pointed at the screen.

"See that? An invalid code again, and this time it gives me a warning along with the option of quitting or trying again."

"I see that. What happens if you put in the wrong code the third time?"

"All hell breaks loose, Mike. The alert goes out, my system freezes and they automatically trace me. I'm not exactly sure what the INS would do, but I've heard horror stories about people who've tried to crack the CIA data bank. It's every bit as illegal as physically breaking into an office building to steal their files."

"Oh, well!" Michael sighed. "I guess we can forget about locating Jose Sanchez through his wife."

"That would be the intelligent thing to do. I've written a program to crack access codes, but I'm not sure I've got all the bugs out yet. Since we're just playing around, I'll save it for something more important."

"Like what? Transferring funds at the bank?"

"Oh, no. That would be incredibly stupid, and I'm no criminal. I'd only try my program in case of a life-threatening emergency."

"Like what?"

"How should I know? I'll recognize it when it comes up. But just having that program makes me feel safer, more in control of my world. Does that sound crazy to you?"

Michael nodded, and Toni laughed. "I know. It sounds pretty crazy to me, too. Actually, I was just playing around one day, and the idea came to me. I've always been a nut for solving the impossible puzzle. Harry said I would have made a good cop."

"You told him about it?"

"Sure. He got a huge kick out of it, said he'd know exactly where to look if anyone ever messed with the Treasury Department's computers. But I don't think he actually believed I could do it."

"That's a relief."

"It certainly is." Toni laughed. "Harry'd lock up his own mother if she broke the law. We'd better stick to the straight and narrow to find your Jose Sanchez. Does he have a police record? Harry gave me an access code to their setup."

"I don't think so, Toni."

"Too bad. I'll try DMV, then. Everyone in L.A. drives a car." Toni typed some numbers on her screen and leaned back. "Jose Sanchez. That name's so familiar, Mike. I wonder if I've ever met anyone named . . ."

Michael pointed as a list appeared on the screen and started to scroll. Toni took one look and laughed.

"No wonder that name seemed familiar! I must have met at least one of them. Over four hundred Jose Sanchez's in California alone. But don't panic. I'll narrow the field."

The red light flashed on Toni's hard disk as she entered what looked like a foreign language to Michael. There were quotes and equal signs and little marks that looked like miniature corporal stripes lying on their sides. The only thing that seemed to resemble the English language at all was the word QUIT preceded by two question marks.

Toni pressed the send button and leaned back again. "This might take a couple of seconds, Mike. It has to weed out all the ones that don't match. Ah . . . here it is! Jose Sanchez with an address in Venice. That's right by Santa Monica. You've heard of Santa Monica, haven't you, Mike? And this address is . . . uh-oh!"

"What's the matter?"

"According to the DMV computer, Jose Sanchez lives smack dab in the middle of the area hit by the quake two years ago. That building's gone, Mike. I'm almost sure of it."

"We struck out?"

Toni shook her head. "Oh, no. We've barely scratched the surface, and this is just a minor snag: I'll plug into the Maple Grove Center next."

"The Maple Grove Center? Sounds pretty."

"Not really. It's just a big complex of high-rise office buildings. But a whole lot of L.A. department stores use their facility for billing. If Jose's got plastic, he might be listed."

"Plastic?"

"That's slang for credit cards. I keep forgetting you're from Cleveland. They probably don't call them that back there. Look, Mike." Toni pointed at the screen. "There he is. They list the same address as DMV, but now I can bring up his work history."

Toni typed in some commands, and the screen filled with information. "Does this sound like your man? Jose Sanchez, thirty-eight. Wife's name, Marguerite. Six dependent children."

"That's him."

"This Jose Sanchez is employed full-time at the Crossroads Truckstop at the junction of the Santa Monica and Harbor freeways. He's a good credit risk, Mike. See that little symbol after his name? That means he sends his payments on time. Do you want me to print this out for you while you take your call? It's almost nine."

"Great idea. Thanks, Toni." Michael was grinning as he went out the door. Toni was absolutely amazing. In just a couple of minutes she'd saved him the trouble of calling every Jose Sanchez in the L.A. telephone book.

Michael had just enough time to transfer his day's work for Toni before the telephone rang. The call from Stan took fifteen minutes, but it seemed like much longer. Yes, Michael was fine. No, his work on the computer wasn't frustrating. And yes, he'd learned how to underline something in a file. He'd covered that section just this afternoon. Hold on and he'd get the book.

He'd held the phone away from his ear a moment and then came back on the line. Stan should put his cursor on the beginning of the word or words he wanted to underline and then press the F8 key. Then he should use the arrow keys to extend his selection to the end of the underlined section. When he reached the end of the section he wanted to underline, Stan should hold down the key marked Ctrl, that stood for "control", and type a U.

Yes, he was pretty sure it would work on Stan's machine. The instructions he'd read on how to print had worked, hadn't they?

Stan had copied down his instructions and then told Michael all about a complicated legal case that he was handling, something about probate and a will Stan's client was contesting. And all the time Stan had been talking, Michael had been prowling around the apartment, hunting for the phone book to look up the Crossroads Truck stop.

When Stan had let him go at last, Michael still hadn't found the phone book. He opened the refrigerator to get a drink of cold water and frowned as he spotted it on the middle shelf. He must have been sleepwalking last night. And for some crazy reason, he'd stashed the phone book in the refrigerator. Maybe he was a wacko after all

The Crossroads Truck stop was listed, and Michael rehearsed his cover story as he dialed the number. He could hear people talking and silverware clattering as he waited for Jose to come to the phone, "Hello, Mr. Sanchez? My name is Peterson, and I'm a reporter with the L.A, Times, I'm doing a feature on the Lester Robinson case. You've heard about it, haven't you?"

Jose said he knew about Lester's murder, and Michael went on. "While I was doing my background research, I discovered you served on a jury with Mr. Robinson ten years ago, is that correct? Good. I'm always careful to double-check my facts. Now, Mr. Sanchez, are you aware that two other members of that jury have died in the past few days?"

As Jose said he knew about Miss Jantzen and Neal

Wallace, Michael took a deep breath. This was the hard part.

"Okay, Mr. Sanchez. I've already spoken with several other people who were on that jury, and they're afraid there may be a connection. A couple of them are taking precautions. Are you at all nervous about having served on that jury? And have you taken any precautions to insure your personal safety?"

Michael nodded as Jose admitted he'd taken no precautions. He'd been hoping that Jose had taken steps to protect himself. "Off the record, Mr. Sanchez, I think there's a connection. The statistics seem to bear it out. Now, that's my personal opinion, not the opinion of the paper, so please don't mention it. But if I'm right and somebody's trying to kill off the members of that jury, it would be very smart to watch your back, if you know what I mean."

Jose agreed, and his voice sounded nervous. That was great—exactly what he'd been trying to accomplish. But then he asked a question that Michael hadn't prepared for.

"No . . . uh . . . I'm not sure when my story will run, Mr. Sanchez. But I'll be glad to let you know. And naturally, I'll send you a copy. Can I reach you at this number? Or is there another number that would be more convenient for you?"

Michael drew a deep breath of relief as Jose said his work number was fine. At least he hadn't volunteered his home address or telephone number. That was excellent. He'd scared Jose enough to make him cautious.

"Thank you, Mr. Sanchez. I'll contact you if we need to arrange a personal interview. And please be careful."

Michael hung up with a feeling of satisfaction. He'd managed to warn Jose without saying who he really was. And he never would have found him this quickly without Toni's expertise on her computer.

Then he sobered quickly as he remembered how easily Toni had brought up the information on Jose. He'd have to be more careful around Toni. He'd slipped up when he'd mentioned that it had been years since he'd eaten pizza. Of course, he'd covered up his lapse very quickly, but Toni was sharp, and she'd said she loved to solve puzzles. If something he said didn't ring quite true, she might just decide to pull up some personal background on Mike Kruger from Cleveland. And if she did, she'd discover that he didn't exist in any of her data banks.

Cheryl Frasier was ladling brown gravy over a meatball sandwich when Jose came back to the kitchen. She was a plump blond woman in her middle forties, the most popular waitress at the Crossroads Truckstop. When the truckers kidded around with Cheryl, she gave it right back to them in spades. But she remembered every name and every face, and she always had a minute to slide into the booth to look at pictures of kids and grandkids. All her regular customers and every member of the kitchen staff loved her.

"I've got two red flannels with sunny sides up and a C-burger fries, no dill. Make that burger bloody will you, Jose? It's for Herbie Collins, and he wants the moo still in it."

Cheryl turned and caught Jose's worried expression,

"What's the matter, Jose? You look like Marguerite just told you the rabbit died. "

"The rabbit?" It took Jose a moment to get it. "No Cheryl, Marguerita is not with child."

"But that's not for the lack of trying, right, Jose?" Jose smiled, but his face turned slightly red. Even after five years of Cheryl's frank teasing, he still got slightly embarrassed.

"Sweetie Bea?" Cheryl called out to a passing waitress. "Could you be a doll and dump this plate on table fourteen? I've got to talk to Jose for a minute."

Cheryl walked over to the side of the grill and leaned on the counter. "Look Jose, I know I've got a big mouth, but never when it's something important. Then I can be as quiet as a corpse. What happened? Is something wrong at home?"

"No, Cheryl. It is nothing like that. The call, it was from a reporter. He asked questions about Mr. Lester Robinson. "

"The undertaker that was murdered? Why would he ask you?"

"I served on a jury many years ago, and Mr. Robinson was one of the others. Also Miss Jantzen."

"The lady who was murdered in Westwood?"

Jose nodded. "That is true, Cheryl. And also Mr. Wallace, the artist who fell from the platform above the freeway. Three from the jury have been murdered."

"Wait a minute, Jose. That artist had an accident. Nobody murdered him, right?"

"I am not sure, Cheryl. The reporter did not say. But he told me that some of the others are taking precautions. He said I may be in danger, that it may not be a coincidence."

"No wonder you're worried." Cheryl sighed. "But, Jose, maybe this reporter's just trying to stir up trouble. Those guys are always looking for a big story. The first thing we should do is find out if the artist was really murdered. Wouldn't it make you feel better if you found out he wasn't?"

Jose nodded. "Yes, Cheryl. I would feel much better."

"Okay, then. I'll find out for you right now. Did that reporter give you his name?"

"Mr. Petersen. From the *Times*. He said he was writing a feature article."

"I'll call from the office. Tell Bea to cover my tables for a minute, will you?"

In less than five minutes, Cheryl was back. She looked exasperated. "Something's rotten in Denmark, Jose. There's nobody named Petersen who works for the *Times* except for a lady in the want-ad department. And the man I talked to said there are no new developments in the artist's death. It was an accident, just like we thought."

"But why would this man say I should be careful and take precautions? And why would he lie to me?"

"I don't know, Jose. He may be a harmless fruit-cake, but you never know. Somehow he found out where you work, and he knew you were on that jury. That worries me. If I were you, I'd call the cops and tell them about it. And I'd carry a knife or a gun, just in case."

Jose sighed. "I cannot tell the police, Cheryl. They would come to my home and . ."

"And what? You can tell me, Jose. I won't spread it around."

"I have not said this before, Cheryl. My cousin

from Tequila is here, and he has no papers. Please, do not speak of this to any person. Ramone has a wife and four children, and there are no jobs for him in Mexico. His family will starve if he does not send them money."

Cheryl nodded. "It's tough down there now. I've heard about that. And I understand, Jose."

"That is good. I give you my promise that I will carry my knife, Cheryl. Then no bad things can happen to me."

"My lips are sealed. That's a fact. And I never heard word one about that call you got. Jose, did you say your cousin's from Tequila?" She waited until Jose nodded.

"And that's where they make it? The tequila, I mean?"

"That is true."

"Now you've got me going, Jose. I've got to know. Do they really eat those ugly little worms in the bottoms of the bottles?"

Jose laughed for the first time since he'd taken the call. "No, Cheryl. The men from Mexico are much too wise to eat worms. They save them all for your American truck drivers."

CHAPTER 19

It was ten o'clock in the morning by the time Toni finished the last page Mike had written. His main character, Bob, had been confined to a mental institution. Mike had done a masterful job of portraying Bob's rising panic as the door clanged shut behind him and he was forced to enter a hostile and alien world. Toni rubbed her arms and shivered. She actually had goose bumps. Now she was glad she hadn't had the chance to read this section last night when it was dark outside.

Mike had been very productive since he'd started to work on the computer. In only five days he'd turned out fifty-three pages, and there'd be another ten or so today, she was sure. She liked to think that it was due to her influence. Certainly his initial purchase of the computer had been due to her urging. But a computer was merely a tool for accomplishing a task more efficiently. It could run every complicated program in the world, but someone still had to sit down at the keyboard to actually generate the work. Mike would have written the same words whether he'd used the portable typewriter he had in his apartment or a ballpoint pen or even a quill. But the actual process would have taken him much longer.

She reread his description of the mental hospital and nodded. Mike was a natural storyteller. The pages she'd read were exciting and fast-paced. She could hardly wait for tonight's installment. His insights into the workings of a mental institution were nothing short of amazing. His powerful image of Bob's fight to maintain what sanity he had left while surrounded by people who assumed he was insane was truly chilling. He was a talented writer. Why hadn't he made contact with an agent? She'd asked last night, and Mike had told her that it was much too early to think about that.

Toni sighed. She had a good notion to call Muriel Watkins and tell her about Mike's book. Muriel was an editor in New York, and she was an expert at handling the fragile egos of beginning authors. But it wouldn't be fair to contact Muriel without Mike's permission. He'd finally trusted her enough to let her read his manuscript. Now she had an even bigger task. She had to convince him to trust her friend Muriel.

Toni picked up the phone and dialed. "Mike? It's Toni. I just read your last chapter, and I really like it. I think you're ready for a critical reading."

There was a frown on Toni's face as Mike answered. She could tell he would take some persuading. "No, I don't think it needs any revision. Not for a first reading And I know the perfect person to give you some honest criticism."

Toni sighed as Mike gave her his objections. It was too early. He wanted to go over the material again, to add some things he'd just thought of. He was glad she liked it, but he wasn't ready to give it to someone else to read quite yet.

"Look, Mike. I know how you're feeling, but you're going to have to send it off someday. Why not now? I have a friend who's an editor in New York. I know she'll be objective, and she might have some good suggestions for the rest of the book."

It took ten minutes of hard sell, but at last Toni hung up the phone with a smile on her face. Mike had finally agreed. Now she could call Muriel with a clear conscience. Muriel would be at work now, and her office number had just been changed. Toni thought she knew it. She possessed an excellent recall for numbers, but it wouldn't hurt to check it to make sure.

Toni sat down at her computer and typed BLACKBK.DOC to bring up the file containing her personal addresses and phone numbers. She always listed people by their first names, a procedure dia-metrically opposed to everything she knew about filing, but she had a good reason to do things back-wards. Johnny, the man at the garage who serviced her car, was listed under the Js. How could she put him anywhere else when she didn't even know his last name? And the plumber, whose name she never could remember, was entered in the Ps for plumber. It might be a little crazy, and people would laugh if they saw her system, but it worked for her, and that was what counted.

Toni scrolled to the Ms. There were four entries. The first was Manager, Apartment Building. The Ms were a good place to put him because the manager changed every year or so. Then there was Marc Rawls a dentist she'd dated a couple of times. No sense in cluttering up her hard disk with him. Toni erased the entry—scrap was a good place for Marc—and moved on to the next name. It was Mike Kruger. Mike stayed, very definitely. And the last entry was Muriel Watkins in New York. Toni picked up the phone and punched in the number.

"Devonshire Publishing. Muriel Watkins speaking."

For a moment Toni was speechless, but she recovered quickly. "Muriel, it's Toni. My God! You sound so important."

"Hi, Toni. Not really. I just wish they'd give me a secretary to answer the phone. Enough of that. How's the weather out there?"

"Perfect. Blue skies, green grass, temperature in the low eighties."

"Sounds like paradise to me."

"Yes." Toni sighed. "But, Muriel, it's like this every day out here. I'm dying for the excitement of a good blizzard."

"Don't say that. A vengeful God may be listening, and we both know he has a peculiar sense of humor. Remember when we got stuck at the Minneapolis airport, coming home from that conference?"

"With no snow boots? You're right, Muriel. I like Southern California just the way it is. So how's the new job? You wrote that you got a promotion."

Muriel snorted. "That's right. I'm a senior editor now. That means five times more work for the same amount of money. But I'm not complaining, Toni. It still pays a lot better than that first job we had. Your computer business is doing all right, isn't it?"

"It's fine. I got a couple of new contracts last month. A big billing job that's no sweat at all and

another research assignment. I'm happy, Muriel.
And, well, I've met somebody."

"A man?"

Toni laughed. "Yes, Muriel. A man. I've stopped
dating the lower life forms. His name's Mike Kruger
and he's a writer."

"Mike Kruger? I've never heard of him. What
does he write?"

"Fiction. You haven't heard of him because he's
never been published. He's fifty-three pages into his
first book right now. I might as well come out with it,
because that's why I called. I think he's a fantastic
writer, but I might be just a tiny bit prejudiced. I was
curious to find out what you think."

"Send me something. You could email a file, but
I'd really prefer hard copy. And send it to my home
address. I'll read it the moment I have a free
evening, and I promise to call you right after I've
read it. But I'm warning you, Toni. If he's no good,
I'll tell you."

"That's what I was hoping you'd say. Don't pull
any punches. Nothing you can say will change the
way I feel about him. I can take the brutal truth."

"My kind of brutal truth?"

"Well"—Toni laughed—"maybe you'd better
throw in a polite phrase or two, just to be nice. I'll
get his manuscript to you today, Muriel. And thanks
a lot."

After a few more minutes of conversation Toni
hung up and turned on her printer. She'd made a
separate file for Mike's work, and it took only a few
minutes to print out a clean copy for Muriel. Then
she wrote a short note thanking Muriel again, and
stuffed it all into an envelope. How many stamps did

she need? She really ought to buy a postage scale. If she knew what the package weighed, she could stick on the stamps and drop it in the mailbox immediately.

Toni went back to her computer again and loaded a math program. This should be simple, now that she'd thought about it. She'd gone out to buy paper for the printer just the other day, two cases of it. The stock boy had taken it to the car for her, and she'd admired the easy way he carried it, one box on each shoulder He'd told her it really wasn't very heavy. Each case weighed only sixty pounds.

There were twelve reams of paper to a case. Sixty divided by twelve was five. The reams weighed five pounds apiece. She didn't need her math program for that. And there were five hundred sheets to a ream, so a hundred sheets weighed a pound. And fifty-three pages was roughly one half of that. Sixteen ounces to a pound, and half was eight, so Mike's pages weighed eight ounces or so. Then there was her note to Muriel and the envelope to consider, plus the two file folders she'd used to protect the manuscript. At a stamp per ounce, ten stamps should be plenty. But ten stamps would have some weight of their own. Should she add another stamp to cover the weight of the other ten stamps? This was getting ridiculous!

Toni shut off her computer. She hadn't even used the math program. Then she sealed the envelope, stuck on ten stamps, and wrote Muriel's home address on the outside. She was heading for the door when she reconsidered and came back to put on two extra stamps. Why quibble about the price of two stamps? If she sent off the package with insufficient postage, the post office might return it to her, and who knew how long that would take? It was better to be on the safe side.

It only took a moment to dash to the mailbox outside the front door. There was a schedule posted, and Toni smiled as she discovered that the next scheduled pickup was at noon. It was eleven-thirty now, so that was perfect. She dropped the package inside, and as she heard it hit the bottom she had a terrible thought. What if the stock boy at the stationery store hadn't really known how heavy the paper was? She'd accepted his word as gospel, and he could have been off by ten or twenty pounds either way.

Toni groaned. Why was she always so impulsive? She should have driven down to the post office and done the whole thing properly. At least there was a way she could check it.

An hour later, Toni was back. The post office had been a nightmare. It seemed everyone had been sending registered letters or certified mail, and no one had filled out the little slips ahead of time. There had been only two windows open, and three other clerks, standing in the back doing absolutely nothing that Toni could see, had deliberately avoided noticing that the line was long and unbearably slow.

Oh, well. Toni sighed. At least she'd accomplished her objective when she'd finally reached the window. She'd duplicated the package exactly, and the clerk had weighed it. Ten ounces. That meant she'd been right in the first place. If the mailbox outside the apartment building hadn't already been emptied, she would have waited for the mailman and asked for her two extra stamps back.

* * *

Michael dialed the number and waited for his call to go through. He'd sleepwalked again last night, but at least there'd been no more murders in the morning paper, and he didn't remember having the usual nightmare. Last night's dreams had been about his manuscript winging its way to Muriel Watkins in New York.

Why had he agreed to let Toni send it? To New York, of all places? The police were searching for him. Stan had told him that the papers had done articles about Michael Hart, the deranged murderer who had escaped from a mental hospital in California. Of course, he'd changed all the names in the manuscript, but it was still possible that Toni's friend might suspect his story was autobiographical

Michael forced himself to think rationally. The chances of anyone guessing that Mike Kruger was really Michael Hart, simply by reading his manuscript, were so slim they weren't even worth mentioning. There was really no need to worry. But he'd been worried enough, when he'd gone to sleep at Toni's apartment last night, to sleepwalk again and wind up in his own apartment this morning.

He'd covered his nightly disappearance by telling Toni he'd gotten up in the wee hours of the morning with an idea for the next section of his book. It had been pure fabrication, of course, but he was running out of excuses. How much longer could he expect Toni to believe that he'd gone out for Danish, or home to work, or back to his apartment to change into fresh clothes? She was bound to think he didn't want to spend the entire night with her, and that wasn't true at all.

No answer. Michael hung up the phone in disgust. He'd been trying to reach James Zimmer for three days now, but he was never in his office or at his home. Michael could have left a message with his secretary, but what could he say? Would you please tell Professor Zimmer to be careful because he might be murdered? The secretary would assume he was a total crackpot and report the call to the police. No, he had to speak to the professor personally and convince him that he was in real danger.

Michael picked up the list he'd made of the jurors and sighed. Twelve names. He'd remembered them all. Two were circled in green. They were the safe ones, as far as he knew. Stan had told him that Gayle Hochsdorf and Chong Lee were out of the country, and they should be fine as long as they didn't come back before the police had caught the madman who was murdering their fellow jurors. He thought of tipping off the police himself but then they would start looking for Michael Hart again. As far as he knew, he was the only one who'd tumbled to the connection between the murder victims, and he didn't dare tell anyone except the jurors themselves.

Three names were crossed out in black, Helen Sotherby, Oscar Cassinger, and Sylvia Weintrob they'd died of natural causes, two of them before his escape from Oakdale. At least no one could blame him for their deaths. But there were three others with a red line through them. Those were the frightening ones. Margo Jantzen, murdered in her home in Westwood. Neal Wallace was killed accidentally, but then cut up in his casket by a wacko. And Lester

Robinson, stabbed to death in his mortuary right next to Neal's mutilated body. Could they blame him for those? You bet they could! He was an escaped patient from Oakdale with a history of mental illness, a grudge against the jury that had convicted him, and no alibi. Even Stan would refuse to take his case this time around. His brother was too smart to bet on a sure loser. Family loyalty would go by the boards if it would ruin Stan's win-loss record.

Only four names remained on the list, and Jose Sanchez was on top. Michael had placed two check marks after his name. The first check meant that Jose had been located. The second meant that Michael had succeeded in warning him.

The next two names had no identifying marks. That worried Michael. He'd assumed that Sister Mary Clare would be easy. He'd called the Archdiocese and asked for her address, but it seemed it was more complicated than just looking her up in a file. They'd needed more information. Which order was she in? Did she teach? Nurse? Was she cloistered? Michael hadn't known the answers to any of these questions. The man at the Archdiocese had told him that there were over seven thousand sisters in California alone. Almost three thousand of those were in Los Angeles, and there was no way of telling if Sister Mary Clare was still in this area. She could have been sent anywhere in the United States, even overseas if she was doing missionary work.

Michael had thanked him and hung up. Sister Mary Clare was the one juror he had trouble remembering in detail. There had been nothing to distinguish her from any other nun he'd ever seen. She'd worn a black habit, and her veil, or whatever they called it, had concealed her face and thrown her features into shadow. She'd kept her eyes downcast and never looked at him directly. There was just nothing memorable about her.

Rosalie Dumont was the next name on the list, and Michael had spent two whole mornings trying to locate her. He'd called every Dumont in the Los Angeles telephone book, but no one knew a Rosalie. He was tempted to ask Toni to run the name through her data banks, but that wouldn't be wise. He'd come up with a good excuse for wanting to find Jose Sanchez, but Toni would be sure to grow suspicious if he asked her to run any more names.

The last person on the list was James Zimmer. He had one check mark behind his name. Michael had located the professor, but he'd been unable to make contact to warn him. At least he knew where Professor Zimmer worked, and that was a step in the right direction. Could he take the risk of going to the campus and warning him in person?

That was a radical step, and Michael hesitated. He was almost positive he could blend in on a large college campus if he dressed in nondescript clothes and carried books under his arm. He'd just have to try it if he wanted to warn the professor in time. He'd already wasted two days with telephone calls, and there was no guarantee he'd ever reach James Zimmer that way.

Michael grabbed the phone and dialed the college number again. When he reached the switchboard, he asked to be connected to the personnel office. He'd find out the professor's schedule and catch him between classes.

"Personnel office," A tentative voice answered the phone.

"Could you give me Professor James Zimmer's class schedule, please?"

"Professor James Zimmer? I think I can get that for you."

Michael listened as the girl explained that she was only a temporary student helper, so she wasn't really sure where things like that were kept. It might take her a few minutes to locate the file with the schedules. Miss Beemer, the regular secretary, was out to lunch, and the student helper who usually worked in this office had called in sick. Would he rather call back in an hour? When Miss Beemer was back?

Michael told her that he couldn't call back, but he'd be glad to wait while she tried to find it. He listened to recorded music for a few moments, but the sound was so tinny coming out of the receiver that he couldn't even recognize the tune. And then, in much less time than Michael had expected, the girl came back on the line.

She sounded very pleased with her efficiency when she told him that she'd located the schedule and that Professor Zimmer had three classes this semester, plus his conference periods, of course. One class was at 10 a.m. on Tuesdays and Thursdays, and another was at 2 p.m. on Mondays, Wednesdays, and Fridays. The third was an independent study seminar for senior students, and that meets on Thursday evenings from seven to ten. Because this was Friday, Professor Zimmer would just be starting his two o'clock class. If this was an emergency, she'd be glad to send a runner down to call the professor

to the phone. The regular secretary had told her
how to do that.

"No, it's not an emergency. I can catch Professor
Zimmer myself if you can tell me what classroom
he's in. And give me directions to the campus."

The girl seemed relieved that directions were all
that Michael wanted. She told him that she usually
worked in the ticket office, and she was used to
giving directions to people who drove to the campus
for concerts and plays. Michael copied down her instructions as she rattled them off, thanked her for
her trouble, and rushed to Toni's apartment to
borrow her car. It was two o'clock now, and the girl
had told him that Professor Zimmer's class ran for
an hour. He'd have just enough time to drive to
Gateway University and catch the professor when he
came out of his classroom.

CHAPTER 20

Lenny ordered another cup of coffee from the bartender. This was the first hangover he'd had in years.

How many bottles of beer had he gone through last night? Ten? Fifteen? He'd been nearly out on his feet, but at least he'd forgotten how ugly the woman had been until he'd looked at her this morning.

It was a real drag leaving work and going straight to a crummy bar, but he needed an airtight alibi in case there was another murder. Eddie still wasn't back, the little creep, and Lenny had been spending his nights with women who weren't even attractive, just so he'd have someone with him around the clock.

The bartender leaned across the bar. "Let me give you a little friendly tip, buddy. You've been forking out bar prices for my lousy coffee all night, and there's a coffee shop right around the corner with some decent brew. So what are you doing in here?"

"I like the company." Lenny reached over to pat the thigh of the skinny woman sitting on the stool next to him. "And coffee's the only thing I can keep down right now."

"Hangover?"

Lenny nodded. "You got it."

"Coffee's not going to fix it, buddy. Believe me, I know. What you need is one ounce of brandy. No more, no less. You chug it right down, and twenty minutes later, you'll feel like a new man."

Lenny swallowed hard. "I don't know. Hair of the dog never worked for me. I tried it once."

"But not with brandy, right?" The bartender grinned as Lenny shook his head. "This is on the house. I'm pouring you an ounce of brandy—the good stuff—and I want you to drink it like medicine. Got it?"

Lenny nodded and picked up the glass the bartender put in front of him. He took a deep breath, swallowed the contents, and winced as it burned all the way down his throat.

"That's my man," The bartender grinned in approval. "If that doesn't do the trick in twenty minutes, I'll give you free coffee for the rest of the night."

The girl on the stool next to Lenny nodded sagely. "It works, honest. I saw him doctor a couple of guys, and they were raring to go afterwards. Can you buy me another drink while we're waiting, Tiger? I'm dry as a bone over here. And a daiquiri always makes me feel so sexy."

Lenny nodded and motioned to the bartender to whirl up another daiquiri. She'd downed four already, and she was just a skinny little thing. If the bartender had been pouring her real booze, she would have been out like a light by now. Straight mix, iced tea in a whiskey glass, that was the way things were done in a dive like this. But Lenny wasn't complaining. He needed her for an alibi, and that was worth laying out the bucks for a whole night of overpriced Shirley Temples.

"Here you go, babe." Lenny pushed the drink over to her, and she gave him a smile. She wasn't a dog like the one last night, but he never would have gone for her under normal circumstances. There was no meat on her bones, none at all. She reminded him of a skinny little kid. She'd been working the bar when he'd walked through the door, and she'd been only too happy to let him buy her a drink. What was her name again? Elena or Helena or something like that.

"What's the matter, sweetie? You look down in the dumps. Tell Babsie all about it."

Lenny took a big swig of his coffee. Her name was Babsie? Helena must have been the one last night. Babsie's purple eye shadow made her look a little like Vampira on the late show, but she really wasn't all that bad. Nice skin. And nice hair. But looks didn't matter. Right now he'd hook up with the ugliest broad in the world if he thought it would throw the police off his trail.

"Nothing's wrong, babe." Lenny smiled back. "I'm just thinking about the job, that's all."

"What line of work are you in, Tiger?"

"Auto parts. I own a couple of stores. "

Her face lit up with interest, and Lenny almost groaned. He shouldn't have said that. Now that she knew he owned a couple of stores, she'd charge him the going rate.

"Auto parts is a good business, sweetie, if you know what you're doing. Look at the Pep Boys. They started out on a shoestring. Are you strictly domestic? Or do you carry foreign parts, too?"

Lenny took a minute to answer. Babsie's question had taken him completely by surprise. He didn't think she'd known what the word domestic meant. If she really wasn't interested, she sure as hell was doing a good job of faking it.

"I'm domestic, babe. There's no profit in foreign. Too many parts to carry. They take up shelf space, and cost you an arm and a leg to stock."

"I know what you mean." Babsie sighed. "Last time I checked, one of those little cigarette lighters for an MG cost over thirty bucks wholesale"

"You drive an MG?"

Babsie laughed. "Not on your life, Tiger. I need something that runs. English cars are always laid up with electrical problems. I just love sports cars, though. They're fun to drive if you get one that hugs the road."

"I bet you've got a Fiat, huh?"

"Italian engineering?" Babsie made a face. "That's not for me. They overstress everything they build in Italy."

Lenny frowned. "Okay. I give up, Babsie. Tell me what kind of sports car you have."

Babsie looked a little embarrassed. "I don't have a sports car, sweetie. I've got a jeep."

"Those are nice cars. American Motors? Or one of those new Chryslers?"

Babsie shook her head. "Neither. It's military, so there's no manufacturer's markings. But it's a Willies, I can tell. I bought it at one of those big surplus auctions five years ago."

"You got a good buy?"

"Sure did!" Babsie nodded emphatically. "It was dirt cheap because the block was cracked. And speaking of cracked blocks, Tiger, how does your head feel? It's been twenty minutes."

"It has?" Lenny looked surprised. "You know, I feel a lot better. The bartender was right. Now, tell me some more about that jeep of yours. It must have cost you a bundle to get it up and running, huh?"

"Nope." Babsie shook her head. I just pulled the engine and replaced it. No sweat."

"You pulled the engine yourself?"

"Oh, sure. It was easy. I just pushed it under a tree limb and rigged up a hoist with a couple of strong ropes. It lifted right out, slick as a whistle. But I guess I shouldn't have told you all this. I ruined my image as a sexpot, didn't I, Tiger?"

"I guess you did!" Lenny laughed. "So you pulled your own engine. That's pretty good. I never met a hooker that . . . wait a second, Babsie. I mean—you do work here, don't you?"

"You thought you made a mistake for a minute, didn't you?" Babsie laughed. "You can relax, because I'm a hooker, just like you thought. If I sounded different there for a minute it's just because I got too interested in talking with you. Don't tell anybody I blew my act, will you?"

"No. I won't tell."

"Well, see you around, Lenny. I've gotta try to pick up somebody else before closing time or my ass is grass and the bartender is the lawn mower."

As Babsie blew him a kiss and slid off the stool, Lenny wondered where he'd ever gotten the idea she wasn't good-looking. She had a nice little shape, and she'd be real cute if she washed off that makeup. What was she doing working in a bar like this anyhow? She had a lot more class than that.

Lenny reached out and grabbed her wrist. "Where you going, Babsie? We haven't finished our conversation."

Babsie bent over and whispered in his ear. "I know, but I gotta hustle, Lenny. The bartender gets half my take and he won't let me work here unless I bring in cash. And I need my share so I can buy out my regular boss when he goes under. It's crazy, Lenny. I tried to tell him what he's doing wrong, but he's not the type to take advice from a woman. And I think I could have turned things around, I really do."

"Your regular boss?"

Babsie nodded. "I work during the day, Lenny. Answering the phone, ordering stock, waiting on the customers, stuff like that."

"What kind of store, Babsie?"

Babsie looked completely flustered. "It's an auto parts store, Lenny. That's why I was so interested in what you had to say. But don't worry. I'll never be any competition for you. The place I want to buy is strictly foreign."

"Foreign?"

"That's right. I know what you said, that there's no money in it. But it's really not that expensive to stock if you know what you're buying. I've got it all figured out on paper."

"Are you pulling my leg, Babsie?"

"Nope. That's my dream, Lenny. You know the old joke about the whore who's saving her money to buy a chicken farm out west? Well, mine is the same thing, except it's not chickens, that's all."

"You're really serious about this right?"

"I'm serious, but don't tell the customers. I'm supposed to be dumb and fun—that's all they want.

Well, you're a real nice guy, Lenny. I enjoyed spending time with you. And just between us, don't try to pick up that blonde over there in the pink dress. She told me she's got the clap."

She began to move away and Lenny grabbed her arm. "Wait a second, Babsie. You're really serious about this, right?"

She nodded and Lenny patted the stool next to him. "Sit down and tell me how much the bartender usually pulls in from you girls."

"About sixty from each of us. There's five girls, so it's a nice little profit for him. But I don't mind. He protects us if a customer gets too rough, and he's a real nice guy. Now let me go, Lenny. I can't afford to get him mad at me. This is a good place to work, and I don't want to lose it."

"Hey, barkeep!" Lenny tightened his fingers around Babsie's wrist and motioned for the bartender. "We got to have a little talk."

The bartender came up, and Lenny fanned three twenties on the bar. "How about if I take off with Babsie here? Does that give you a problem?"

"No problem." The bartender looked down at the money and smiled. "Have fun, buddy. Babsie's a real nice girl."

"Oh, yeah. I almost forgot," Lenny took out his money clip again and peeled off another twenty. "Here's a little something extra for that hangover cure. It worked just like you said."

As the bartender reached for the money and pocketed it, Lenny pulled Babsie to the door. When they got outside, she turned to him with a puzzled expression on her face.

"He's got rooms. You don't have to spring for a motel."

"Forget the motel. Not that it wouldn't be fun, babe, but I got bigger things on my mind right now. I figured we'd take a spin to the store so you can eyeball my inventory. I'll give you two big ones for a couple hours work. What d'ya say, Babsie?"

"Two hundred dollars?" She waited until he nodded, and then she gave him a happy smile. "I say you're on, Lenny. But what do you want me to look for?"

"Just tell me what I gotta do if I decide to expand to foreign. And if you got some real good ideas, I might just let you handle that part of it. How does manager of foreign parts sound to you? I can make it worthwhile."

Babsie chewed on her lower lip. Lenny could tell she was debating whether or not to tell him something.

"Look, Lenny, you're a real sweet man, so I gotta tell you that I don't have the qualifications for a big job like that. What if I mess it up for you?"

"You don't exactly have the qualifications for being a hooker, either." Lenny looked her up and down and grinned. "But you did it, didn't you, Babsie? Now, that shows guts, and I like guts. Just say, 'Yes, thank you,' and then shut up. I got a lot of admiration for a lady who's smart enough to take advantage when opportunity knocks. You know what I mean?"

"Yes, thank you."

Babsie gave him a brilliant smile. The expression in her eyes made Lenny feel good all over for the very first time since Margo had been murdered.

* * *

This time he was driving in his dream, being very careful to stop at every red light and observe the traffic regulations. There was a map open on the seat beside him, and once he pulled over to the side and parked under a street light so he could check his progress. He sat there for what seemed like hours, hands gripping the wheel, staring out at the yellow circles the headlights made as they tunneled out into the blackness and overlapped on the pavement ahead.

Was he dreaming the dream, repeating it in his mind like a zealous film editor? Running and rerunning a tricky segment until it was perfect? Or was he remembering what he'd dreamed before? It was all very confusing, and the answer eluded him, hovering just on the border of consciousness and then slipping away when he attempted to reach out and grab it.

He was standing in a courtroom on a perfect Southern California afternoon. Huge rectangles of sunlight washed in through the long, high windows. He could see the wood gleaming, smell the furniture polish they'd used to rub down the fences. Fences? No, that wasn't quite right. The structure was more like a large open box made of gleaming oak with a rail running around it. The rail was the object that caused him to think of fences. But this one was heavy and sturdy, and it ran all around the box.

There were people inside, many people. He could count them if he wanted to be sure, but he already knew their number. Twelve. A perfect dozen.

The light was growing fuzzy now, and the image became diffused like a picture shot through a certain kind of lens. What was it called? Wide angle? No, that wasn't right. It was a vignette. But there was something that made his heart pound and his hands tremble as he held them clasped behind his back. Was he praying? No, his hands were clasped behind his back. And there were bracelets around his wrists, but they weren't bracelets exactly.

That was later. He was getting ahead of himself, or maybe the editor had made a bad jump cut. Back to the robe, a long black robe. And the man who was wearing it was walking across the stage. He was of some importance. Every member of the audience rose as he made his entrance. Was he royalty, perhaps? Everyone in the cast and the audience seemed to know exactly who he was.

That wasn't important. He was getting side-tracked, and the dream was playing on. The twelve were the principal players. This was their scene, and he had to be very careful not to step on their lines. But there had been no rehearsal, at least none that he remembered.

What was his cue? Who was he playing? Too late to attempt to remember that now. The curtain had already gone up. It was show time.

The twelve were magnificent. Their faces were huge and hard, like the sculptures of the presidents at Mount Rushmore. Their eyes were flat, gleaming stones that accused him. He was playing the con-demned man. Thank God he'd remembered in time.

Guilty. Guilty. Guilty. Their voices were slow and measured. They rang with the deep, resonant tones of a bell. A death knell. For him. But he was inno-cent! They had given the wrong interpretation. The author had never intended the play to end this way!

And then he was moving, hurtling over the rail in

one soaring leap, right into the jury box. But they had vanished, and he was alone on the stage, alone in the bright white eye of the spotlight.

And then he was on a table—a metal table that was so cold, his body was numb. The light was still above him, and he was pinned in its icy glare. The actors that suddenly surrounded him wore masks to hide their identities. One had a knife with a blade that came closer, closer. Just as it was about to cut into the flesh of his face, the stage was plunged into sudden, devastating darkness.

Oh, God! They'd missed a light cue. And the knife— But it was no longer a knife. It had changed to a spoon. A bent metal spoon, filed down to a killing edge. There was breathing in the darkness. Coming closer. Hoarse laughter. Danger! He was not alone on stage any longer. Someone was approaching. Shh! He'll hear you! And another. And yet another. They grew to a ring of fearful shadows. Shadows that had the power to hurt. And maim. Cruel and unusual punishment, but that didn't matter. No one played by the rules in this place. And then he was falling, knocked almost to the point of unconsciousness. But not enough, not nearly enough.

The scene shifted in its cloak of inky blackness. Forces of evil were torturing his body. His flesh was tearing, ripping apart in bloody tatters. His warm red blood was raining down, filling his mouth and his eyes and his ears.

He screamed, but the director didn't hear him. Or perhaps he hadn't screamed at all. He couldn't play this scene. Not ever again. They had to pull the curtain to end the play.

The lights came on, so bright they blinded him. The green masks reappeared, wavered, and then reversed their direction so quickly they were gone in a blink of the eye. The scenes were out of order as they flickered past, fleeing double-time, even faster across the screen.

There they were the twelve. The hard, solid, chiseled twelve in their box of gleaming wood. It was starting again. Another performance. The long black robe had entered, and everyone rose as the curtain went up.

Oh, no! He couldn't! The twelve were the key. If he could still their lips before they could speak the first line, the play would be finished before it had started.

He jumped the fence. There was no time to wait for his cue. One of the twelve crumpled to dissolve into empty, benign space. And then two. And three. How clever he was, how fast he moved, to catch them before they could elude him. He'd learned their tricks. Another. And another. Until only the four were left. But where were they? Hiding.

And then he was driving, driving to find them as the houses rolled past his car, all shuttered and dark. Four beacons to guide him. Four places to go. Four players left to silence before he could sleep.

And he knew that he would rewrite his part. Triumphant, the way it was meant to be played. But there were miles to go, speeches to utter, actions to perform.

Only when the stage had returned to a mute, peaceful void could the curtain fall with a whispered finality. And the play—the chronicle of his pain that seemed destined to go on forever—could mercifully end.

CHAPTER 21

It was almost four in the morning. Jose Sanchez yawned as he flipped a hamburger on the grill. The past few days had been exhausting, but it had been worth it. His cousin had found a job.

Three days ago, at six in the morning, Jose had taken Ramone to the place on Pico Boulevard where the men lined up to look for work. It was cold in the morning darkness, and many of the men shivered because they had no jackets. As the men waited, stamping their feet to keep warm, a fog crept in from the ocean. It mixed with the fumes from the early morning traffic to cover them all in its damp, foul blanket.

Pride was difficult to maintain as the cars and trucks drove up. They loomed out of the wet gray fog like beasts with shining yellow eyes, and their drivers examined the line of workers on the curb, on display like so many pieces of beefsteak in a market. One by one they rolled down their windows to point at those they wanted to hire. "Hey, you! Okay. And you. Get in back."

The lucky ones jumped quickly into the truck beds or back seats to be driven away. There was no minimum wage for this kind of work, no protection if they were treated unfairly. Most of them had no papers, so they could not work legally in this country. The workers would be paid at the end of the day, and they would accept the amount they were given without protest. Whatever it was, it would be more than they could earn back home in Mexico.

Ramone was discouraged. There was an unwritten law among the men that could not be broken. Certain ones took the best places in line, and they were the first to be chosen. When they were gone, certain other men moved forward to fill their places. It was late by the time Ramone was given his turn to stand close to the street. And no one chose him. He was too puny to lift heavy concrete blocks, one driver said. Several others claimed he looked sick. Another wanted a worker who could speak English, and Ramone had learned only a few phrases. By then it was eight o'clock, and the best jobs had already been taken. Most of the workers who were left wandered away to try again the next morning.

Jose and Ramone stayed, along with a few others who were equally desperate. And then, very close to nine in the morning, a man in a shiny new pickup truck pulled up to ask if anyone knew how to paint a house, inside and out. The gringo's Spanish was so bad that no one could understand him, but Jose recognized his Texas drawl. So Jose asked in English if the senor was from El Paso. And the man smiled and turned friendly as he said yes, he sure was. Jose said that El Paso was beautiful country, not like Los Angeles, and the man agreed. He was going back someday, just as soon as he saved enough money to buy a good ranch. Did Jose know how to paint? He would be happy to hire him if he did.

Jose said that he was not there to look for work, since he already possessed a full-time job. He had come only to help his cousin, who spoke very little English. But Jose's cousin had been a painter back in Tequila, Mexico. And if the señor would hire Ramone, Jose would come along and lend a hand for no pay.

The Texan was very happy to get two men for the price of one. He said to jump in; they would get started right away. But when Jose and Ramone started to get in the back of the truck, the man said no, they could ride up front with him where it was warm. He didn't want them to freeze their patooties off before they had done any work.

Jose and the man laughed. And then Jose told Ramone to laugh also. It was Texas humor, impossible to translate, but the gringo seemed like a nice man, and there was a good heater in his truck.

The painting was not difficult. With both of them working, they had made good progress by the time the man came back at noon. He brought a bucket of chicken and a six-pack of beer. Corona. Why did gringos always assume they liked beer? Jose didn't drink it often, but when he did, he preferred Budweiser. Marguerita teased him and said he thought he was too much of a honcho to drink anything but imported beer. Budweiser was imported beer to them.

The Texan was happy when they showed him what they had done; he told them that it was not necessary to call him Señor Rawlins. His name was Rollie. And he said he wanted to pay Jose for working also. It wouldn't be fair if he took advantage. Texans did not operate that way.

As they ate the chicken and sipped the beer, Rollie paid Ramone a compliment. He said he admired the careful way that Ramone had masked the windows and the molding. He could tell that Ramone was a fine painter. Perhaps, if Jose could act as his interpreter and tell Ramone what work he wanted done, he could hire Ramone for the six other houses he owned that needed to be painted.

Six houses? Jose was suitably impressed. Rollie was a landlord then? No, not exactly. He was in the business of buying old houses and fixing them up for resale. And that meant he always had work for a good painter to do.

Jose said that was wonderful. Did Rollie also need a gardener? Ramone had a great talent with trees and plants, and he had also done landscaping back in Tequila.

Rollie slapped his knee and laughed. He said that he had never expected to find a gem like Ramone standing in line on Pico Boulevard. What other talents did his cousin have? This was getting good.

Jose told him about Ramane's last job as a maintenance man repairing the trucks and machinery for a construction company. He told Rollie that Ramone also had the knowledge to fix electrical wiring and that he had done some fine carpentry, although it was only in his home in Tequila, not for pay.

Rollie slapped his knee again and offered Ramone another beer. He said Ramone was a Jack-of-all-trades, a phrase that meant he could do most anything he set his mind to. Ramone was a valuable man, and he could put him on his payroll full-time, if he had his papers.

That was a problem. Jose sighed and admitted that his cousin had no papers. They were very difficult to obtain. Ramone had to prove he had a job to get his papers, and he could not accept a job unless he already possessed them.

Rollie laughed and slapped his knee again. Wasn't it the truth? They had a phrase for that kind of situation back in El Paso. They said you were between the stampede and the stockyard door, stuck in the middle of the shit and the stomping.

Jose laughed. Rollie's phrases were very colorful. He had to remember that one. But what should his cousin do about the green card?

Keep right on working and not worry about it, Rollie advised. He would pay Ramone in cash every day and start pulling some strings with La Migra. He was sure he could get his hands on a green card as long as Ramone was careful not to get picked up and shipped back before the paperwork could go through.

Then Rollie went to his truck and came back with something he called red-eye. He poured a little in each of their beer bottles and said they were going to celebrate, by God. The beer with the red-eye was called a bulldogger in El Paso. What did Jose think of it?

Jose told Rollie that it was very good. And Ramone had caught on right away when he saw Jose's gesture. He pretended to enjoy the vile drink so much that Rollie had slapped his knee again.

Then Rollie said that since they were all good

buddies now, he wanted to ask Ramone a personal question. It had been itching at the back of his mind ever since he found out that Ramone was from Tequila. Would Jose please ask his cousin if they ate those worms in the bottom of the bottles?

"Jose? I think that burger's done by now" Jose looked up, startled, to find Cheryl laughing at him. The hamburger he had been frying had a small black lump of charcoal on the grill.

"You're tired, huh? Cheryl shook her head. "Still helping your cousin with that painting?"

"Today was the last day, Cheryl." Jose plopped another hamburger on the grill and scraped the incinerated lump into the trash. "Now Ramone can work alone. He has succeeded in understanding Spanish spoken by a Texan. And Mr. Rollie Rawlins has submitted papers, so my cousin will soon be legal."

Cheryl nodded. "That's good. Now all Ramone has to do is lie low until it comes through. I'm glad this whole thing is almost over, Jose. How much sleep did you get last night?"

"Less than three hours. My eyes closed during Marguerita's excellent dinner, and she made me go straight to bed."

"Why don't you take a break, Jose? Catch forty winks back in the storeroom. I can handle the grill for a while."

"Thank you, Cheryl. You are very kind. But it would not be right for me to ask you to do my work."

"Yes it would if you do me a favor."

"What is this favor?"

Cheryl smiled. "I'm just dying for some of Marguerita's salsa. If you bring me a batch as a favor, then I'll handle the grill for you as a favor. Have we got a deal?"

"Of course, Cheryl. But I will bring you the salsa anyway. Marguerita is proud that you like it."

"A favor for a favor, Jose. It's only right." Cheryl smacked him on the rear and pushed him toward the door. "Now go sack out, and I'll wake you if things get too busy."

Jose smiled as he stepped out of the kitchen door. Cheryl was a good friend. He took a deep breath of the cool night air and yawned again. Then he headed straight for the supply shed. Cheryl was right. He was exhausted.

The storeroom was on the far side of the building, a long metal shed that had a creaking metal door and a padlock. It was never locked during business hours, and since the truck stop was open twenty-four hours a day the padlock had rusted open on its hinges.

As Jose stretched out between two sacks of flour, he felt something hard and uncomfortable in his pocket. For a moment he was puzzled, but then he remembered. It was his knife. He had carried it with him since the telephone call, but nothing—absolutely nothing—had happened. There had been no more calls, and no new murders of jury members had been reported in the papers or on the television.

On the first day after the call, Jose had been very frightened. Even though Marguerita had known that something was wrong, he had not spoken of it to her. But that night he had decided that he must try to face his enemy alone and force him to show his face. He had walked down a deserted street, watching

every shadow cautiously, but no one had come
forward to try to harm him. He had walked three
nights more, and then he had stopped. When he
had asked Cheryl what more he could do, she had
said that the man was probably a harmless crackpot
after all, but it couldn't hurt to keep carrying his
knife.

Jose slipped the weapon out of his pocket and
rested with his fingers touching the handle. He listened to the sounds of the darkness, but there was
no sense of approaching danger. The night was as it
always was, disturbed only by the hissing of air brakes
as truckers pulled into the parking lot in front, and
by the low rumble of traffic from the freeway interchange. There was a radio playing somewhere,
barely audible, and Jose recognized the song. It was
a country-and-western standard, something about
having a satisfied mind.

He dozed off then, dropping deeper and deeper
into a sleep so heavy it was almost drugged. The
noise of the traffic dulled into a whisper and then
faded into silence. He did not hear the sound of
approaching footsteps or the creak of the supply
room door as it was opened. And he did not wake
as the sharp blade pierced his sleeping heart and
stilled it forever.

Toni woke up with a groan. Only one thing could
wake her in the middle of the night, and this was it.
When Mike had gone out to do his errand, he'd
come back with at least a dozen cartons of take-out
Chinese from a Szechwan place. Toni loved Szechwan,
and she'd really gorged herself. Then she had been

thirsty all night, and she'd downed a full twelve-ounce tumbler of ice water right before they'd gone to bed. No wonder she was uncomfortable.

She slid quietly out of bed and hurried to the bathroom. What time was it? She shut the bathroom door and turned on the light, squinting at the sudden illumination. The old Burma Shave clock she'd taken as a memento from her father's house told her it was four in the morning. They'd gone to bed at eleven, but it had been an hour before they'd gone to sleep so that meant she'd totaled only four hours.

Toni padded back to bed, but she didn't climb under the covers. There was no way she could go right back to sleep. She should have gone to bed thirsty instead of drinking that water. But now that she was awake enough to think about it, this whole phenomenon might have some practical value. Twelve ounces of water at bedtime woke her up in four hours. She'd never realized it before, but she owned a built-in alarm clock, one that would be sure to wake her no matter how soundly she slept. Of course, she'd have to run a few tests to see exactly how it worked, but it ought to be every bit as consistent as her internal plumbing.

She sat down on the edge of the bed and figured it out in her head. If she drank two glasses of water instead of one, it should shorten the time she would be able to sleep before nature called. And less water should lengthen the time. All she bad to do was measure her bedtime fluids intake exactly, and she could wake up any time she wanted.

Toni got up and hurried to the office to write herself a note. She'd call her discovery the internal water clock. The mechanism was simple, and she'd repeat it tomorrow night, just to be sure. And then she'd experiment with larger and smaller amounts of liquid until she had a workable model.

When she'd written it all down, Toni sat there for a minute, reading it over. She hoped it would still make sense in the morning. Once, a couple of years ago, she'd gotten up in the middle of the night to write down something she'd thought was truly profound. But when she'd read it the next morning, there had been only seven words on the page. It said, *Jogging through an hourglass in a storm*. She'd framed it and hung it above her computer. So much for solving the world's problems while she slept. She still hadn't a clue to what it meant.

Toni was smiling as she went back to bed and crawled under the covers. She was getting sleepy again now. She slid over toward Mike's side of the bed, intending to cuddle up next to his warmth and drift back to sleep, but . . . Toni patted the blankets. He was gone! It was only four-thirty in the morning, and he'd already left her. Was she really that ugly when she woke up in the morning? No, that couldn't be the reason. Mike had never stayed around long enough to see what she looked like in the morning.

That did it. Now she was wide awake again. Toni switched on the light and slipped into a warm quilted robe that had belonged to her mother. It had once been royal blue, but it had been washed so many times over the years, that it had faded to the color of sun-bleached denim. She was really getting a complex about Mike's disappearances. She had a lover who refused to spend the whole night with her.

Was she doing something wrong? Did she snore? Did she have dragon breath in the middle of the night? Or, God forbid, did she pass gas in her sleep? There was some reason Mike always left before morning rolled around and she wanted to know what it was.

Toni left her door wide open and walked down the hall in her fuzzy blue slippers to ring Mike's doorbell. She had to get this whole thing settled right now, before it really became a problem.

No answer. He'd probably gone back to sleep in his bed. She knocked very loudly, considering the hour, and rang the doorbell repeatedly. In spite of her persistence, she heard no one moving inside, no footsteps approaching to open the door. Was Mike home? And if he wasn't, where had he gone with no car? Had he given back her keys? Toni rushed to look, but they weren't on the hook where she usually kept them. She'd have to leave her door open while she checked the garage. Her door key was on the ring. Forget worrying about burglars. This was more important, and she'd only be gone a second or two.

Toni raced down the stairs and pushed open the garage. Her parking space was empty. There was probably a reason why Mike had taken her car in the middle of the night, but she couldn't think of what it could be.

Back up the stairs to her apartment. Toni did her best to remain calm and sensible. What should she do? If a stranger had taken her car, she'd call the police, but that didn't apply to this situation. She'd told Mike he could use her car anytime he wanted.

Then she spotted his wallet on the kitchen table and flipped it open. This was bad. He was driving her car and he'd forgotten to take his driver's license. She hoped he didn't get pulled over by the police.

A note. He might have left her a note. She hadn't even looked for one. Nothing in the kitchen. No note on the table beside the bed. Nothing next to her computer, or anywhere else she could think of to look. Of course, he'd probably figured she wouldn't wake up. She'd told him that she could sleep through anything.

Toni made herself a cup of cocoa that was spiked with a shot of brandy to settle her nerves. Mike would have an explanation when he came back. If he came back.

She had to stop thinking like this. It was much too early to start calling around looking for him, even if she'd known where to look. She'd give Mike until daybreak before she took any action. But where was he? And what was he doing? Did he have another girlfriend stashed away somewhere? She'd heard about men who divided their time between two women, but Mike didn't seem to be that type of man. Of course, the successful two-timers wouldn't appear to be two-timers, or they couldn't be successful.

Toni took another big swallow from her cup. The brandy didn't seem to be helping. If Mike was involved with another woman, how would he explain his absence to her? An extra night job, she supposed. That was a pretty good excuse as long as the other woman didn't try to reach him at work. Or maybe she did. He'd said that his regular nine o'clock call was from his brother, but it might be from her rival. What would she look like? Toni was willing to bet she was a blonde. They were always blondes. And she had huge breasts, much bigger and firmer than Toni's. Mike would go home to his other apartment . . . or maybe it was a house in the suburbs . . . and there she'd be, the Playboy Bunny blonde, waiting up for him. She'd pour him a drink and rub his back. Poor baby. He worked so hard. And he'd say she looked gorgeous in that peek-a-boo black negligee. If she promised to spend the extra money he earned on sexy clothes like that, he wouldn't mind taking on a third job. Come to think of it, maybe he wasn't as tired as he'd thought he was. And she'd laugh and kiss him, and then they'd . . . Cocoa sloshed out on the table, and Toni went to get a sponge to wipe it up. Her little scenario had been ridiculous. She was sure Mike wasn't with another woman. There had to be a good reason why he was gone, and if she used her brains, she'd be able to figure out what it was.

Perhaps Mike hadn't been able to sleep in the first place. He'd told her that he wasn't used to Szechwan cuisine, and he'd eaten a lot of fiery dishes. Those little peppers could really play havoc with the digestive system. He might have gotten up and looked in her bathroom medicine cabinet for some Alka Seltzer. And she knew there wasn't any because she never needed it. She'd always been able to eat anything she wanted with no side effects. But if Mike had been desperate for something to settle his stomach, he might have dashed out to one of those all-night convenience stores. She'd told him that there was one only a few blocks down, but he'd probably forgotten. So he'd taken her car and decided to drive around until he spotted one. That was it. She just knew that was it. She could picture him now, driving through the dark streets until he saw the sign. AM/PM Market or 7-Eleven. Now he was pulling into the parking lot, getting out of the car, and locking it behind him. He would lock it she was sure. Mike was a careful person.

The Alka Seltzer would be right there on the shelf behind the checkout counter. He'd only buy one envelope. There'd be no need for a whole package because he'd vow never to eat Szechwan again. And the old man behind the counter would say, "Stomach problems, fella?" And Mike would say, "Szechwan food. I guess I ate too much of it." The man would nod and get him a cup of water so he could get instant relief right there in the store. And then he'd suggest that Mike pick up something else to settle his stomach for the rest of the night. Yogurt or ice cream. They always worked. Mike would remember that they'd finished the last of the ice cream two nights ago, and he was crazy about Rocky Road, so he'd buy more. And then he'd drive back and park in her parking spot and come up the stairs. And he'd come through the door carrying a carton of Rocky Road ice cream. Of course, he'd be happy that she was awake, so they'd sit down at the table and gorge themselves on big bowls of Rocky Road.

Toni sighed. Wrong scenario. Drinking a bromo and buying ice cream wouldn't take this long. It was after five-thirty in the morning, and Mike had been gone at least an hour and a half. What if he got into an accident on the way back to the apartment building? A drunk might have plowed straight into him, and he might be lying in a hospital right now, uncon-

scious and needing her. Since his wallet was here, he
wouldn't have any identification, and they'd never
find out who he was.

Toni reached for the phone book. She'd waited
long enough. At least, she could call the local hospitals
to see if anyone of Mike's description had been admitted. She was just dialing the first number when she
heard the key in the lock.

"Mike?" Toni threw down the phone and raced
into his arms. "Thank God you're back! I was so sure
you'd had an accident!"

He hugged her, and Toni hugged him back. She
was so relieved.

Michael wasn't relieved; far from it. He sighed
and held Toni a little tighter. He'd have to tell her.
It was only fair. She'd obviously been worried sick
about him.

"Toni? Sit down a minute. There's something I
have to tell you, and it may take a while."

"It's the blonde." Toni sank into a chair. "I knew it.
I just knew it."

"What blonde?"

"The one in the black negligee. Your other woman."

"What are you talking about, Toni? I don't have
another woman. There's no one but you."

Toni let out a deep, shuddering sigh. "Thank
God! I didn't think you did, but I wasn't completely
sure. Uh . . . Mike? Tell me the truth now. Do I do
anything disgusting in my sleep? Like . . . uh . . .
snore or whatever?"

"No, Toni. You're very sweet when you sleep. And
you don't snore."

"That's a relief! Then I guess you must have gone

after the bromo and Rocky Road. And since you didn't bring the carton back with you, you must have eaten it all on the way home."

"Rocky Road? No, Toni. I didn't go after ice cream."

"The drunk hit you before you got to the store? Don't worry, Mike. I've got insurance. I've even got a rider for uninsured motorists. I'm just glad you're not hurt. Anyone can have an accident. And I'll bet it wasn't your fault in the first place."

"Nobody hit me, Toni. The car's fine. I checked it over when I got back and there's no sign of an accident.

"You checked to see if someone hit you? I don't understand. If someone hit you, wouldn't you know it?"

"Not unless it woke me up." Michael walked to the cupboard and took out two brandy snifters. He poured a generous portion into each of them. "I don't know who's going to need this more, Toni, you or me. Take a sip and don't ask any questions. I'll tell you everything. "

"But . . ." Toni opened her mouth, and then she thought better of it. She clamped it shut again and waited.

"I sleepwalk, Toni. That's why I'm never here when you wake up in the morning. Sometime during the night I get up and do whatever I do in my sleep. I don't know why I sleepwalk, but I can't seem to stop doing it. I've tried everything I can think of. And tonight I found out that I sleep-drive, too."

"You drove in your sleep? Toni took another sip from her glass. "Isn't that . . . uh . . . dangerous?"

"It must be. It certainly sounds dangerous to me. But I did check your car, Toni. And there's not a scratch on it."

"Where did you drive, Mike? Do you know?"

"Not really." Michael shook his head. He had a hunch that he'd driven back to Gateway University, but that was only a guess. He'd been thinking about Professor Zimmer right before he'd gone to sleep. When he'd gone to the college in the afternoon, he'd found the professor's class had been canceled. There was a note to that effect on the classroom door. Michael had called the personnel department from a phone booth on campus, and this time he'd reached Miss Beemer. Yes, Professor Zimmer was on leave this week, but he was scheduled to return for his class on Monday. In a way, Michael had been relieved. If the Professor was out of town he'd be safe until Monday, and Michael would make sure he was right there on campus to warn him before his class.

"Mike? Are you all right?"

Michael realized that Toni had asked him a question. "What was that, Toni? I guess I was falling asleep. "

"I asked where you were when you woke up."

"On the Santa Monica freeway, just before Lincoln. I had to get off and check the map to get back here. It's a good thing you had one, Toni. I was totally disoriented. "

Toni tried not to show how shocked she was, but she knew she wasn't pulling it off very well. Driving on a Los Angeles freeway while you were wide awake was bad enough. But driving while you were asleep at the wheel? It was amazing that Mike hadn't been killed.

"Mike? Do you know if you do other things in your sleep besides walk? And. . . . uh. . . . drive on busy freeways?"

Mike nodded. "I know I dress and undress. And once the towels in the bathroom were wet, so I must have taken a shower."

"Oh." Toni shivered a little. "How . . . interesting."

"You meant to say how frightening, didn't you?" Toni nodded, and Michael took her hand. "It scares the hell out of me, too. I wake up in the morning and wonder what I've done and where I've gone. And I can't remember, Toni. There are hazy images once in a while, but I'm not sure whether I dreamed them or whether they've really happened."

Toni swallowed hard, "When did you start sleep-walking, Mike? Do you remember?"

Michael shook his head. "I was too young to remember, Toni. I must have been about three or so. But I know it was right after I moved in with my Aunt Alice. She was so worried she took me to a doctor, but he said it was just a reaction to my new environment. It stopped after a couple of months when I got used to the house."

"That makes sense." Toni nodded. "Your apart-ment is a new environment. But don't you ever hurt yourself, Mike? I should think you'd bump into the furniture or fall down the stairs in your sleep."

"My aunt used to worry about that, but I've never hurt myself. It's as if I'm on automatic pilot. My eyes are open, so I assume I see any objects in my way and avoid them."

Toni really didn't know what to say. Of course, she'd heard stories about sleepwalking, but she'd never actually met anyone who did it. There should be something she could say to comfort Mike. He looked really down.

"Well . . . at least we've got something else in common, Mike. That thing you said about automatic pilot reminded me. Sometimes I get up in the morning and put on the coffee without waking up. And once I got halfway through the dishes before I woke up and realized I was washing them. That's not so different from your sleepwalking, is it?"

"Maybe not." Michael frowned as he pushed her car keys across the table. "You'd better take these back, Toni. And I understand if you don't want me to spend the night anymore. My sleepwalking probably makes you nervous."

Poor Mike. Toni's heart went out to him. He thought she wouldn't like him as much now that he'd admitted his problem. That was absurd. She had problems, too. Everyone did. And maybe they could help each other out.

"Let's go back to bed, Mike. You must be tired. Should I hide the car keys, just in case?"

"You don't have to do that, Toni. I'll go home. It'll be easier for you that way."

"Oh, no, it won't!"

"What if I wander around your apartment or something? Won't that upset you?"

Toni kissed him. "No. It might just be fun, in a crazy kind of way. If I do things half-awake and you do things sleeping, it could be a lot of fun if we bump into each other on the way. Say, Mike . . . do you ever do any housecleaning in your sleep? Like washing the dishes or vacuuming the floors?"

"I don't know, Toni. I might."

"Good, from now on I want you to think about refrigerators right before you go to sleep. My freezer hasn't been defrosted in over a year."

CHAPTER 22

It was two in the afternoon before Michael got back to his own apartment. It had been wonderful waking up with Toni for the very first time. They'd gone out to run and then eaten a leisurely breakfast. She'd been very understanding about his sleepwalking. Of course, he hadn't told her everything, but it was a real relief to have someone to confide in, even halfway.

Michael took a quick shower and dressed in jeans and a yellow sweatshirt he found in a drawer. It said THE UNIVERSITY OF AUCKLAND on the front. As far as he knew, Stan had never been to New Zealand, so he must have picked it up at a store.

There was a whole pile of sweatshirts, and Michael lifted them out to examine them. There was a red one from Moscow University. That was an appropriate color. And a black one from the University of Tasmania with a lion holding a torch. The blue one was from Swaziland. And there was a white one with a blue tree on the front from Beirut, Lebanon.

There were twelve sweatshirts in all, some from universities Michael had never heard of, like Bophuthatswana and Senegal. It was kind of interesting, in a way. He remembered meeting a couple of people who'd collected college sweatshirts, but either they'd had friends who attended those universities or they'd gone there themselves. This set appeared to be a strange mixture of unrelated colleges.

Stan had never been the type to collect things. Perhaps that had been a reaction to the stuffed animal collection that Aunt Alice had started for Michael. For whatever reason, Stan had always claimed that collectors were anal retentive. Michael was positive that the sweatshirts had never been part of a collection belonging to Stan. It was much more likely that Stan got a really good buy on a dozen assorted college sweatshirts that no one else had wanted to buy.

Michael was about to go into the office to work on his book when the telephone rang. Toni or Stan. No one else ever called him. He was betting on Toni. Stan never called him during the day unless there was a crisis. And so far the crises had all been murders. Mike picked up the phone to answer the call. The moment he heard the voice on the other end of the line, he started to frown.

"Mike? It's Stan."

"Oh, hell!" The words were out before Michael could stop them, but Stan laughed.

"Oh, hell? Is that any way to greet the brother who's been burning the midnight oil to push through your appeal?"

"Sorry, Stan. That just slipped out. Please tell me that there wasn't another murder."

Stan sighed. "Sorry, Mikey. There *was* another murder. Remember the Mexican guy on your jury?"

"Jose Sanchez? But that's impossible!"

"I'm afraid not. He was stabbed this morning at the Crossroads Truck stop. Why did you say that it was impossible?"

Michael thought fast. "I'm just shocked, that's all. I was hoping that no more jury members would be murdered. How did it happen?"

"The police figure Sanchez tried to stop some itinerant who was stealing food from the supply shed. He had a knife, but the other guy was quicker. Sanchez never even had a chance to defend himself."

Michael's mind was spinning. Another murder. And he'd warned Jose Sanchez himself. After this, Stan just had to believe there was a connection between the jurors and the murders.

"Listen to me for a minute, Stan. Margo Jantzen, Neal Wallace, Lester Robinson, and now Jose Sanchez. That's four out of twelve, and they can't all be coincidences. It's got to be part of a crazy scheme to murder off the jurors at my trial. What else could it be?"

"Don't get so upset, Mikey. I admit you've got a point. But don't forget that Neal Wallace wasn't murdered. My contact at the police station said they went over that scaffolding with a fine-tooth comb, and it snapped from stress. They're sure of it."

Michael did his best to keep his voice calm. There were times when Stan could be remarkably dense.

"That could be true, Stan. But you're ignoring what happened to his body at the mortuary. Maybe his death was an accident, but someone sure hacked him up afterwards. And that's the reason I think we've got to count him in on the four."

"Well, maybe. I guess I'm beginning to believe your theory, Mike. It makes sense in a weird kind of way. But why would anyone want to kill off your jury?"

"I don't know, but the killer must have a reason. What can we do about it, Stan? I know we can't tell the police. If we point out the connection, they'll start looking for Michael Hart. But don't you think that I should at least warn the rest of the jury?"

"Don't talk crazy, Mikey!" Stan sounded angry. "You just sit tight and leave that up to me. I know where they are. I already told you I've kept track of them. You've got to promise me to stay out of it completely or you'll ruin all the work I've accomplished so far. You see that, don't you?"

Michael backtracked fast. Stan really sounded upset. "I see that, Stan. You're the boss, and I promise not to move a muscle. But you really will warn them?"

"Of course I will." Stan sounded a bit mollified. "I'll start on it right away, Mike. By the time I call you tonight, everyone who's left will know to be extra careful." There was a pause and then Stan spoke again. "Mikey? You're all right, aren't you? I mean, you sounded a little strange when I told you about Sanchez."

"I'm okay, Stan. It was just the shock, that's all. I remember thinking that Sanchez looked like the type of man who could handle himself in any situation."

"He did look that way, didn't he?" Stan sounded pleased. "You've got an incredible memory for those jury members, Mike. I think you remember more about them than I do."

Michael was silent. Of course he remembered them. He remembered them so vividly that he saw them in his dreams every night.

Stan cleared his throat. "I'll sign off now, if you're sure you're all right. I've got tons of work to do. You know how that goes. Right, Mike?"

"Right, Stan. How's the appeal coming? When you called, you said you'd been burning the midnight oil, working on it."

"That's right. I should have mentioined it before I told you about the Mexican juror. I'm sorry, Mikey. I know it's always on your mind, but I've got a million other things to handle and sometimes I forget to give you a progress report."

"It's okay, Stan. I know you're very busy."

"That's true. There's good progress on your appeal, though. I went over that footage I told you about with an expert, and he's agreed to testify that it's you. I had a lab blow up the best freeze frame, and the resolution is nice and sharp. My guy compared it to that last photo you had taken for your portfolio. Remember?"

"I remember. The photographer charged a small fortune. Which pose did you use?"

"I don't remember off the top of my head, Mikey. I think you were wearing a blue shirt. Anyway, there's no doubt in my expert's mind. And there won't be any doubt in the judge's mind either. How does that sound?"

"Just great, Stan." Michael frowned. He remembered those photos very well, and none had been taken in a blue shirt. Oh, Well. Stan had never paid much attention to color. "My appeal will be coming up pretty soon, then?"

"That's right. If they schedule right away, and I'm pushing for that, it could be by the end of the month. So what do you think of your older brother right now, Mikey?"

"I think mom and dad were wrong. They should have named you Clarence Darrow Gerhardt." Mike waited until Stan chuckled. "That's fantastic, Stan. This is the twenty-third already, so that means I could be cleared in a week!"

"Hold on a second, Mike. I said it could be *scheduled* by the end of the month. There'll be a delay. There always is. But even at the worst, it ought to come up within three or four weeks. You can be patient for that long, can't you, Mikey?"

"You bet I can, Stan. I was patient for years. Patient fifteen sixty-three, as a matter of fact."

"What was that, Mike?"

"Just a joke, Stan. Fifteen sixty-three was my patient number at Oakdale."

"Oh, very funny, Mike. Are you sure you're all right?"

Michael sighed. He'd have to remember not to try anymore jokes with Stan. His brother had never developed a good sense of humor.

"I'm fine, Stan. Don't worry about me. And thanks for working so hard on my appeal."

"No problem, Mikey. Your case is my number one priority. I'm a little concerned about you, though. You sound tired. Maybe you should take a couple of aspirin and nap for a while. You had a real shock there with the news about Sanchez and the appeal and everything."

"I'm not that tired, Stan, but maybe I will. Are you still planning to call me at nine tonight?"

"On the button. Okay, Mikey. You take that nap now, and I'll talk to you later, check?"

They said goodbye, and Michael hung up. The way he'd figured it, he'd gotten at least two hours sleep before he'd driven off in Toni's car, and another six after they had gone back to bed. Eight hours of sack time was enough for anyone. He felt more rested today than he ever had before, and he was sure he hadn't sounded tired. Not only had Stan turned into a paranoid, he was a worrywart, too.

Michael turned on his computer and sat down. He really shouldn't be so hard on his brother. Stan had his faults, but he had a brilliant legal mind. And he'd promised to warn the rest of the jurors. Michael just hoped that Stan's warnings would be more effective than his had been with Jose Sanchez.

Toni finished the calculation she was doing on the percentage of women in managerial positions from certain target areas, and inserted the figure in the proper table. She'd made great strides with the research project this afternoon. Now all she had left to do was to tally up some other statistics, draw up a projection graph, and print it all out. As she saved her work, she realized that the radio station she had selected on her office stereo was running the news. Because it was impossible for her to concentrate on figures while someone else was talking, she got up to put on one of her favorite CDs.

She listened to the news as she pulled Vivaldi's Four Seasons out of the drawer and slipped it into

the machine. Trouble in Lebanon again. And Iran.
And El Salvador. Another drug ring had been
busted in Los Angeles, and a big jewelry store on
Ventura Boulevard had been robbed. This city was
just one ball of laughs. A murder, of course. There
weres always murderers, child molesters, car jackers,
and robbers in a city the size of Los Angeles. The
news was so depressing, she seldom listened to it.

What was that? Toni turned up the volume, but
all she got was the tail end of the story. Someone
named Sanchez had been murdered last night. That
name was very familiar. Where had she heard it
before?

Toni switched to her CD and gave a big sigh of
relief as Vivaldi's "Winter" came on. Or was it
"Summer"? She could never tell the four seasons
apart unless she read the description inside the
cover of the CD. Why had the name of the murder
victim been familiar? Sanchez. Wasn't that the name
Mike had asked her to run through the data banks?
Of course, there were lots of people named Sanchez.
She knew that by the number of hits she'd gotten
in the data. And even if the murder victim had been
Jose Sanchez, it could be one of the other hundred
or so who lived in this area. She'd ask Mike about it,
if she remembered.

Now that Vivaldi was playing and she could concentrate on work again, Toni found she didn't want
go back to her projections. Perhaps she needed a
break. She went to the refrigerator to get herself a
glass of iced tea, but that didn't really help either.

Mike's sleepwalking had been bothering her.
She'd made a pretty good show of being nonchalant

about it, but that purely was for Mike's benefit. Was there anything she could do to help him?

The moment she thought of it, Toni attempted to connect to the state computer bank in Ohio. She knew she was prying into Mike's personal life, but perhaps she could discover something in his past that was causing his sleepwalking. Then they could confront it together and resolve it. Of course, she didn't have any credentials for that sort of thing, but she'd heard about a study some prestigious university had done where bartenders and hairdressers had turned out to have a higher quotient of helping people with their problems then trained therapists did.

Toni sat back and waited to be connected. It seemed everyone was using the system today. She was lucky that she had a habit of memorizing numbers without realizing she was doing it. She could rattle off Harry's old badge number and the number of the workman who had inspected the elevator, even though she had no reason at all for remembering either of them. Her selective memory for numbers was usually a worthless talent, in fact, this was the very first time it had actually come in handy.

Last night, when she'd flipped through Mike's wallet, she had memorized the numbers on his drivers' license and his social security card. By plugging those numbers into the Ohio state computer system, she could find out more about Mike Kruger's life without coming right out and asking him.

At last she got through. It was a simple matter to access DMV files. Anyone with a little know-how could do it. She typed in Mike's name and his driver's license number and waited as the search

began. In a moment, a message flashed on the
screen. NOT FOUND. TRY AGAIN? She typed it in
again, but she got the same message. Fine.

The Ohio DMV computer bank was obviously
messed up. She'd try just the name. At least she knew
that was right. She typed in KRUGER, MICHAEL S.,
exactly the way it had been written on the license
and waited. After a moment, the same message appeared. NOT FOUND. TRY AGAIN?

Toni sighed. All right. She'd try it the other way
around. Someone had probably made a typo, and
the name was misspelled in the data bank. It happened all the time, sometimes with disastrous results
when mistakes were made in entering credit information. She typed in the number and waited. There
was always a way around a glitch if you knew what
you were doing.

Aha! There it was! Toni leaned forward as a name
appeared on the screen. The license number had
been issued to Harriet B. Mathews in Akron, Ohio.

Toni frowned as she hit the print screen button
and got the sheet on Harriet Mathews. She had a
good notion to call the Ohio DMV and tell them
that they needed someone to straighten out their
computer. She'd try Michael's social security number
and hope the Federal government had been more
careful about inputting data.

Social Security was a more difficult bank to crack,
but Toni managed to sneak in the back door. Their
files were confidential, but they weren't guarded as
rigorously as some of the other data banks. She
typed in Mike's name and number and waited.

This one took a while. More entries to search.
With the new IRS regulations, most parents applied

for their children's social security numbers shortly after their birth. Finally, after what seemed like several hours but was probably less than a minute, a message appeared on her screen.

ENTRY UNMATCHED. INPUT FIRST PARAMETER ONLY Toni typed in Mike's name without the number. Another long wait, and then a list appeared. There were over forty entries under the name Michael Kruger, and they were from all over the United States. She printed it out and studied the list carefully. None of these birth dates were even close. If she couldn't find anything with the first parameter, she'd try the second.

She was very careful as she typed in the nine digit social security number that had been printed on Mike's card. The search began again, and eventually the information for that number appeared on the screen. Toni frowned as she scanned it, and then printed it out. Mike's social security number belonged to Harriet B. Mathews.

"Oh, brother!" Toni signed off and read the information she'd printed. According to the Ohio DMV, Miss Mathews was thirty-nine years old. Thirty-nine was about right for Mike, now that she thought about it. And Harriet was single, with brown hair and brown eyes. She was a big woman, one inch over six feet tall, and weighed one hundred and sixty pounds, according to her driver's license. Toni thought she probably weighed more. Most women lied about their weight on their driver's license. Harriet Mathews had received two parking tickets in the past year, one of them in Cleveland, and she'd paid promptly. She had no moving violations. That was nice.

Toni shrugged and turned her attention to the social security printout. Miss Mathews had begun working right out of high school. She hadn't earned enough to qualify for Social Security benefits during her first five years. Since her earnings had been so low during that period, she'd probably been attending class and working part-time.

There was a lot of information on Miss Mathews, and Toni scrolled through it. Then she noticed something interesting. For the past ten years, she had shown no regular withholding for social security. Instead she'd paid a lump sum that was a little over twelve percent of her applicable income. She had to be employed, because most people paid roughly half that and their employer paid the rest. It was another fact Harriet B. Mathews had in common with Mike. The only thing that seemed to set them apart was their sex.

"Oh my God!" Toni gasped as she had a terrible thought. Could Mike have had a sex change? She'd met a man who'd been turned into a woman, but she hadn't thought they could do it the other way around. Of course, with the miracles of modern medicine, there was no telling what they could transplant, or implant, or whatever.

"No way!" Toni spoke aloud. It was impossible. She'd slept with Mike, seen every inch of his body, and there was no way synthetic plastics could be that advanced!

Toni thought it over and there was only one sensible conclusion. Mike was using fake ID, and both numbers belonged to a woman in Ohio who had a lot in common with him. Could she be Mike's sister? Harriet B. Mathews was single, so the last name would probably be the same, barring divorce or name changes. She'd try a search for Michael Mathews and see where that got her.

Thirty minutes later, Toni gave up. She'd established Michael Mathiews didn't exist in any data bank she could access. Kruger was obviously an alias, but why was Mike using fake ID in the first place? Did he have a family somewhere that he was running away from? Was he in trouble with the mob? Or the law?

Toni used the number that Harry had given her, and plugged into the police data bank. There was no listing for Michael S. Kruger or Michael Mathews. Harry had told her that the names in the data bank were cross-referenced with known aliases, so that meant she'd struck out cold. For some reason, Mike was hiding his past, and she couldn't find out why unless she knew his real name. She supposed it was possible that he'd been a federal witness and the Feds had changed his identity. But they certainly wouldn't use numbers that belonged to someone else when they could give him a whole new identity and plug it right into the appropriate data banks.

What should she do? She didn't want to confront Mike with what she'd learned. He'd told her about sleepwalking and about his Aunt Alice. It was the first time he'd confided in her, and if she admitted she'd dug into his past, he'd never trust her again. There could be a very good reason why Mike was hiding his true identity, and she'd just have to wait until he trusted her enough to tell her.

Toni sighed. She knew what it was like to have

the urge to confide in someone about her past. She'd gathered the nerve to try it once, but the other person had drawn away, shocked. And their relationship had never been the same again. Toni had learned her lesson. There were some things that were better left private. Mike might have had a similar experience. Wouldn't it be wonderful when they both felt safe enough to be completely honest with each other?

CHAPTER 23

Professor James Zimmer pulled into his parking spot at Gateway University and shut off the engine of his car. A week in the lot at the Los Angeles airport didn't seem to have hurt the Mazda at all. The manufacturer's advertising had been quite accurate. It was a great little car.

It had been exactly 6:59 p.m. when Professor Zimmer's flight had landed at the airport, forty-four minutes behind schedule. He had been delayed another thirty minutes at the baggage carousel, and then he'd waited thirty-five minutes for the airport shuttle bus, which was scheduled to make a complete circuit of the airport every ten minutes. He'd finally arrived at Lot C to find his Mazda sandwiched in between a black Cadillac and a dusty yellow Winnebago, right where he left it.

The Mazda had started right up, and at a quarter to ten he was back where he belonged. If he were the type to indulge in anthropomorphism, he would have said that his Mazda was also glad to be back.

It had seemed to purr like a kitten when he'd pulled into the entrance to the campus.

The professor locked his car and started to walk away before he remembered what was in his small travel bag on the passenger seat. Perhaps it would be a good idea to take it with him. His application for tenure would be processed soon, and if some crazy student broke into the Mazda and discovered what he had in his bag, the rumors would surely reach the University governing board. Vandalism wasn't a big problem on campus, but Gateway University still attracted some students who were a little off-center. Their parents hoped that sending them to religious college would straighten them out, and sometimes that did happen, but more often than not, it didn't.

When Professor Zimmer crossed the commons carrying his briefcase and his travel bag, he realized that he was very glad to be back. Things had not gone well in Washington. Morals and the Media had been an exciting and timely concept, but the structure of the conference had left much to be desired. The individual meetings had been held in separate buildings, and the directions the professor had been given at registration were sketchy at best. He'd almost missed an important panel because two digits had been reversed in the building number and the students he'd asked had known nothing about the conference or the buildings where it was being held.

There had been several other negative aspects, factors that were indicative of the degeneration of his profession. A shamefully large percentage of his colleagues had regarded the convention as an excuse to vacation on the honorarium given by the sponsoring institution and the per diem expenses they would receive from their home colleges.

Professor Zimmer had spoken to one immensely popular academician who had attended only the meeting at which he was scheduled to speak. The man had openly admitted that he'd spent the rest of the time in his hotel room with his mistress, who had been flown to Washington at the sponsoring institution's expense.

Professor Zimmer did not approve of such behavior, but he could empathize with his colleagues' hunger for some sort of remuneration. The life of an academic in today's world carried little in the way of compensation. Teaching was a life of quiet disillusion, and, for many, the only high spots were the honoraria they received for attending conventions, and the opportunity to taste the good life on someone else's expense account while enjoying the company of their peers.

A full professor's salary was laughably low compared with those for other fields that required terminal degrees. Medical doctors made over ten times a college professor's annual salary, and the length of their training was comparable. To Professor Zimmer's dismay, he had found several students in his classes this semester who had made more money than he did. And those students were working only part-time!

Why then, did anyone choose to enter a field with such low pay, long hours, little opportunity for advancement, and ridiculously rigid rules? To mold bright young minds, of course. That was the standard altruistic reason most dedicated teachers gave. Unfortunately, the bright young minds of today seemed to have lost all respect for the lowly academician. He'd heard one young student remark that if the professors had any real talent; they'd be pulling in a decent salary doing, rather than teaching. Students listened more attentively to their stereos and their televisions than they ever did to their teachers.

This was precisely the reason Professor Zimmer had gone to the governing board of Gateway University and petitioned to attend the Washington convention. The media had such a great impact on youth of today that they must be forced to recognize their moral obligation to act in a responsible manner.

The board had been astounded by his request. It was uncharacteristic for the professor to be so passionately vocal. They hadn't heard a peep out of James Zimmer since they had hired him.

There had been the standard objections, which Professor Zimmer had anticipated. Gateway University was a private religious institution that attempted to maintain a low public profile. Publicity was unseemly, and this conference would certainly be covered in the newspapers.

Professor Zimmer had argued eloquently. Wasn't a moral issue of this magnitude precisely the type of thing on which they should take a firm stand? Their image would surely suffer if other religious universities were represented and Gateway deemed it unnecessary to participate. He had read them a list of colleges who were participating and saved the best for last. Gateway University's arch rival, King's Hall, was sending three delegates.

This put a different light on things. They had hastened to assure him that they were favorably impressed with his staunch moral stand, but Professor Zimmer suspected that they'd been even more impressed with the fact that the convention's sponsoring institution had offered to pay him a small honorarium. It meant that they could send him to the convention without pulling out the college checkbook.

There had been a vote, during which he'd left the room, and when he was called back into the inner sanctum, they announced that they had unanimously decided to give him leave. Unfortunately, they didn't have the budget to provide per diem. Or travel expenses. But if the professor still thought it was his moral obligation to attend, they'd arrange to reschedule the classes he would miss during the week he'd be gone. The bells began to chime as Professor Zimmer walked past the cathedral. That meant it was almost ten o'clock.

The chimes were two minutes early. Everyone on campus knew that, and the reason the tower clock was set early, to make the students hurry to class, was effectively defeated. Professor Zimmer walked briskly to his office building, climbed the stairs, and unlocked the door to his office. It was getting late and he had some work to do.

When the professor pushed open his door and switched on the lights, he thought he was in the wrong office for a moment. Dorothy's desktop, which had always been immaculate, was now piled high with magazines and books.

He smiled as he walked closer to inspect the clutter. There was an untidy pile of magazines, the type one would find at supermarket checkout stands. "Popular Soap Star Claims Husband Dressed in Her Clothes" was the headline. He'd certainly never suspected that Dorothy read the celebrity scandal sheets!

There was a well-thumbed astrology paperback on the corner of the desk and a horoscope worksheet filled out in Dorothy's careful hand. Professor Zimmer was so shocked that he almost missed the ashtray filled with cigarette butts. He hadn't known that Dorothy smoked. Or wore lipstick, but the evidence was there on the cigarette butts. Or painted her nails with the Passionate Plum nail polish he spotted on the corner of her desk. He was certain the administration didn't know any of these things either, or they never would have hired Dorothy in the first place.

Professor Zimmer surveyed the evidence of his secretary's secret life and chuckled. Dorothy had always made such a point of being a paragon of virtue. There must be an unwritten code of conduct for secretaries as well as professors. Dorothy had certainly succeeded in fooling him until tonight!

Should he mention this to Dorothy and share a laugh with the secretary he'd occasionally suspected was a spy for the administration? No, that wouldn't be wise. He would only embarrass her, and it might actually hinder their working relationship. There was no reason for her to know that he'd taken an early flight. She could go on with her act, and he'd go on with his. But it made the professor feel good to know that at least one other person at Gateway University had a secret vice to hide.

Professor Zimmer went into his office and sat down at his desk to call a number that wasn't listed in his office phone list. He frowned when he got the answering machine, but he reminded himself that he had not been expected back until tomorrow. Was it safe to leave a message? Yes, as long as he was careful how he worded it.

"Hello, this is Jamie." Professor Zimmer's voice took on a much younger tone. "I'm back early, darling. Its ten-fifteen, and I've got a little work to do at the office, but I'll call you when I get home. I brought you something. It's what we were talking about the last time we saw each other. And yes, I did have the nerve to buy it!"

Professor Zimmer hung up and patted the bag he'd carried in from the car. It had taken all the courage he'd possessed to walk into the store, even though he'd assured himself that no one could possibly recognize him. Perhaps he was much more risqué than he thought. And now he'd better think about other things or he'd never get ready to resume his classes.

There was one more call left to make. Professor Zimmer dialed the number and reached another answering machine. He'd anticipated that no one would be in this office. It was long past regular business hours. He left his message and immediately felt better. One more task accomplished. Then he picked up the folder his secretary had left on his desk and opened it.

Last week Dorothy had proctored the midterm he had written before his media class met on Monday. The papers had to be corrected, and he'd never finish at a reasonable hour unless he got started.

The exam was multiple-choice, with sixty questions. Since he had a template, it was no trouble to correct. The essay question at the end, however, would take some time. Professor Zimmer worked for an hour and he was over halfway through when he heard a cautious step in the outer office. Just as he was about to get up to see who was there, the campus security guard came barreling in.

"Aw, shucks! Sorry, professor. I thought you weren't going to be back until Monday."

"I wasn't, George. But I managed to catch an early flight"

George, a well-built young man with a limited vocabulary, looked sheepish. "Sorry I crashed in here like that, professor, but I thought you were a burglar."

He gave an understanding nod. "Of course you did. That's perfectly all right, George. It's good to know that you keep your eye on things. I'll be leaving in less than an hour, so if you spot anyone in here after that, it'll be a real burglar."

"Okay, professor. I'll keep my eye out. You want me to bring you something? I got coffee out in the guard shack."

"No thanks, George. Coffee would just keep me awake when I get home. I'll see you on Monday."

George backed out, and Professor Zimmer shook his head. The campus security guard wasn't the brightest young man in the world, but he took his responsibilities seriously. If push came to shove, he'd rather have George around in an emergency than anyone else he could think of. The night guard was quick on his feet, and he seemed to have no fear at all. Professor Zimmer certainly wouldn't have had the courage to crash into an office, armed with nothing but a rubber gun, if he suspected a burglar was inside.

It was almost midnight by the time Professor Zimmer tallied the results of his exam. He tried the phone number once more, but no one answered. He left another message, shorter this time, saying he'd call again tomorrow. It was too late to see his lover anyway. He was exhausted, and he wanted to go straight home and climb into bed. Even though he knew there was only a three-hour difference in the time zones between Washington D.C. and Los Angeles, he suspected he had some type of jet lag.

Professor Zimmer put the folder with the exams into his briefcase. His media class hadn't done all that badly, considering what they'd had to work with. They certainly were not the brightest students he'd ever taught. Then he picked up his travel bag, doused the lights, locked the office door behind him as he left, and walked out into the quiet darkness.

As he exited the building, he smiled. Gateway University was beautiful at night without the throngs of noisy students. It was built on a section of land consisting of gentle rolling hills and ponderosa pines. The tract of land was so large, it was still partially undeveloped, and it had been donated to the Reverend Esmond Heath long before the turn of the century to house a university devoted to religious study. The original architect had done an excellent job of designing the buildings to blend with the surrounding countryside, and Professor Zimmer hoped that an architect of similar persuasion would be hired when Gateway started its projected expansion.

Rather than walk past the cathedral again—it

always made him feel vaguely guilty—Professor Zimmer decided to take the long way around through Statuary Walk. This section of the campus belonged to the fine arts department, and it was always featured in the full-color brochures the college sent out to recruit new students in the fall.

If a student's artwork was deemed worthy, it was placed along the winding walk for future generations of students and professors to admire. Statuary Walk covered approximately two city blocks, and it was heavily wooded. It was designed so that walkers came upon the statues almost by accident as they followed the decorative flagstone path. Strategically placed spotlights enhanced the beauty of the sculptures as well as illuminating the walkway after dark.

Professor Zimmer smiled as he passed the first statue, a granite Madonna and child that looked to him like a large blob of rock holding a smaller blob of rock. There were many Madonna's on Statuary Walk, along with a plethora of Christs, some on the cross, others off. It was predictable that the sculptures created by Gateway art students should have predominantly religious themes. There had been quite a scandal last year when one of the most talented graduate students had submitted his sculpture entitled *Whore of Babylon*, an extremely realistic bronze nude. The *Whore of Babylon* had not been assigned a place on Statuary Walk, even though Professor Zimmer had seen it and thought it really quite beautiful.

The most famous of the statues on display was called *Revelation*. As far as Professor Zimmer could make out, it was a crouched figure with multiple limbs and a huge head with multiple faces representing the major ethnic groups who lived in Los Angeles. The student who had sculpted it had come from a wealthy family who had purchased an enormous block of expensive black marble for their son to chisel away. Professor Zimmer had seen the marvelous block of stone when it had been delivered, and he wished the student had called his statue *Revelation Hidden in Black Marble* and left it just as it was.

Revelation had been featured in a television series last year, and Professor Zimmer had gathered with the other professors in the fine arts department to watch it on the university's large television monitor. The husband and wife in the episode had owned a detective agency and their son was a talented magician. The son's task was to create the illusion that the statue had been stolen when it was actually right there on Statuary Walk. If the son could do this, the bad guys would be fooled into letting their hostage go. The board of Gateway University been paid ten thousand dollars a day to allow actors and crew on the college campus for the three days it took to shoot the episode.

Professor Zimmer walked past *Revelation* and sighed. Perhaps he just didn't understand modern art because he thought the acclaimed statue was ugly. It certainly looked both ugly and threatening tonight. In the shadow from the floodlights, the multiple limbs seemed to be reaching out for him, moving closer and closer like some prehistoric beast on the prowl. Even when the statue was behind him, he could still see the grotesque shadows it cast on the walkway, growing larger as he walked away from the light source. Perhaps it had been a mistake taking Statuary Walk tonight. For a moment there, he'd actually imagined that one of the elongated shadows had moved.

There it was again! Professor Zimmer whirled around, but no one was in sight. He must be more tired than he'd thought. Not only was he experiencing visual hallucinations, but now his auditory senses had come into play. He was almost positive he'd heard stealthy footsteps in the area just beyond the light. His imagination, coupled with exhaustion from his week at the convention, was affecting his mind. His instincts told him to flee for the safety of his car, but he knew he'd feel foolish if George were watching, and he burst out of Statuary Walk as if demons were chasing him.

Deliberately, the professor walked forward, keeping his steps measured and even. There was nothing beyond the floodlights except his own over-active imagination. The last sculpture on the walk, a cast bronze called *Pagan*, was one of his favorites. It had been installed only a month ago, and it was a composite of many ancient gods. Professor Zimmer didn't know that much about mythology, but he enjoyed trying to identify the gods that were represented. Since the feet of the statue had wings, he assumed they indicated the Roman god Mercury. The figure was in a crouch like the Titan Atlas, supporting the world on his shoulders. And here was something he hadn't noticed before—there were several places on the statue's head where the hair was coiled in ropelike strands. Was that Gorgon Medusa's influence? Of course he recognized the Norse god Thor, holding his hammer. What was it called? He had looked it up just the other day. Oh yes, Mjolnir. And then there was another god, one he couldn't quite remember that . . .

The professor stopped abruptly. Something behind the statue had moved. He was sure of it. The hell with decorum. Something was there!

Professor Zimmer broke into an awkward run, his travel bag and his briefcase banging against his legs. The exit to Statuary Walk was in sight, just past the next tree. He had covered almost three quarters of the distance when something faster and much more powerful grabbed him from behind. The professor fell heavily to the flagstone walkway, breaking his left kneecap on the rough-hewn stone. He had no time to feel the intense pain such an injury would cause. The last sight his terrified brain could process was that of the huge black shadow of Thor's mighty hammer crashing down on his skull.

CHAPTER 24

"You have a great apartment, Lenny." Babsie flipped eggs onto a plate, added four strips of extra-crispy bacon, and set it down in front of him. "A disposal, a dishwasher, a built-in microwave. You sure know how to live in luxury."

Lenny grinned as he dug into his breakfast. It had been a lucky night when he'd picked up Babsie. Not only was she a hell of an organizer at the store, but she could cook like a dream, and she loved his apartment. He hoped that Margo was twirling in her grave about now. The last time he'd brought her here, she'd called it a dump

Babsie thought his apartment was wonderful, and Lenny could understand why. He'd seen the hole where she lived when he'd followed her home that first night. The neighborhood was anything but safe, and she had four locks on her door just to protect the few things she had. Babsie didn't have much. He'd checked it out while she was in the little closet she called her powder room. He'd poked around, checking out the place. She owned four little skirts, four blouses, one dress, and two pairs of shoes. That was all she had in her closet, plus the hooker outfit she'd been wearing the night he'd met her.

Her place was clean. Lenny had noticed that. The old linoleum floors sparkled, and there wasn't a speck of dust anywhere. Babsie was a very good housekeeper, but she didn't have much to show for it. Her furniture was so old and rundown, Lenny doubted Salvation Army would take it as a donation. Come to think of it, that was probably where she'd gotten it in the first place. She'd tried to fix it up with covers she'd made, but the couch cushions still sagged, and you could tell it was cheap stuff. She didn't own a television and the only thing she had to play music on was an old portable radio with a busted antenna. No wonder she thought his place was nice. It was the Ritz compared to hers.

Babsie poured his coffee, strong and black just the way he liked it, and sat down beside him. He was toying with the notion of kissing her from across the breakfast table when she jumped up again.

"God, Lenny, I'm such a dummy! I went out to get you a paper while you were sleeping, and I almost forgot it."

"Hey, thanks." Lenny grinned even wider as she came back with the morning paper, "you didn't have to go to all that trouble, babe. I could've lived without it until we got to the store."

"A man should have his coffee and his news first thing in the morning. That's what my daddy used to say. And he should have it before either one gets a chance to get cold. Don't you think that's cute, Lenny?"

"Huh?" Lenny looked up from the first page. Eddie's hit man had struck again. This time it was

Professor James Zimmer at Gateway University. Babsie looked concerned. "What's the matter, Lenny? Your face is all white."

"Somebody I knew just died, that's all."

"I'm sorry, Lenny. Was it a close friend?"

"Not really, babe." Lenny sighed. "Just somebody I sort of met once, that's all." Babsie got up from her chair and moved over to stand behind him. As she reached around to hug him, Lenny grabbed her hands. What a nice lady Babsie was. She wasn't the least bit bitchy like Margo, and she had a real good heart. But now Lenny knew, for sure, that he wasn't in any position to make a move. He could be nailed for five counts of murder any day now and it wasn't over yet. If it wasn't for the really bad mess that Eddie had gotten him into, he'd be seriously considering getting something permanent going with her.

It was almost noon and Mike was still sleeping. Toni tiptoed past the bed to get her shoes. She'd never slept this late before either. Perhaps it had something to do with how nice it had been to cuddle up next to Mike under the blankets. She'd opened her eyes at seven-thirty just as she'd always done, but once she'd made sure that Mike was still in bed with her, she'd gone right back to sleep.

She looked over at Mike and smiled. He was sleeping on his side with his knees bent up, and his hair was tousled like an innocent little boy's. He certainly hadn't acted like an innocent little boy last night! Toni felt her face growing warm, remembering. It was nice having a sleeping lover in her bed, one that had stayed with her the entire night. Toni noticed his sweatshirt on the floor and picked it up to hang it over the back of the chair before it could get impossibly wrinkled. Then she realized that it wasn't the same color as the one he'd been wearing last night. He'd been sleepwalking again, and he must have gone home to change clothes.

Toni glanced around the bedroom, but nothing seemed to be out of place. Then she checked the office, but she didn't think he'd been wandering around in there. The living room was fine, and so was the kitchen. No, Mike hadn't defrosted the freezer in his sleep. But he must have done something in the middle of the night. He'd been wearing a black sweatshirt. They'd joked about the fact that it was from the University of Tasmania, and she'd called him her little devil all night. The one she'd picked up this morning was light blue.

She didn't start to panic until she saw the car keys on the table. She was sure they'd been hanging on the hook by the door last night. Mike must have driven her car in his sleep again. Thank God he was all right!

Toni put on her shoes and ran down the stairs to the garage. Her car was there, in its proper space, but it was much closer to the pole than she would have parked it. She inspected it carefully, but it appeared to be fine. No dents anywhere. Nothing broken that she could see. At least he hadn't been in an accident. But where had he driven? What had he done? Toni felt her head spinning. He'd come back to her, not to his own bed. Did that mean he was getting better?

"Hi Toni."

Toni whirled around to see Harry getting out of his car. "Hi, Harry. What are you doing home so early?"

"It's not early to me, kid, it's late. I've been down at the precinct for the past ten hours."

"What happened, Harry?" Toni did her best to put on a friendly smile. She was so worried about Mike's sleepwalking that it was difficult.

"Murder. They called me in at one in the morning." Harry sighed. "I'm getting to the point where I hate to hear the phone ring. We figured it started out as a mugging, but the victim must have fought back. If you ever get mugged, Toni, just hand over your wallet or anything else the perp wants."

"Anything, Harry?"

"Anything you figure isn't worth losing your life over. And there's not much that fits into that category."

"Okay, Harry. I'll keep that in mind. But we don't have many muggings around here. This is a low crime neighborhood, isn't it?"

"So far it is." Harry shrugged. "That doesn't mean much, Toni. Look at what happened in Westwood last year. Gang warfare right on the streets. And the little bastards are committed to do it. As long as they've got wheels, they can get out of the slums and go to a nice neighborhood to commit their crimes."

"Where was the murder, Harry? In Westwood?"

"Not this time. It happened out at Gateway University, right in the middle of the campus. That used to be a low-crime area, too, until this morning."

"Gateway? Isn't that the religious college out on the 118 Freeway?"

Harry nodded. "Say, Toni, maybe you can help me out on something. I need a woman's point of view. Why would a perfectly ordinary college professor carry around a bag full of women's lingerie?"

Toni thought fast. Why would a college professor

carry lingerie on the campus? "I'm not sure, Harry. Maybe he had a fancy girlfriend. Or maybe he wanted to be somebody's fancy girlfriend."

"Toni!"

Harry looked shocked, and Toni laughed. "Okay, I'm just being realistic. He could have been a closet cross-dresser. Are you sure it belonged to the professor?"

"No." Harry frowned. "It was brand new, Toni."

"Well? Was it his size?"

Harry's face turned red. "I should have called you when it happened, Toni. You're better at this kind of thing. I'll call and have them check it out right away. Anything else?"

Toni noticed that Harry pulled out his notebook, and that made her feel good. She had to concentrate on the problem at hand even though she was still worried about Mike.

"Okay. Let's assume that it didn't belong to the Professor. The killer could have planted it on him to start a scandal. After all, Gateway's a religious college."

"Yeah. That's a good one." Harry wrote it down and looked at her for more.

"Maybe it wasn't a mugging at all, Harry. The killer might have made it look that way to throw you off the track."

We thought of that, Toni. We're not locked into the mugging concept, but everything fits into the pattern except for those pink satin panties with the little . . ." Harry stopped and cleared his throat. "Never mind Toni, It's not important."

"If you say so, Harry. Tell me what you've got so far."

"Okay. The professor was murdered between midnight and twelve-thirty this morning. A blow to the head with a blunt instrument." Harry cleared his throat again. "I don't need to go into all the gory details. He was walking across campus to his car, and someone hit him and cleaned him out. Wallet, credit cards, everything was missing. And they got into his office on campus and messed that up too."

"What did the Professor teach?"

"Three classes in something called media, one each on radio, television, and newspapers, and its effect on society. The secretary went through his office and said there was nothing missing in there."

"Your killer must have been looking for something. What kind of man was the professor? Did the students like him?"

Harry nodded. "He was a real prince of a guy, according to everyone we talked to. The students liked him a lot, but they said he was a tough grader. And all the staff liked him, too. Nobody we talked to could think of a reason why anyone would want to kill him. Oh yeah, one other thing. He'd just come back from a convention in Washington D.C., and the security guard said no one expected him back until Monday. That cuts down on the probability that he was a specific target."

Toni frowned. "Three questions, Harry. Does Gateway have any night classes? Were there any special functions going on last night? And do you know which buildings are open at night?"

Harry patted his notebook. "We thought of that, Toni. There were no night classes, so the campus was practically deserted by the time the professor got there around ten. And there were no special functions last night. The only building open was the library, and it closed at eleven."

"How far is the library from the professor's office? Could someone have seen the light in his window?"

"That's possible."

"All right, then. A student at the library sees the Professor's light and hangs around after the library closes. You said the professor was a tough grader, so maybe the student was trying to steal one of his tests. Or change a grade. He might not have wanted to hurt the Professor, just knock him out so he could steal the keys to his office."

"Yep." Harry made another note. "That's good, Toni. We'll interview every student enrolled in his classes. And I guess we'd better check around for the kids that flunked out, too. That lingerie could've been a way to get even. And the kid could have messed up the office for spite."

"That sounds good, Harry. Could a former student have driven on campus without a pass? Or a gate card? Or whatever they use to get in?"

Harry laughed. "You could drive a tank right onto that campus and no one would notice. There's no security system at the gate, and it's a big place. There are a lot of back ways to come in."

"How about security guards?"

"There's only one guy on at night. And he spends most of his time chasing off the high school kids who come out there to drink and mess around."

"That doesn't help much, does it, Harry?"

"Not at all." Harry sighed. "We're going to concentrate on the students and the staff, but that's really just a fielder's choice. Our guy could be someone from outside with no connection to the college at all. Anybody who was out for a midnight drive last night could have zipped onto that campus and killed the professor."

CHAPTER 25

Ebony Rose woke up to the musical peal of her alarm clock at one in the afternoon. It played her theme song, "Second Hand Rose." Her boyfriend had given it to her for Christmas. She'd slept for seven hours. That was enough. She had to get up. It had been daybreak before she'd come home to her penthouse apartment. She'd thrown a prenuptial party for one of the girls.

There was a smile on Ebony Rose's face as she pushed back the pink satin sheets and got out of her canopied bed. She slept in the nude because she loved feeling of satin against her skin. It was her favorite material, and she'd never been able to afford it when she was young. Now she surrounded herself with it. Her cocoa-brown skin glistened in the sun as she slipped into a rose-colored satin kimono and walked down the hallway to the kitchen. The party had been sensational. They'd locked the doors of the club at 2 a.m. on the dot, and then they'd given Rennetta a real send-off. Ebony Rose always threw a lavish party when one of her girls got married. The stripper she'd hired had been the best, handsome and rugged enough to have been a movie star. He'd performed his regular act, and the girls had all shrieked and applauded. It was a reversal of roles, and they had loved it. Then, for his finale, he'd lifted Rennetta right out of her chair and carried her off to the waterbed they'd set up in the back room.

Ebony Rose figured that Rennetta wouldn't forget her party in a hurry. It would be a long time before she was treated like that again. The man she was marring today was sixty-five years old, filthy rich, and completely impotent. He wanted Rennetta around for window dressing. It was a status symbol for him to have a beautiful young wife. Unfortunately, he was also the jealous type and he'd threatened to divorce her at the drop of a hat if she ever played around. Since he was as healthy as a horse in every other way, Rennetta could look forward to a celibate life for the next twenty years or so. Ebony Rose figured that Rennetta would earn every penny of the inheritance she'd eventually get.

There was a time when Ebony Rose had harbored a similar ambition for herself. A rich older man and an easy life of luxury. But now she was very grateful that things had turned out the way they had. She liked being her own boss, and she was sure she wasn't good wife material. She was now thirty-two years old, and she'd never met a man she'd wanted to marry. Except one, of course. And that was completely impossible.

Bridget, her housekeeper, had prepared a pitcher of freshly squeezed orange juice, and Ebony Rose poured herself a Waterford tumbler full of the delicious liquid. That, with one piece of whole-grain toast, would be here only meal until the light dinner that Bridget would fix tonight. Ebony Rose ate her toast and sipped her juice. Even though she was way behind schedule today, she had to spend at least an hour working out in her dance and exercise studio. She didn't perform at the club except on very special occasions, but she still kept herself in prime condition. After all, her nude dancing had earned her the down payment on the club she now owned free and clear. And it had paid for this luxury penthouse and the custom rose-colored Jaguar she drove. At one time her body had been her most valuable asset, and it was only right to treat it well.

Her breakfast finished, Ebony Rose set the crystal tumbler on the pink-veined marble counter, where Bridget would find it and wash it. Then she picked it up again and rinsed it out. Even though Ebony Rose, the daughter of a black domestic, had an Irish maid of her own, she still rinsed out her glasses.

It was time to get to work. She walked back to her bedroom and chose a leotard from the long rack of clothes in her walk-in closet. She had at least thirty exercise outfits, ranging in color from the palest cotton-candy pink to vivid fuchsia. Today she chose one that was the color of the pink geraniums her mother had grown in a cracked ceramic pot on their kitchen windowsill. Then she put on matching satin dance slippers and hurried down the hall to her dance studio.

For her first set of exercises she used the ballet barre that ran the length of the room. The muscles in her left leg were painfully tight, and no amount of stretching seemed able to loosen them. Her old injury had come back to haunt her. She'd have to start doing the therapy exercises she'd learned from the doctor, and avoid wearing her favorite high-heeled shoes for a month or so.

Ebony Rose had been only ten when her mother's friend had pushed her down a flight of stairs, and she'd torn some ligaments in her ankle. The doctor at the emergency room had taped it, and she'd had to wear a brace for six months. She'd never told her mother exactly why the boyfriend had pushed her, but her mother must have suspected because the boyfriend had disappeared that night, and he had never come back.

Ebony Rose remembered crying because she couldn't roller-skate any longer. Her mother had dried her tears and told her that her injury could be a blessing in disguise, if she got in the right frame of mind. She could have been killed on those steep steps, and she should think of that. And now, because she couldn't run around with the neighborhood kids for a while, she should concentrate on getting the best marks in the class, and maybe she could win a scholarship to college. Wouldn't that be wonderful?

So Ebony Rose had studied instead of doing everything else she'd wanted to do. And she'd discovered that she liked being the smartest kid in class. She won a scholarship, just as her mother had wanted. And she'd finished two years of college before she'd been forced to drop out to take care of her mother.

Now she'd strained her ankle again, and it was her fault for not being careful. Why had she worn those ridiculously high-heeled satin shoes? And she'd let the girls talk her into drinking a whole bottle of champagne. And after that, she'd attempted to do an acrobatic disco dance with the male stripper.

Ebony Rose sighed. She'd broken a lot of rules

last night, and now she was paying the price for it. Her regular regime was very stringent. She ate the proper foods, and she didn't smoke. She never touched drugs of any kind, and she took no pills unless her doctor prescribed them. She limited herself to one glass of premium wine a day, and she only drank that on special occasions.

She supposed the girls regarded her as a bit of a prude, if that was possible for a woman in her line of work, but Ebony Rose followed her self-made restrictions for a very good reason. It was a rough world out there and there were plenty of people who'd like to knock her down a peg or two. She had to be healthy and alert if she wanted to stay on top.

An hour later, finished with her workout for the day, Ebony Rose tossed her special blend of herbal essence into the Jacuzzi and climbed in to relax her tired muscles. She loved her Jacuzzi. The closest she'd ever been to a Jacuzzi in her childhood was the lukewarm bath she'd taken once a week in the old-fashioned tub at the end of the hall.

Ebony Rose sighed deeply as she remembered those occasions. Almost every time she'd climbed in the tub, the man in the next apartment had banged on the wall to use the toilet. She'd suspected he did it on purpose, watching her go down the hall, giving her enough time to get in the tub, and then pounding on the bathroom door to yell that he had an emergency. The bath water had always been cold by the time he came out, and there was never enough hot water to run more.

She'd known it would do no good to complain to her mother. They couldn't afford to move into a place with its own private bathroom. But she remembered sitting at the old kitchen table and dreaming over the glossy decorator magazines her mother had brought home when her ladies had thrown them out. Jacuzzis, swimming pools, decks, and tennis courts. Kitchens with butcher-block tables and a whole array of copper pans hanging from the beamed ceilings. A dining room with crystal goblets and a lace tablecloth. A master bedroom suite with an enormous round bed covered with a pink satin coverlet, and huge walk-in closets with mirrored doors holding more clothes and shoes than you could find in a store. And if you actually owned a mansion like the ones in the magazines, you didn't have to lift a finger. There would be a housekeeper to clean, and a cook to prepare the meals, and a maid to help you dress, and a butler to answer the door, and a chauffeur to drive you wherever you wanted to go. Ebony Rose was determined to have all that someday.

Her mother's dreams hadn't been that elaborate. When Ebony Rose had asked, she'd said all she wanted was a nice two-bedroom apartment with wall-to-wall carpeting and a bathroom with a tub and shower.

It gave Ebony Rose satisfaction to know that she'd made a few of her mother's dreams come true during that last painful year of her life. Her mother had loved the apartment Ebony Rose had rented for her with the view of the park and the full-time maid who was a registered nurse. It had been proof that her daughter had made it up out of poverty, the first of the family to go to college and the first one ever to make that much money.

Even though Ebony Rose had some regrets, she was glad she'd dropped out of college and gone into the business so she could give her mother a little of what she deserved. It was just a pity her mother hadn't lived a few years longer. Now she could easily afford to buy her a big house and staff it with plenty of domestics. Her mother would probably have insisted on doing most of the work herself, but Ebony Rose knew she would have loved sitting in the back of a limousine for a drive through the old neighborhood.

A few minutes later, dressed in a shell-pink caftan, Ebony Rose sat down at her French provincial desk to make out the daily schedule. The red light on her answering machine was blinking, and she pressed the play button. She'd been too tired to take her messages when she'd come home, and she'd forgotten all about checking it earlier.

"Hello. You have eight messages."

Ebony Rose stifled the urge to say thank you to the recorded voice and picked up a pen to write down her messages. The first was from Miles, her hairdresser. He'd be here at five this afternoon to do her hair, if that was acceptable. It was. The second message was from a client who wanted Giselle and Leona to work a party tonight. Ebony Rose checked their schedules, booked them, and made a note of the time and the address. The third message was from her boyfriend and it made her laugh in delight. He was very naive sometimes, and she found that refreshing. He was also the brightest man she'd ever met, and he treated her like a lady, even though he knew damn well she wasn't. He was the only person she still saw from her old life.

The fourth and fifth messages were just heavy breathing with a couple of extremely rude phrases that where far from original. It was probably the usual hassle from some joker down at the police station. They were still mad that she'd walked away from their last attempt to bust her.

The sixth message was from her lawyer, and it was important. He said there was no problem he could anticipate with the corporation she wanted to form, Ebony Rose smiled. It really paid to hire a high-priced, powerful attorney. He had connections, he kept her out of trouble, and his advice was always sound. It was definitely worth the five-figure retainer that she paid him.

The seventh message presented a problem. It was a dinner invitation from an important private client, eight o'clock this evening at Le Petite Chateau, a well-known French restaurant in Beverly Hills. Ebony Rose shook her head as she listened. She was spending the evening with her boyfriend, and there was no way she'd break that date. Even if she'd wanted to go, and she didn't, her lawyer had advised her never to appear in public with a client, especially a private client.

Ebony Rose stopped listening to her messages and called Chloe to book her for the client. Her client had admired the color of Chloe's aquamarine eyes. The tinted contact lenses had been a wise investment.

Chloe was thrilled with the invitation. Eight o'clock? That was perfect. What should she wear? The little black dress, Ebony Rose advised her, with a rope of pearls. Real pearls, not that costume junk that Chloe liked to wear. She could drop by at seven to get something out of the safe, and Ebony Rose would help her choose the correct accessories. This was an important evening, and if Chloe played her cards right, she could make a real conquest.

A moment later, Ebony Rose had her client on the phone. She was sorry to tell him that she had a touch of the flu and she wouldn't want him to catch it. It was really quite a coincidence that he'd mentioned Le Petite Chateau. She'd heard Chloe say just the other day that she'd always wanted to go there. Chloe would fit right in with his sophisticated crowd, and she'd tell her to wear something very special. She was certain that they'd have a wonderful evening. And she'd be sure to get some rest and drink plenty of liquids. It was very sweet of him to be so concerned.

When Ebony Rose hung up, she gave a big sigh of satisfaction. She was free and clear, if Chloe did things right. He'd been the last of her private clients. She'd managed to refer all the rest to other girls without causing any hard feelings on anyone's part. It just went to prove that she was a great matchmaker. Her boyfriend would be relieved to know that she was finished with that aspect of her life. Not that he hadn't understood, but he'd been concerned for her safety in spite of her lawyer's expertise and the other precautions she'd taken. Ebony Rose knew she'd been playing on the edge. Now she'd be legal, completely and totally legal. There was one last call on her answering machine, and Ebony Rose smiled as she listened to it. It was her boyfriend again, promising to call her today and reminding her that they had a date for tonight.

The recorded voice came on again. "That was your last message. To save your messages, press nine. To erase your messages, press seven. Edony Rose pressed the button to erase her messages, and the voice spoke again. "I will erase your messages."

The machine made a mechanical sound as it erased everything except her outgoing message. Her lawyer had been very emphatic about erasing her messages after she'd played them. She'd almost been caught in a very bad situation when she'd forgotten to erase a couple of messages in the past. Luckily, her client hadn't left a number and her lawyer had convinced the police that it had been a crank call.

Ebony Rose glanced at the diamond wristwatch she'd bought right after she'd formed her first corporation. It was almost four o'clock and she had just enough time to drink a cup of herbal tea and read her morning paper before Miles arrived to make her pretty for the man she loved.

CHAPTER 26

Michael made himself another cup of coffee and sat down at the table. He had run with Toni at one-thirty and had breakfast at her apartment. Then he'd come back to his place to shower and dress in clean clothes. Right now he was about to read the morning paper, even though it was after three-thirty in the afternoon.

He leaned back in his chair and groaned. Even a twenty-minute shower under water as hot as he could stand it hadn't taken the kinks out of his back. He felt like he'd been chopping wood in his sleep. Maybe he had. At least Toni hadn't noticed that he'd gone out to drive her car again last night. And just like the other times he'd driven in his sleep, he didn't have the slightest notion where he'd gone. The only thing he'd been able to remember was a sign for a freeway with two numeral ones in it. That didn't help much. He'd checked the map, and it could have been the 110, the 118, or the 101. And it was always possible he'd seen the sign and not taken the freeway. Not being able to trust his sleeping body to stay in bed was driving him batty.

Michael took the little red rubber band off the newspaper and hung it over the kitchen doorknob. He had quite a collection of red rubber bands by now, one for each day that he'd been out of the hospital. They represented his freedom, or he supposed he should call it semi-freedom. He didn't feel free enough to go outside the apartment without being extra cautious, and he had to be home for Stan's call at nine every evening. But it was a far cry from the hospital, with its rigid schedule and restrictions. Now he could be by himself whenever he needed solitude, and work whenever he wanted, even at midnight. And he could see the people he really cared about at any time.

That meant Toni. He cared about her more than anyone else. Michael was sure he'd be content to live the rest of his life with Toni, but it was much too soon to tell her that. He hadn't even mentioned the word love. When his appeal was decided and he was truly free, he'd confess everything about his life that he'd held back, and tell her that he loved her.

The front page of the paper didn't hold any surprises. The president was trying to push his current legislation through Congress. There was a big picture on the first page of the nation's leader squaring off against one of the more vocal Congressmen. Michael stared at his face and remembered that he hadn't known who the president was until he'd escaped from the hospital. Maybe there was some truth to that adage, "Ignorance is bliss." There was trouble in the Middle East again. That seemed to be a constant. And there was a feature story about a man who'd won over four million dollars in the Powerball lottery. They hadn't had that lottery before he'd gone to prison. Perhaps it had begun when he was in the hospital. He had no way of knowing. Every time he saw an article about the lottery, he had the urge to run out and buy a ticket. But if, by some strange miracle, he won anything big, they'd have to know who he was. The lottery was something else that would have to wait until Stan got the verdict on his appeal.

Michael skipped the comics and the editorial page. He'd come back to those later. Metro was the section he needed to read. If he'd done anything at all while he was driving last night, it would be reported in Metro.

"Death at Gateway University." The headline caught his eye. Michael felt sick as he read the article. Professor James Zimmer had been killed last night, the victim of a violent mugging. Why hadn't Stan called to warn him? Perhaps he had, but the professor had ignored Stan's warning.

Michael felt sick as he finished the article. He knew a mugger hadn't attacked Professor Zimmer as he walked across the college campus. It had only looked like a mugger, the perfect cover-up for the deliberate murder of another juror. He wanted to call Stan to find out when he'd warned the professor, but he couldn't call from the phone in his apartment. Stan had been very specific about that. But he could call from a pay phone at the shopping center. Toni had told him about the mall that was only a few blocks away. Not even a paranoid like Stan could object to that.

He grabbed his keys and ran down the hall to

Toni's apartment to borrow her car. At least he'd be asking this time, instead of commandeering it in the middle of the night.

Toni frowned as she picked up Mike's keys and headed for the door. She'd told three lies. First, she said her house keys were difficult to take off her key ring, although they snapped right off.

Then she asked Mike if he could please leave his keys since they could unlock the laundry room door and some of her clothes were drying downstairs. That was lie number two. She never used the apartment laundry room. She had her own washer and dryer hooked up in the hallway closet. Fortunately, Mike had never noticed.

Finally, she asked Mike to drop by the stationery store in the mall to pick up some paper for her printer because she'd just used the last ream. She had another case and a half on the shelf in her office, but she needed some time before he came back. The clerks in the stationery store were always slow about getting things out of the back room.

Just as she was about to go out the door, the telephone rang. It had been sitting there as mute as a giraffe for hours. But now, the moment she'd mustered the courage to do a little snooping, it was ringing its little bell off. Was it a sign from above that she should leave well enough alone? Unlikely. It was probably another wrong number, and if it was, she might just say something positively rude.

"Hello?" Toni answered, but there was silence. It was a long distance call. She could hear static on the line. Even though each long-distance carrier claimed their system was superior to every other carrier, they all had a certain amount of static on the line. Toni was about to hang up when she heard a series of clicks and then the static abated somewhat.

"Toni? Is that you?"

Toni smiled as she recognized Muriel's voice. "Yes it's me. Hello Muriel. Are you having trouble with your office phone? Your voice is really faint."

"No, Toni. I'm not calling from the office. It's past seven in New York, and I don't work that late."

"Of course you don't." Toni felt silly for making that mistake. "I always forget about the time difference."

"That's okay. Everyone else forgets about it, too. You have no idea of the number of calls I get at the office after five. I have to make this fast, Toni. I've got a train to catch if I ever want to get home tonight. Your guy is good, really good."

For a moment, Toni was confused and then she caught on. "You mean Michael?"

"Yes. I started reading those pages you sent me on the train this morning, and I got so involved that I rode right past my stop. I talked to my boss about it, and he said to have Mike's agent call him to discuss terms. Just don't, and I repeat, do not send me any more of Mike's pages at the office. Send everything to my apartment. It's going to take me an extra hour to get home tonight and I'm just lucky I didn't end up in—"

There was a loud burst of static and then Muriel's voice came back on the line. "It's definitely good, Toni. Mike reminds me a lot of James—"

The line went dead before Muriel could finish. Toni stared down at the phone and listened to the dial tone for a moment. Then she hung up. James who? James Joyce? James Fennimore Cooper?

James Baldwin? James somebody-or-other she'd never heard of? It didn't really matter which James it was. Muriel had loved Mike's book and Devonshire Publishing wanted to buy it!

Toni glanced down at the keys in her hand. Should she? Or shouldn't she? She should, of course! Now that Mike would soon have a book contract, he needed his wits about him. If she could figure out whatever thing in his past was causing his sleep-walking, he'd be better able to concentrate on giving Muriel his best work.

Was that a rationalization? Toni hurried out into the hall and unlocked Mike's door. Of course it was a rationalization, but that didn't matter. She wanted to do everything she could to help the man she loved. If she could satisfy her own curiosity in the process, so much the better.

Michael held the phone away from his ear as his brother ranted and raved. He'd known that Stan would be upset at his call, but he hadn't expected him to fly so completely off the handle. He waited for a break in the conversation and then he jumped in before Stan could get started again.

"Stan, calm down a minute. I'm calling from a phone at the mall. You know the one. It's only a couple of blocks from the apartment. It's perfectly safe."

That set Stan off again, and Michael sighed. If he'd known his brother's reaction would be this bad, he would never have called. Finally, after another few minutes, Stan slowed down a little.

"You're sure no one spotted you, Mike? Absolutely positive?"

"I'm sure, Stan. There's about a million people out today. It's some kind of giant sale, and all the stores have tables set up in the mall. Nobody's interested in looking at a guy using the phone when there's a whole lot of bargains out on the tables."

"Okay, okay. I'm sorry I yelled, but you can understand my concern. What's this emergency, Mike?"

"Professor Zimmer."

"Oh, hell, Mike! I really am sorry. I made a mental note to call you, but it just slipped my mind. The police think it was a mugging, so you don't have to worry about it. Now go right back home and don't stop off anywhere. You can't be too careful."

"Stan?" Mike couldn't believe his brother was being so casual. "That's not the point. I need to know if you warned the professor."

"Warned him? Of course I warned him! I said I would, didn't I? But I'm afraid he didn't take my warning seriously, Mikey. He said I didn't have any proof that someone was after the jurors."

Michael frowned. That was strange. Four people out of a group of seven had been killed. Maybe it wasn't exactly proof, but if Michael had been in that group, he certainly wouldn't have taken the statistics lightly.

Had Stan done a good job of warning the professor? "How about Rosalie Dumont and Sister Mary Clare? Do you think they took you seriously?"

"I'm sure they did, Mike."

"But are you positive? The killer's going to try to get them next. We both know that."

"Relax, Mikey. Take a deep breath. That helps to lower blood pressure. I don't want you getting sick on me. Not now. The minute I heard about Zimmer's death this morning, I ordered twenty-four-hour bodyguards for each of them. My men are in place right now. Does that make you feel better?"

Michael let out a long sigh of relief. "Yes, Stan. Thanks a lot. At least they'll have a better chance than Professor Zimmer did."

"You bet they will! Is that all, Mikey? I've got a client waiting."

"Just one more thing. Why do you think he's doing it Stan? I've been trying to figure it out, and I can't think of a reason."

"I don't know. You're right, Mikey. It doesn't make sense, but the killer's reason doesn't really matter, does it?"

Michael frowned. It certainly mattered to him! There was a killer out there who was setting him up. He'd be crazy if he didn't want to know why!

"Sorry, Mike." Stan broke the silence. "Of course it matters a lot to you. I just wasn't considering it from your perspective. But I've got a hunch it'll all be over this time tomorrow."

"A hunch, Stan? I didn't think you believed hunches."

"I don't, not usually. You'll have to trust me on this one, Mikey. It'll all be over by tomorrow. Just keep that in mind."

At first Michael was puzzled. What was Stan talking about? Then he remembered that his brother had ordered guards. "I get it, Stan. If the killer tries it again tonight, your guards will pick him up."

"Affirmative. This whole thing will be wound up tonight. That'll be a relief for both of us. Right, Mikey?"

"Right, Stan."

Michael frowned. Stan sounded really strange. He was beginning to wonder if his brother was coming unhinged from the pressure.

"Mikey? I just want you to know that I'm sorry about Zimmer. He was a bit of a stuffed shirt, but he wasn't all dry and academic. Joyce said he really gave her the once-over."

Michael's brain kicked into high gear. Joyce was Stan's secretary. How did she know Professor Zimmer?

"Professor Zimmer must have been the juror who brought you that footage. Is that right, Stan?"

"You're batting a thousand. And Zimmer did me one heck of a favor, Mike. Most people would have taken it straight to the police. Now go home. And stop worrying. Everything is under control. Maybe I'll drop in on you tonight, just to calm you down. You'd like to see your old brother again, wouldn't you, Mikey?"

"You know I would, Stan. But I thought you said it wasn't safe."

"Oh, it's not. It's definitely not. But maybe I'll decide to live dangerously." Stan chuckled. "If things work out the way I plan, I might just ring your doorbell instead of your phone. Now say good-bye, Mikey. And get your tail back home behind locked doors. I've got a lot of work to do."

Michael said good-bye and hung up. What a weird conversation! Could Stan be on drugs? It wasn't so much what Stan had said as the way he'd said it. Of course Stan had a lot on his mind, and Michael had interrupted him in the middle of a client meeting, but he'd never known Stan to be quite so manic before.

He was still puzzling over his brother's curious state of mind when he walked back out into the center part of the mall. He'd go buy Toni's printer paper, and then, since he was already here, he might as well pick up a couple of other things he needed. It was nice being out in the world again.

CHAPTER 27

Ebony Rose got into her car and pulled out of the underground garage. She hadn't even had time to make her tea before the phone rang. And then she'd run around like crazy dressing in street clothes and yelling to Bridget to keep Miles there if he came before she got back. She could have saved a little time by calling down and telling the garage attendant to bring her Jag around to the front entrance, but she didn't like the way he drove. She'd worked hard for the car, and she didn't want some pimply teenager to squeal all the rubber off the tires.

The counter was flashing when she pulled onto the Wilshire entrance to the freeway. Traffic was heavy this time of day, and the last thing she wanted to do was drive across town. Why had he insisted on seeing her immediately? And in a crowded shopping mall, of all places!

Freeway conditions were bumper-to-bumper. She didn't have to be careful about keeping her speed down to the posted limit. No speeding tickets for her today. She'd be lucky if she could get out of second gear.

After what seemed like forever, Ebony Rose got off the freeway and drove to the mall. She took her ticket from the machine at the entrance to the parking garage and drove all the way to the top to park. She always parked on the roof level when she came to the mall. Most people wanted to be inside the parking structure, and that meant there was usually plenty of parking on the roof. Today it was completely deserted except for a couple of panel trucks.

The elevator took forever to get to the top level. Ebony Rose pressed the button and waited, tapping her foot impatiently. Then she noticed the shoes she was wearing. Deck shoes didn't really go with her fuchsia designer pantsuit, but she'd been in so much of a hurry, she'd grabbed the first pair of low-heeled shoes in her closet.

While she was here at the mall, she might as well dash into the wine shop on the fifth floor to pick up some of the Chardonnay Jamie liked. She'd already decided to drink Perrier tonight, but just because she was watching her intake didn't mean that Jamie had to be deprived.

He enjoyed the expensive wine she served and Ebony Rose knew that he could never afford to buy it on his salary. She smiled as the green light flickered on the elevator. She could hear it coming. She wondered if Jamie would have any news about the footage he'd found. The man in the background had been Michael Hart, she was sure of it. She hoped they'd do something for him soon. The poor man had spent ten years locked up for a crime he hadn't committed, and she'd voted guilty just like

Jamie and all the rest. The only holdout had been the little nun. Ebony Rose had wavered a little when she'd seen how troubled the sister had been. But then the foreman had reminded them of reasonable doubt. And even Sister Mary Clare had finally decided her doubts weren't reasonable.

The elevator bell rang. Ebony Rose stepped to the side and put a friendly but neutral expression on her face. If there were other passengers inside, she hoped they wouldn't look down at her feet. Then her expression turned to terror as the doors opened and the man burst out to grab her.

These elevators were the worst he'd ever been in. Michael took a deep breath as he got off at the fourth floor and headed left toward the stationery store. Elevators had always bothered him, and he'd felt dizzy and slightly disoriented when the cage had risen all the way to the top, even though he was sure he'd pushed the button for the fourth floor. He'd almost lost it there for a minute, and he wasn't entirely sure he hadn't passed out. Elevators reminded him of the rides at the county fair he'd gone to with Stan and Aunt Alice. And the man in the tent who had tried to molest him. He'd told Aunt Alice and she'd been so furious at Stan for leaving him alone, that she'd caused a big scene right there on the midway. And Stan had been so angry at Michael for getting him in trouble with Aunt Alice that he'd taken him up on the Ferris wheel and rocked the seat to scare him. It had frightened Michael so badly, he'd balked at riding elevators all his life until now.

Michael knew he'd been hyperventilating when

he got off at the top floor and waited for another elevator going down. But he'd been determined to lick his problem once and for all. He'd forced himself to ride the elevators several times. And now that he'd proved to himself that he could do it without freaking out, he felt good. He had conquered his fear in less than twenty minutes.

Waiting in line at the stationery store, Michael was smiling. It would be great to see his brother again. And Michael's long ordeal was almost over. Stan's guards would pick up the killer, he would win his appeal, his sleepwalking would stop once the pressure was off, and then, with all those problems behind him, he'd be free to tell Toni what had been on his mind during the last couple of days.

It seemed to take forever for the stock boy to check on the printer paper. Michael didn't really mind. He browsed around the store, looking at the racks of paperback books. Would his book be published someday? It was an incredible long shot, but if it ever happened, he'd dedicate it to Toni. She was the one who'd given him the idea to write in the first place.

The stock boy came back at last. The truck had just pulled in with supplies, and it would take another fifteen minutes or so to get it unloaded.

Now that he was inside the mall, surrounded by people who couldn't be as much of a threat as Stan thought they were, he'd take advantage of the opportunity to wander around a little. And he'd be sure to stop in at that flower shop he'd spotted to buy Toni some roses. She'd been a real help in a lot of ways, and he might just get the nerve to write those three little words on the card.

Toni sat at Mike's desk, holding the list in her hand. Twelve names and eight of them were crossed out. She knew every name on the list, but she hadn't made the connection until now. They were the jurors from the Michael Hart trial. That was one of the reasons the name Jose Sanchez had seemed so familiar. She would have caught on a little sooner if Harry had mentioned the name of the professor when he'd told her about the murder this morning, or the name of the mortician who'd been killed.

She looked down at the list again. Two names were circled in green ink. The first had "China" written under it, and the other had the word "Northumberland." They must be out of the country. That left ten, and eight of them were dead. Five of the jurors had been murdered. Mike had crossed out those names in red ink. Two were left. Only two. Rosalie Dumont and Sister Mary Clare.

Toni was close to a state of shock. It had started when she'd found the clippings of the murders. There were frequent murders in a city the size of Los Angeles and she'd never guessed that these seemingly unrelated acts of violence could affect her personally. Now that Toni thought about it, she lived a very isolated life. She didn't watch television often, and she seldom listened to the radio. She never read the daily newspaper, and her world really revolved around her computer and the people who lived in her apartment building. It was a very closed environment. Of course she hadn't known the jurors on the Hart trial were being murdered. She'd paid absolutely no attention to what was going on in the world outside her safe little seven-story island.

Only two jurors left, Rosalie Dumont and Sister Mary Clare. How strange it was. Her mind was working as clear as a bell, but her body felt frozen. Everything made perfect sense. It just had no impact for her. Mike had wanted her to locate Jose Sanchez because he'd been a juror on the Hart trial. And when he'd asked her to run her stat program on his new book idea, he'd really been doing research on the murders of the Hart trial jurors. But why was Mike so interested? And why had he lied to her about his real reason? She had to find out.

Toni reached into the desk drawer and felt around in the bottom. The clippings were the first piece of the puzzle, and the list was the second. There had to be more pieces and her job was to find them. She had a lot at stake. Because she loved Mike, this was one puzzle she had to solve.

There was something shoved all the way back in the drawer, something that felt like a piece of soft plastic. Toni drew it out and turned it over in her fingers. A bracelet. The kind they clamped around your wrist when you were admitted to the hospital. And the name on the front was Michael Hart.

Suddenly, Toni felt a chill rush through her body. Michael Hart—the man who had murdered his wife ten years ago, or the man who'd been convicted of murdering his wife ten years ago. She still wasn't sure whether he'd actually done it. But why did Mike have Michael Hart's hospital bracelet? It seemed to take forever for her to form that question.

Only two jurors left, Rosalie Dumont and Sister Mary Clare. Her legs carried her out of his apartment and back down the hall to her own. Good thing she'd left the door unlocked. Mike had her keys. She locked the door behind her and went straight to her computer. The modem. The police data bank. What happened to Michael Hart? It sounded like the title for a movie.

Michael Hart had escaped from the Oakdale Facility for the Criminally Insane. That was fascinating. And Mike Kruger had moved in that same night. He was writing a book about a mental hospital that read so real, it sent chills down her spine. Muriel had felt the same way. If Toni didn't know better, she'd suspect that the reason she couldn't find Mike Kruger's name in any of her data banks was that Mike was using a fake name and he was really Michael Hart.

But that was impossible. She *did* know better. Mike didn't look anything like Michael Hart. Harry had shown her Michael Hart's mug shot, and she'd been very careful not to let on that she'd already seen his face. Harry would have wanted to know all about it, and she avoided anything that had to do with her past. No one knew, not even good friends like Harry and Doris. But even without that mug shot to refresh her memory, Toni knew that Mike didn't resemble Michael Hart in the slightest. People couldn't change the shape of their faces. Unless, of course, they'd undergone some sort of massive reconstruction.

Toni loaded the program to crack access codes. She'd told Mike she'd never use it except in a real emergency that was a matter of life or death. But there were only two jurors left, Rosalie Dumont and Sister Mary Clare. That *was* a matter of life and death.

The program worked, but Toni felt no thrill of accomplishment. Nothing seemed to affect her one way or the other. There was something dead, something deep inside her that was numb and frozen, and she doubted that anything could ever bring it back to life again.

There it was. Toni hit the proper sequence of keys to request a complete review of the file on Michael Hart. The screen scrolled past, and she caught certain phrases. Plastic surgery. Extensive. A year to complete. Cheekbones. Nose. Shape of the jaw. All the things that made a person's face uniquely his own had been changed for Michael Hart. It reminded her of an old television show. Would the real Michael Hart please stand up? And now, would he tell the panel his secret? Was he murdering the jurors who'd served at his trial?

As she gazed at the screen Toni realized that she had all the evidence to solve the puzzle. And every bit of it was circumstantial, exactly as it had been ten years ago. Mike had taken her car the night that Jose Sanchez was murdered. And he'd told her he'd been on the Santa Monica freeway. He could have killed Jose Sanchez. That was the first piece.

There were thirty extra miles on her odometer today, exactly the distance to Gateway University. And Harry had told her that it was possible for a tank to drive onto the campus without being noticed. Had Mike murdered Professor Zimmer last night and then come back to sleep in her bed? That was the second piece, and she didn't want to go over the rest. There were only two jurors left, Rosalie Dumont and Sister Mary Clare. What could she do?

Toni tried to think, but something seemed wrong with her head. Perhaps the numbness that affected the rest of her body had spread to her mind. And then there was a knock on her door. Was he back? The man who was Mike Kruger or Michael Hart? As her icy legs carried her across the floor to answer the summons, she reminded herself that there were only two jurors left for him to kill, Rosalie Dumont and Sister Mary Clare.

CHAPTER 28

Harry rang the doorbell again and knocked a little louder. He hoped Toni wasn't sleeping or anything like that. Then he heard footsteps, and the door inched open.

"Hi, Toni. Jesus, kid! You look awful. It isn't catching, is it?"

Toni blinked, and then a little color started to come back into her face. "Oh, Harry! I think I'm coming down with a cold. I was just napping, that's all."

Harry nodded. He knew what it was like to get up out of a sound sleep and try to function. He'd been doing it a lot lately. "Everything's all right, isn't it, Toni? I mean with Mike and all?"

"Sure, Harry. Everything's just peachy. Do you have time for a cup of coffee?"

She seemed to be better now, and Harry began to breathe easier. "Can't do it, Toni. I've got to get down to the station. They just called me in."

"Another murder?"

Harry shrugged. "Maybe, maybe not. We're checking it out right now."

"You don't know if it's murder?"

"Not yet. This woman fell off the roof of the Triangle Mall. Twelve stories, right there on La Cienega. Are you sure you want to hear this, Toni? You don't look so hot."

"I want to hear it. Tell me, Harry."

"Well . . . okay. We don't know whether it was suicide or if she was pushed. That's always a possibility considering the line of work she . . ."

"Who was she, Harry?"

Toni looked like she really didn't feel well at all. Harry wished he hadn't said anything now.

"Nobody you'd know, Toni. She ran a high-class hooker operation. You want to sit down or something? You look like you're ready to pass out on me."

"I'm fine, Harry. You know how it is when you first wake up. What was her name?"

"Ebony Rose. She owned a nude dancing place on Sunset."

"Was that her real name?"

"No, it was Dumont. She took the name Ebony Rose when she first got into the business. We've been trying to pin something on her for . . . Toni, I really think you'd better sit down." Harry grabbed Toni's arm and sat her down in the chair. She was shaking like a leaf in the wind. "You want me to call a doctor, Toni?"

Toni swallowed hard. "No, Harry. I'm all right, really. I was just thinking about somebody jumping off the top of that mall. Heights scare me, Harry."

"Me, too. Just between you and me, I don't think

she jumped. She knew a lot of big people, and some of them aren't exactly law-abiding citizens. You know what I mean?"

Toni nodded. "Mafia?"

"Oh, maybe not as big as that, but guys with enough money to arrange a convenient suicide if they thought she knew too much. She was playing in the big leagues, Toni."

"So you're going to write it off as a suicide, Harry? To keep from stepping on any toes?"

"Not me. You know how I feel about that, Toni. No one's big enough to ignore the law. But I can't guarantee what the boys who pull our strings are gonna do. If you're sure you're all right, I really have to get my tail in gear."

Harry was halfway to the door before he remembered what he'd stopped by for in the first place. "Toni?"

"Yes, Harry."

"I'm expecting a package and Doris won't be home until late. If UPS comes by, will you take it in for me? I left a note on my door."

"Sure, Harry. And thanks for telling me about Rosalie Dumont"

Harry walked down the steps to the garage and climbed into his car. He was halfway to the precinct before it struck him. How the hell had Toni known Rosalie Dumont's first name?

"Hiya, Lenny. How's it hanging?"

Lenny stared at Eddie in absolute shock. He'd never thought the little creep would have the nerve to come back after what he'd done!

"What's the matter, Lenny? Your mouth's open wide enough to catch flies. You must of thought I was never coming back, huh, Lenny?"

Lenny snapped his jaw closed and dragged Eddie into the apartment. Then he realized that Babsie was here. He didn't want her to hear the load of stuff he was going to lay on Lenny. "Babsie, honey? You suppose you could go in the bedroom for a minute or something? I gotta talk to my guy here in private."

"Sure, Lenny. You want a beer before I go?" Lenny shook his head. He was too mad to drink beer, and he'd sort of lost his taste for it anyway. As soon as the bedroom door shut behind Babsie, he threw Eddie down in a chair.

"You little creep! Do you know how much trouble you made for me? Call off your guy right away!"

"What guy, Lenny?" Eddie looked completely puzzled, "I don't know what you're talking about."

Lenny lowered his voice. "The guy you called that night we were talking about Margo. You know. The hit man"

Eddie frowned. "I didn't call any hit man, Lenny. Maybe I'm stupid, but I'm not *that* stupid."

"Then who did you call that was such a big secret you couldn't do it from here? Huh, Eddie?"

"God, Lenny! You really thought I called a hit man? Let me go out and drag in that box I left in the hall. That's who I called."

Lenny stared at Eddie to see if it was some kind of cop-out, but he looked serious. Was it possible he was wrong? Lenny nodded, and Eddie went to bring in the box.

"Open it, Lenny," he said once he'd set it down in front of Lenny. "It's a present I got for you."

"What's this?" Lenny opened it and drew out a DVD. *The Untouchables?*"

"Yeah, Lenny, with Eliot Ness." Eddie looked proud. "I met this guy who had fifty-five episodes. And I remembered you told me you loved it when you were a kid. That's who I called that night, Lenny. Honest. I talked the guy into duping his whole collection as a favor for you."

He pulled over to the side of the street and parked under a tree. He'd never been this exhausted before. This whole thing was a terrible strain. He shut his eyes for just a moment and tried to push back the panic that threatened to render him immobile. He'd been fine a few minutes ago, looking forward to the point where all the loose ends were wrapped up. But now the hounds of panic were nipping at his heels again. What if something went wrong? What if he couldn't find the last juror tonight?

He forced himself to rest and relax. He wasn't in any condition to drive right now, and he might be pulled over for a traffic violation. He'd wait a bit until the worst of the rush hour traffic was gone. Luckily, no one would notice him here. And if they did, they'd assume he was waiting to pick up someone at one of the factories that lined the street. Just a few moments and he'd be fine. All he needed was some time to collect his thoughts.

The headrest felt good, and he leaned back against it. At last his body was beginning to relax. Now all he had to do was think about something pleasant. A kiss. Warm arms around his body. Sleeping under blankets, with someone he loved.

Carole had been that someone. Beautiful Carole,

with warm breasts and a warm heart. He'd loved her right from the beginning, but then she'd done something so treacherous, she hadn't deserved to live.

Night began to fall, but he didn't notice. He was thinking about Carole and the time, ten years ago, when she'd told him that she was pregnant. She'd stood there, hips canted forward as if she were already heavy with child. She'd never looked more beautiful than she had at that moment. At first he'd been speechless, but then he'd recovered enough to ask if she was sure. And she had smiled the smile he'd thought was for him alone and said yes, the doctor had confirmed it. She was six weeks pregnant. Wasn't that wonderful? She'd known that he'd always wanted to have a child.

Choking a bit on the words, he'd asked the important question, the one that had decided everything. He hadn't wanted to ask, but his obligation was clear. He had to know the truth about the woman he loved. Truth was the highest priority. Was she sure it was his baby?

She should have been an actress. She'd done such a superb job of faking her injured outrage. Looking at him with wounded eyes, tears glistening in the corners. Of course the baby was his. How could he even think otherwise?

He had left quickly, before she could see his reaction. Her lie had acted as an icy slap to make his mind function clearly again. So he had planned and waited. And then he had come back to put an end to all the lies. Only after it was done, as he had gazed down at her still-beautiful dead body, had he told her why. She had deceived him. The dead baby inside her dead womb was not his. He'd caught German measles when he was in law school and missed two weeks of his second year. It was all because Aunt Alice hadn't believed in inoculations for older kids, just little ones like Mikey. The campus doctor had checked him out and given him the bad news. The virus had rendered him sterile.

It was dark outside, but she didn't get up to switch on a light. She was still sitting in the chair where Harry had placed her over an hour ago. This whole dilemma reminded her of the trial of some saint—she couldn't remember which one—and she had to be ready to declare her choice. Ethics or love. Love or ethics. A casuistic conundrum that was typical of the Jesuits. She wasn't prepared. God help her, she couldn't choose.

There was a key in the lock. No time left. The clock had run out.

"Toni?" Michael came in and switched on the light.

She didn't say anything. How could she speak? All she could do was look at him, and then her decision was made.

"Toni!" He rushed over and put his arms around her" What's wrong?"

"Love. I choose love."

He frowned. He probably thought she was crazy, and maybe she was. Then he picked her up and carried her to the living room couch. A murderer? Never! Not with these arms that spoke of love. Not with these lips that kissed her so gently. Not with these anxious but innocent eyes. She could hear the words in her head, and they sounded like lines from a romance novel, so she laughed. But she was right. She knew she was right!

"What is it, Toni? Were you worried about me?"

She nodded. Oh yes, she had been worried. But not in the way he meant. Mike Kruger or Michael Hart. It no longer mattered. All the evidence in the world couldn't convince her that the man she loved was a murderer. Even if he drew out a gun and ended her life at this moment, she'd go to her grave believing in his innocence.

"Are you sick, Toni? Is there anything I can get you?"

He was so concerned, she had to tell him. "I was. But I'm fine now. I think it was a crisis of faith, and I won."

He frowned. She could tell that he really didn't know what she was talking about. How could he?

"You'll have to explain that one to me, but this should help. I brought you something, Toni."

He handed her a bouquet. Roses. Deep red velvety roses, sprinkled with dew. It was glycerin, of course. She'd worked in a flower shop once, and she knew the tricks of the trade. But it could just as well have been dew. And there, tucked among the roses, was a card that said, "I love you."

"Mike?" Her voice was stronger now, more in control. She'd made her decision, and nothing could make her change it.

"Yes, Toni?"

"Do you love me? Really?"

He kissed her then. It was a promise, a covenant. Yes, he loved her. She could tell. So she smiled, suddenly at peace with all the dilemmas the world could shower on her. They didn't matter. They weren't important.

"I love you, too, Michael Hart," she said.

* * *

Harry Evans was confused. Toni had obviously known Ebony Rose when she was Rosalie Dumont. His records showed that Ebony Rose had started the business eight years ago, so it had to be before that. How had Toni met her?

He sat at his gray metal desk and reviewed what he knew about Toni. Nothing, really. Antonia Novak, computer whiz. She was a good friend, but he knew nothing about her background and neither did Doris. He remembered when she'd moved in six years ago. He had asked where she came from, and she told him that she'd been living in her father's house in the valley for two years, nursing him through a terminal illness. That accounted for eight years, but where had she been before that? Not in college. He knew that for a fact. She enrolled as a freshman when she started taking those computer classes. Maybe it would be a good idea to run a background check on Toni. And while he was at it, he'd run a check on Ebony Rose, too. There had to be some period when their paths had crossed.

Harry turned on his computer and punched in the codes. Now he was glad that Toni had given him some tips on using it. It was ironic, in a way. He was using the skills she'd taught him to check up on her. Maybe he was just wasting his time, but he had a hunch it might be important.

"I still can't believe you were that little nun. Why didn't I recognize you?"

"How could you? We wore full habits, and I always kept my eyes averted. It was the way we were taught."

Michael gave her a hug. "I'm certainly glad you're

not a nun anymore. And I'm grateful that you're on my side this time. Why do you believe me, Toni? All the evidence points straight to me. For all I know, I might really be the one who's killing off the jurors. I told you what the psychiatrist said about my sleep-walking."

"You're not killing anybody, Mike. You couldn't be, not even in your sleep."

"Okay. If I'm not doing it, then somebody's setting me up. We've got to figure out who it is, and then we can call Harry and ask for his help."

Toni shook her head. "It won't work, Mike. Harry's a friend, but not even a friend would believe a crazy story like this. He'd have to do his duty and lock you up again. And even if your brother wins your appeal, they'll just try to convict you for the murders of the jurors. We've got to find some sort of evidence that the police will believe."

"There's the footage the professor found. That'll help. Thank God. There's a guard out there, Toni. If I thought that you re in any . . . oh, my God!"

"What is it?"

"I just remembered. Stan told me he warned the last two jurors personally."

Toni raised her eyebrows. "Then your brother lied to you, Mike. He didn't warn me. And I'm willing to bet there's no guard, either."

"But why would he lie? Is there any way you could use your computer to find out about my appeal, Toni? It's important."

"Sure. Come with me."

It seemed to take hours to access the court calendar. Toni scrolled through the cases on the docket, but they couldn't find anything scheduled for Michael Hart's appeal. Stan had lied about that, too.

Toni turned to him with a frown. "Why did he lie, Mike? What reason could he have?"

"He must have wanted me to sit tight while the killer finished off the jurors. That's the only conclusion I can come up with. Toni, I think we should call Harry. Even if I get sent back to Oakdale, it'll be worth it if I'm sure you're safe."

Toni dialed Harry's number at the precinct. "Captain Evans, please. This is Toni Novak."

She frowned down at the phone. "He's not? When do you expect him back? I see. No, there's no message. Just tell him that I'll call back."

"Harry's not there?"

Toni shook her head. "They expect him back late, but they're not sure when."

"Let's go, Toni. I'll turn myself in to whoever's there, and we'll get some protection for you. You're a sitting duck in this apartment."

"No, Mike. I won't let you turn yourself into anyone but Harry. Without Harry, no one would take our story seriously. They'd think we were both insane."

"Maybe we are." Michael frowned. "I just wish I had that footage, if there ever was any."

"What do you mean?"

Michael sighed. "Maybe Stan lied about that, too."

"I don't think so." Toni looked thoughtful. "It wouldn't serve any purpose for him to do that."

"You're right. If that footage does exist and I had it, I could prove to the police that I was innocent ten years ago. If I could do that, they might just believe me now."

"Do you think the footage would be in your brother's office?"

"Maybe, but I doubt it. If Stan had it in the first place, he's probably destroyed it by now. He never wanted to clear me, Toni. And now he wants me to take the blame for all these other murders. He's protecting the real killer but I can't figure out why."

"Forget that for now. Do you know who gave Stan the footage? Maybe that person kept a copy."

"It was Professor Zimmer. Stan mentioned it on the phone this afternoon. I don't think he was lying. It just sort of slipped out."

"Let's go, Mike. I think the professor kept a copy. I'm willing to bet on that."

"How can you be that sure?"

"Professor Zimmer made copies of everything. That was one thing I noticed about him during your trial. He even made copies of the daily notes he took during the trial. I asked him why he copied everything and he explained that he wanted a record of everything in case the original got lost. That copy will be in his office on the campus, Mike. That's something else I'm sure about."

"Why are you sure about that?"

"Because Harry told me that the killer broke in there, looking for something. It must have been the footage."

"What if he found it?"

"Don't bother me with details. We've got to assume it's still there and find it." Toni tossed Mike her keys and grabbed a revolver from the drawer in the kitchen. "You drive. I'll ride shotgun. I always hated this ugly thing, but now I'm glad that Harry taught me how to use it."

CHAPTER 29

Stan watched them pull into the parking lot and get out of the car. Had they solved the puzzle? Yes, they were walking across the commons, past the cathedral toward Professor Zimmer's office building. They had no trouble getting inside. Once he'd realized where they were going, he'd driven ahead to unlock the door. If they found what they were looking for, that was wonderful. But even if they didn't, he'd put an end to this whole case when they came back to the car.

At first the police would think that there'd been two more violent muggings on campus. And then they'd find the suicide note and identify the bodies. It wouldn't take any clever detective work to tie it all together. Michael Hart had escaped from the hospital to commit his insane revenge. Tonight he'd killed the last juror, and then he'd turned the gun on himself. It would be a horrible end to a tormented life. All the pieces fit perfectly. It was brilliantly planned. No one would ever suspect him.

He frowned, thinking about the tasks he had left

to accomplish. He could kill her with no problem.
But him? That would be much more difficult. He'd
just have to do it the way he'd intended. There was
no escape, and he'd make it quick and painless. It
was kinder that way. And it was much more humane
than forcing him to live out the rest of his life in a
mental institution.

It would have been easier if he'd hated him, or
resented him, or even disliked him. But he didn't.
It was all circumstance, nothing but unfortunate
circumstance. He hadn't started out to set him up
ten years ago, but that's what had happened in the
course of events, and now he was locked into a situation he'd never anticipated. He was trapped by fate,
and he was as much a victim as all the others.

Would they find the footage? It was possible,
although he'd searched very thoroughly. He could
end it all right there in the professor's office, but it
would be more prudent to wait and see. If they
found it, things could be tied up much more neatly.
Of course, no one would realize the significance of
the footage if they stumbled across it later, but it
would give him a great deal of satisfaction to know
that there were no loose ends.

He got out of his car. No need to take the gun.
He'd leave it under the seat until it was time. He
doubted the security guard would spot him, but it
was better to be safe than sorry.

The night was lovely. Calm. Cool. Very peaceful.
The campus was deserted. It was Sunday night, and
not even the library was open on the Sabbath. It was ·
pleasant to walk across the beautiful campus and
past the towering spires of the cathedral. He was
so busy admiring the glint of moonlight on the

polished stone that he didn't notice the dark, silent shadow that slipped into his car.

"Mike!" Toni pulled the DVD out of the drawer. "Let's have a light. Quickly."

Michael aimed his penlight at the label, and Toni swore softly. "Oh, no! I thought I had it for a minute, but it's only a segment of that PBS series on the first amendment. It's got the library seal right on it. He must have used it in his class."

"Hold on, Toni. Didn't you tell me that Professor Zimmer was the most organized man you'd ever met?"

"That's true, Mike."

"There's the rest of that series right over there on his bookshelf. With covers. Was he the type of man who'd let a loose DVD kick around in his desk drawer without a protective cover?"

"No. Check it out, Mike. This is segment three."

Michael flashed the light on the bookshelf. "One and two are here. And so are four through six. Did you say that disk had the library name on it?"

"That's right. It says Property of Gateway University Library, Audiovisual Department. "

"Did Harry say anyone had broken into the library?"

"No."

"Okay, then the footage is still there. It's inside the cover for segment three. Let's go!"

They were running across campus toward the library, two fleeting shadows in the dark night. Stan just hoped the security guard wouldn't spot them. And now they were standing by the side door, where the shadows were deepest. After a few moments, the door opened and then shut again quickly. Gateway University had terrible security, but they probably weren't too concerned about their students breaking into the library. Why should they be? The last thing a student at this fourth-rate college would want to steal was a book. Would they think to lock the door behind them? Of course. But it would be easy to get in with Professor Zimmer's keys. He'd kept them all, just in case.

He grabbed the gun and stuffed it in his pocket. It was time. Just as soon as they'd handed over the footage, he'd kill them. Two more deaths and he'd be finished.

"This is it!" Michael let out a long sigh. "Look at the label, Toni. It's the original from KLAX."

"Let's get it to the police right away, Mike. I'm not the type to have premonitions, but I've got this terrible—"

"And you're right, Sister. Turn around very slowly. Both of you. Mikey, hand me that footage."

Michael turned to face his brother. "Stan! What are you doing here?"

Stan stood there in the light from the dim bulbs that were left on at night. He was holding a gun, and there was a sad but determined expression on his face. "Sorry, Mikey. Give it to me. I need it."

"Give it to him, Mike." Toni's voice was shaking. "Do exactly what he says."

"That's good advice, Sister. Come on, Mikey. Delaying now won't solve anything."

Michael moved forward slowly and held out the jacket with the footage inside. "Why are you doing this, Stan? I don't understand."

"Oh Mikey." Stan shook his head. "Can't you see that I don't have any choice? She had to die, you know. There was no other way."

"Who?"

"Carole." Stan sighed. "She fell in love with the wrong man, Mikey. And when she realized her mistake, it was too late. She tried to make me think it was my baby, but I knew that was impossible. You're better off without her, don't you see? She cheated. She was nothing but a whore at heart."

"Carole told you that she was pregnant with your baby?" Michael asked. He knew that he had to keep Stan talking. If they were lucky, Stan would get caught up in his own rhetoric and relax his guard. Then they might have an opportunity to grab the gun, or knock him down, or take some action to try to save their lives.

"She swore it was my baby. She said she wasn't sleeping with you anymore, but I knew that couldn't be true. I'm sterile, Mikey. My doctor said I'd never be able to be a father."

"I'm sorry, Stan."

"So am I, Mikey. But I'm even sorrier that Carole lied to me. Now you can understand why I had to kill her, can't you? I couldn't let her get away with—" Stan whirled and aimed his gun at Toni "Drop it, Sister. Now!"

Toni wavered, and for a moment Michael thought

she was going to raise the gun and shoot to save him. "Drop it, Toni! Don't be a fool!"

The moment the words were out of his mouth, Toni let the gun clatter to the floor. The noise was loud in the huge, silent room. Then she looked at him expectantly, waiting for a cue. What could he do? The only thing he could think of was to keep Stan talking. Questioning might work. Stan loved to explain things.

"Raise your hands, Sister." Stan gestured with the gun. "That's it. A little more. And now I think it's—"

"I don't understand why you had to kill all the jurors, Stan." Michael interrupted. "Wasn't it enough to just kill Professor Zimmer?"

"That's not important, Mikey. There's no need for you to—"

This time Toni interrupted. She'd caught his unspoken prompt. "But it's important to us, Stan. Mike said you always had a good reason for everything you did. I know it really bothers him that we couldn't figure it out."

"Is that true, Mikey? Do you really want to know?"

"Yes, I do." Toni had asked just the right question and in exactly the right way. "It was just too complicated for us, Stan. Can you explain it?"

"It is rather complicated, isn't it?" Stan started to smile. "It's like this, Mikey. Professor Zimmer told me that he'd shown the footage to another juror."

There was a library cart only a foot or so away. Michael inched a little closer to it. It was the rolling type, and it was filled with heavy books. If Toni could only keep Stan talking, maybe he could reach it.

Toni came through, right on cue. "And he wouldn't tell you which juror?"

"That's exactly right. I tried every trick in the book, but I couldn't get it out of him."

"Well, it wasn't me. I didn't know anything about the footage until tonight. Did you try to figure out which juror it was?"

Stan was facing Toni when Michael's foot touched the cart. Now all he had to do was locate the lock on the wheel and release it. As he felt around with his toe, Stan laughed.

"Of course I didn't try to figure out who the juror was. That would have been wasted effort. I knew if I killed them all, I'd be safe. I suppose you would have tried to locate the juror. Right, Sister?"

Toni sighed. "I'm afraid that's exactly what I would have done. But I can see your way is much more efficient. Did you expect the police to blame Mike?"

"Of course. I read the psychiatrist's report about his dreams and the sleepwalking. It fit right in. Do you understand now?"

Michael's toe inched down. The brake released with an audible click, but Toni was talking again and Stan didn't hear.

"Yes, I see. Or at least I'm beginning to see. The police would look at the psychiatrist's report, and assume that Mike killed the jurors in a fit of revenge. Do I have that right?"

"Precisely. And now, that's enough talking."

"Just one more question, please, one that really puzzles me. If you kill Mike, won't the police look for his murderer?"

That's the clever part." Stan smiled. "Mikey's going to commit suicide right after he kills you."

"I don't understand that at all." Toni shook her head. "How can you make Mike's murder look like a suicide when it's not?"

Michael managed to get one hand on the cart. Just another inch closer, and he could—"

"That's the easiest part," Stan went on with his answer. "You see, Sister, I typed a note on that typewriter I put in Mickey's apartment. And once the police find that, they won't bother to—"

It was now, or never. Michael pushed with all his strength and the cart took off like a rocket. Stan whirled at the sudden motion, and Michael yelled for Toni to run. She didn't waste any time ducking behind the stacks, and then the room plunged into darkness. She'd hit the light switch. Good girl! Now if she only had the presence of mind to sneak out the back way and go for help.

It took a moment for Michael's eyes to adjust to the sudden blackness. There was a dim light coming in through the windows, but all he could make out was the shape of the hulking bookcases. He had the advantage now. Stan had to find them to kill them. All he had to do was stay very still and pray that Toni had escaped.

Someone was moving. He could hear a rustle. The noise seemed to be coming closer, but it was difficult to tell. Was it Toni? Or Stan?

Then his eyes adjusted. A figure was huddled, crawling slowly toward the bookcase. Toni. She was going back for the gun.

Another rustle. The sounds seemed to come from all around him. But then he saw it—a shape moving fast, heading for the same bookcase. It was Stan. He'd spotted Toni, but he wouldn't dare shoot wildly. The security guard might hear, and he had to make it count.

Suddenly Michael had a flash of insight. Stan couldn't get both of them at once, and he had to kill Toni. She was the last juror. Even if Michael escaped, he couldn't go to the police. No one would believe his crazy story without the footage, and he'd be no threat to Stan if he was running from the authorities all his life. Stan would never expect him to stay and save Toni, so he wouldn't be cautious about looking behind him. That was exactly the advantage Michael needed.

The library shelves were divided, and when they'd first entered the room, Michael had noticed that they'd attached them to the ceiling with eye hooks. It was a sturdy enough method if they were evenly balanced, but one section wasn't. They were rearranging the philosophy section. Four shelves were empty on one side, down at the bottom, where it counted. And Stan was crawling right in front of it.

Michael hurtled forward and pushed with all his strength. The bookcase swayed and toppled with a crash. There was a scream of pain. Toni? No, not Toni. And then the lights came on to blind him.

"Jesus, Mike! Did you leave anything for us to do?" It was Harry Evans, helping Toni to her feet and grinning like a Cheshire cat. "We had you covered all the time, Mike. No problem, until Toni switched off the lights."

"Harry!" Toni looked dazed, "But how did you—"

"Brilliant detective work on my part. Take care of her, will you Mike? I've got things to do."

Michael heard Harry tell all his men to take Stan to the station and book him. And not to forget to read him his rights, because he was a lawyer and they didn't want this one dismissed on a technicality. And then Toni was in his arms, warm and safe and whole. How close they'd come! He'd never let her go again.

"Well, how about that?" Harry came up to them and slapped Michael on the back. "Busy night, huh, Mike?"

Toni was laughing hysterically, and Michael couldn't blame her. He tried to kiss her, but she just laughed harder and pointed down at the floor. Books were scattered all over, heavy philosophy books that had to weigh at least ten pounds apiece.

"Good thing it wasn't filled with your books, Mike. They're going to publish it in paperback. I'll tell you later. Oh, God!"

And then she was laughing even harder while Michael and Harry stared at each other in consternation. Both men were trying to figure out some way to stop her when she leaned over to pick up one particularly heavy book.

"It's Wittgenstein. He saved my life, Mike. My father always told me I'd learn to appreciate Wittgenstein someday."

Harry watched them for a moment. Mike was a real nice guy. He was kissing Toni, and she was kissing him back. He opened his mouth to tell them that they'd never been in any danger. He'd taken all the bullets out of Stan's gun. But then he decided not to spoil the moment. Wasn't love grand? The moment he got home he'd tell Doris to start planning the menu for a wedding reception. By the looks of those two, it wouldn't be a very long wait!

A KILLER IN THE DEAD OF WINTER . . .

As a family clinic administrator, Michelle Layton
has seen her share of suffering. But never anything
like this. Not here in St. Cloud, Minnesota.
A local activist has been found murdered,
his body frozen like a statue and placed in a
Winter Carnival ice sculpture display.
Next a vicious hate crime puts a man in the ICU.
And locked away in the Holy Rest mental ward,
a deranged man of the cloth prays
for more sinners to be punished—
and waits for a sign from above.
These seemingly random acts lead
police chief Steve Radke to Michelle,
who could be the next pawn in a madman's
chess game of life and death,
good versus evil . . .

**Please turn the page for an exciting sneak peek
of Joanne Fluke's**

VENGEANCE IS MINE

coming in December 2015!

PROLOGUE

"Zina, heel!" Bonnie Novak jerked back on the leash with all her strength and dug her heels into the deep snow flanking Twelfth Avenue. Her thirty-eight-pound Siberian husky strained on the leash, eyeing the park across the street eagerly, but Bonnie managed to hold her in check until a yellow school bus rumbled past. Obedience training had been a waste of money. Walking Zina was still a test of brute strength.

The street was clear now, and Bonnie let the dog pull her across the slippery asphalt and into the snow-covered park. The freezing rain last night had coated the snow with a hard crust of ice, and Bonnie's boots crunched as she hurried to keep up with Zina. She caught a quick glimpse of the American National Bank sign before Zina pulled her behind a snowbank. It was seven forty-five and minus nine degrees in downtown St. Cloud. Bonnie gave an automatic shiver until she realized that the temperature was in Celsius. It was really fifteen above, and that was a balmy day for February in Minnesota.

Zina stopped to sniff at the base of a tree, and Bonnie stood silently, enjoying the peaceful morning.

Flanked by tall pine trees, the park was effectively cut off from the noisy traffic on Division Street. It was an island of serenity in the center of the bustling city. The sky above was still gray, but the sun struggled to peek through the low clouds. This might turn out to be a nice day after all.

"Come on, Zina. Let's go." Bonnie jerked hard on the leash and began to walk through the crusty snow bordering the small lake. In the summer Lake George was filled with rented paddleboats, but now it was the municipal skating rink. As Zina sniffed at the frozen bushes Bonnie followed along slowly, examining the ice sculptures that were already beginning to line the shore. On Monday WinterGame would start, and this peaceful little park would be filled with people. The fundraiser would run for a week with figure skating competitions, ice hockey play-offs, snowman building contests, and the ice sculpture exhibition.

"Zina! No!" Bonnie attempted to pull the husky back, but Zina barked sharply and strained toward one of the ice sculptures. It was the most hideous thing Bonnie had ever seen, a statue of a man dying in agony, his skull crushed in. The artist had added plenty of realistic touches. There was even red poster paint for the blood that covered the man's face. Bonnie certainly hoped that this sculpture didn't win the contest.

The Siberian husky began to whine as Bonnie held her tightly by the choke chain. The sun peeked through the clouds for a moment, and Bonnie gave a sigh of relief as she realized that this statue couldn't possibly win the contest. There was something inside, covered by a coating of ice. The rules clearly stated that all entries had to be carved freehand.

Just as Bonnie was ready to turn and start toward home, the clouds rolled away and the winter sun hit the statue fully, highlighting it in grisly detail. Bonnie's mouth opened in a scream, and she swayed on her feet. This was no ice sculpture. It was real. And there was a dead man inside.